DEOSIL

JORDAN L. HAWK

Deosil © 2019 Jordan L. Hawk

ISBN: 978-1-941230-38-1

Cover art © 2019 Lou Harper

Edited by Annetta Ribken Graney

To everyone whom Widdershins has collected on this journey:
You are seen.
You are important.
You are loved.
Welcome home.

CHAPTER ONE

hyborne

I WAS PRECISELY on time for my meeting.

I needed no alarm. At the proper time, I simply awoke. I dressed, combed my hair, and straightened my freshly starched collar. Every motion was practiced, without either haste or slowness.

Perfect.

I departed Whyborne House just as the trolley came to a halt outside. No one spoke when I climbed aboard. I took my place among the other riders, all of us silent, save for the whisper of clothing and tap of shoes when taking or leaving our seats.

The trolley passed smoothly through Widdershins, drawn by some force I couldn't see. It wasn't my place to wonder about such things, however, so I didn't.

"Come to me," a voice whispered in my ear.

I tensed, and on instinct I glanced to the left, where the voice had come from. No one sat there, and my view out the window was unobstructed. People—or things very much like people, or that had once been people—walked up and down the street, avoiding one another as skillfully and silently as ants in a nest. Their clothing consisted of drab browns and grays, with plain suits for the men and unadorned dresses for the women. A cannery worker might wear a heavy apron, or a fisherman an oilskin coat, but otherwise they were variations on a theme.

I returned my attention to the fore and let the momentary tension slip from me. There was no need for concern.

The trolley halted in front of what had been the Nathaniel R. Ladysmith Museum, and now was...something else. Exactly what eluded my mind, like a fish slipping from my grasp in a murky pond.

No matter. I disembarked the trolley and walked up the steps, merging with the flow of people or things. Some of them looked familiar: the woman with her dark hair, who walked a few feet away from the bronze-skinned man, neither glancing the other's way. I did not speak to them, nor they to me, and soon I lost sight of them amidst the throng.

"Come to me," the voice whispered again.

This time, I stopped and looked around for the source of the anomaly. A man with chestnut hair and green eyes barely avoided bumping into me. I felt a strange twinge in my chest at the sight of the spray of freckles across his tanned skin. He passed by, continuing on whatever business he had, without so much as a glance in my direction.

Unease awoke deep in my belly. Something was wrong. Very wrong.

Yes—and that something was me. Standing here, blocking the way so everyone else had to divert around me. I was in danger of becoming the grain of sand in the oyster shell—an irritant to be walled away for the good of the host.

I forced myself to move. To go where I was appointed. Through the museum that was no longer a museum. Through shadowy corridors that grew impossibly larger as I walked, until the architecture towered over me. Carved murals covered the walls, the writing on them in strange clusters of dots I could not understand. Something that was like an umbra, but not, slipped past me without acknowledgement.

At last I came to a hexagonal room. A column of blinding light pierced the center. Before it stood a ketoi man. Arcane fire spilled through his skin, and the dark markings along his back and arms writhed. I froze, unreasonably afraid he'd turn toward me, and I'd have to see his face.

"Come to me," he said. "Before it's too late."

I WOKE WITH A GASP.

For a wild moment, I didn't know where I was, the room around me taking on unfamiliar dimensions. The floor heaved beneath me, and I clawed instinctively at the bedsheets.

Bedsheets. The roll of the sea.

I was in my stateroom aboard the *Melusine,* making my way home to Widdershins with the remaining Endicotts in tow. Cool, salty air flowed in through the open skylight, a welcome break from the summer heat, which had plagued us since leaving the Isles of Scilly in our wake. I breathed deep, willing my thundering heart to settle.

Griffin stirred in the bed beside me. "Is everything all right, my dear?" he asked sleepily.

"Just a dream. A nightmare."

At one time, those words would have been a comfort. Now, they only roused Griffin further. "Are you certain that's all it was?"

We'd both had nightmares that were anything but. I when the dweller in the deeps reached out to my mind, and Griffin after his encounter with an umbra in Egypt. "It wasn't a sending of the dweller," I said. "That much I'm certain of, at least." I related what I could recall of the dream to him; even as I spoke, parts of it began to fragment.

"You didn't know me," I finished. "Christine, Iskander, we were all there, but we walked past one another as if we were strangers."

He rubbed my bare arm comfortingly. "It sounds disturbing."

"It was."

Griffin wound his arms and legs around me, hugging me tight. "I could never forget you, Ival. Or Christine, or Iskander. You've had a great deal on your mind. It's no wonder you'd dream such troubling things."

He was right, of course. It had just been a fancy of my anxious mind, nothing more.

"We're almost home," he went on. "Hopefully, being on dry land once again will ease your mind."

We'd put in to Widdershins by sunset tomorrow. Or rather, today, given the hour. Once there, Griffin would take on the task of settling the Endicotts on the old Somerby estate. I'd already begun decoding the Wisborg Codex, using the fragment saved from Balefire's vault. Back in Widdershins, I'd have the museum's complete copy of the Codex to work on. Hopefully, it would tell us what we'd need to either keep the masters from returning, or to defeat them if that was our only option.

And hopefully, Persephone and I wouldn't die in the process.

I sat up and reached for the clothing I'd hung over a chair when we put out the lights. "I'm going up to the deck for a bit."

"Do you want company?"

I did. I had the sense of our time together slipping away, the grains of the hourglass running out. I wanted to spend every possible second with him, just in case Nyarlathotep hadn't lied. In case my sister and I really were doomed.

But I couldn't say that to him. So I just leaned over and kissed him on the forehead. "Try and get some more sleep. I'll rejoin you soon."

I STOOD for a time near the prow of the ship, watching lightning dance on the horizon. The storm hadn't reached us yet, and hopefully wouldn't, but there was something about seeing those distant sparks of light amidst the utter blackness of the sea. Thick clouds covered the stars, and the moon was waning fast.

Lanterns glowed from the other ships in the flotilla. After the destruction of Balefire, the Endicotts needed somewhere new to settle, and for better or worse I'd invited them to relocate in Widdershins. Whether they would stay after we faced the masters' return remained unclear. At least I now felt relatively certain they wouldn't try to murder me, whatever else they decided.

I hoped they wouldn't, anyway.

I preferred this sort of night at sea, if only because the darkness hid the vastness of the water all around me. A youthful accident had instilled in me the fear of drowning, and even though it had been eroded somewhat by various sea voyages—not to mention several dunkings in the ocean at Balefire—it would never truly leave me.

The salty air filled my lungs, and I clasped my hands behind my back. I hadn't told anyone about the prophecy Nyarlathotep had made to me upon the heights of Carn Moreth, with Morgen's Needle looming over us both. It claimed the maelstrom created Persephone and me to die, presumably as some sort of necessary sacrifices. That the only way to survive was to turn against the maelstrom and side with the masters.

Which of course was out of the question. Neither of us would even consider such a thing, no matter the personal cost. Besides, Nyarlathotep likely had been lying, just as it had lied to Justinian Endicott and so many others. It had been a thing of chaos, the first servant created by the masters, bound utterly to their will and their existence. Why *wouldn't* it have lied?

I only wished I knew for certain whether there was any hope for survival. Or if my time on this earth—my time with Griffin—was truly winding down. If I might hope to see Christine's child born.

Persephone's failure to propose to Miss Parkhurst had annoyed me. But perhaps she'd made the right decision after all. Would Miss Parkhurst's grief be less, than if she lost a wife?

I let out a long breath. There was no profit in such thoughts. If I could not sleep, I could at least work on decoding the fragment of the Wisborg Codex in my possession, rather than wallow in self-pity.

Though I would have preferred to stay in the fresh air, the lighting below was better at this hour, so I retired to the room that served us as parlor, library, and dining area. My notes and the tattered fragment of the Codex were secured behind a brass bar on one of the shelves, and I settled myself with them at the table.

The Wisborg Codex had been written—or perhaps copied from some older text, for all I knew—in the fifteenth century, and every replica I'd seen dated from that time. To preserve its secrets, the unknown scribe had used a complicated system of symbols, impossible to decode unless possessed of the correct key. Once decoded, the tome proved to be written in Aklo, the language used by sorcerers from medieval times on.

I lost myself in decoding and translating. Time passed without meaning, my focus entirely on the aged pages in front of me.

"What do you think, Whyborne?" Christine demanded.

I started, pencil scrawling a mark across the paper. The gray light of dawn struggled through the portholes, and my neck ached from hours spent in the same strained position. Christine and Iskander had emerged from their stateroom at some point, but I'd not even noticed their presence until she spoke.

"Think about what?" I sat back and rubbed at my neck. My eyes felt gritty, and I longed for a cup of coffee rather than tea.

Christine dropped into a chair across from me. "Narmer if the baby is a boy, and Sobekneferu if it's a girl."

"Er..."

"I'm not entirely certain about naming our child after one of the pharaohs," Iskander said as he seated himself beside her. "I thought perhaps, if it's a boy, we might honor my paternal grandfather, Murgatroyd. What do you think, Whyborne?"

Dear God. The poor child was doomed before it was even out of the womb.

Rupert Endicott chose that moment to put in his appearance, saving me from answering. "Ah, good," he said, spotting the partial

Codex and my scribblings on the table. "You're making progress, I take it?"

"I am."

"Excellent." He rubbed his hands together. "Then you can enlighten us all over breakfast."

CHAPTER TWO

riffin

WE SAT CROWDED around the small table, breakfast laid out in front of us. Whyborne had chosen only toast, a sure sign he was troubled. Beside him, Christine cheerfully shoveled eggs off her overflowing plate and into her mouth. The rest of us contented ourselves with porridge, rashers, and eggs, except for Heliabel, who nibbled delicately on a raw fish.

Though we all bore bruises and scrapes from our sojourn through Carn Moreth, my mother-in-law had taken the worst injury. Many of the stinging tendrils on the right side of her head had been reduced to blackened stumps by an Endicott sorceress. Those on the other side curled idly as she ate, her eyes fixed on her son.

"What have you discovered, Dr. Whyborne?" Rupert asked.

Whyborne sipped his tea, made a face, and set it aside. "I'll know more when I have an entire copy of the Codex in hand."

"We're quite aware of that," Christine said impatiently. "Surely there's *something* of use in this fragment, though."

Whyborne shot her a testy look. He'd never returned to bed after his nightmare in the early hours, but then, he hadn't been sleeping well ever since the events at Balefire. I'd hoped the sea voyage home might give him some chance to relax, before plunging back into his responsibilities in Widdershins, but instead he looked more worn than ever. Dark circles showed beneath his eyes, and the weight he'd put on after moving in with me had melted away as he reverted to his old habits of poor eating.

I worried about him. So much rested on his shoulders, but he'd never been one to graciously allow anyone else to help him carry it. Maybe because he'd been so alone as a child; I didn't know. I only wanted him to know the rest of us were here for him. That he didn't have to bear his burdens alone.

I slid my ankle over until it rested against his. He glanced at me; then his sour expression relaxed into a faint smile. "Hear and judge for yourself," he said.

Pushing away his toast, he gathered his notes, tapping them on the table to straighten the edges. "As we guessed from the illustrations in the full Codex, some of it is dedicated to discussing the creations of the masters. The ketoi, the umbrae, the rat-things, the Hounds of Tindalos. In addition to serving as a sort of bestiary, there's a great deal of alchemical ranting about purification."

I frowned. "I thought alchemy was concerned with turning lead into gold, or discovering the elixir of immortality." I glanced at Rupert. "Or sorcery."

Rupert looked faintly pained. "That is a common misunderstanding, I'm sorry to say. Alchemy is the art not only of transmuting the world, but transmuting the self through study. *Solve et coagula*—the dissolving of the imperfections of the soul, reducing it to its base materials, then crystallizing it anew in a more perfect form."

"And in theory, that would result in immortality?" I hazarded.

"In terms of purifying the immortal soul and reuniting with God, yes." Rupert set aside his plate and poured another cup of tea. "Much medieval alchemy is metaphor and symbol, filled with meanings only those in the know can correctly interpret. The lead is the sinning soul, transformed into the purest gold through knowledge and experimentation." He paused as he lifted his cup to his lips. "Needless to say, the alchemy I perform is far more practical, and much less influenced by the Christian concept of sin."

"Which is one of the reasons I'm confused to find so many references to purification here," Whyborne put in. He scowled at his notes, as if they might offer up answers spontaneously. "The Fideles are interested in power. They seem to believe they'll have favored status once the masters return, that they can use to rule over the rest of us. Or, in the case of Mrs. Creigh, to save at least a part of humanity through appeasement. So why is their guidebook obsessed with perfecting humanity?"

"Rupert said alchemy is veiled in metaphors known only to the initiated." I glanced from Whyborne to Rupert and back again. "Perhaps 'purification' in this context means something we can't guess."

"Who cares what the Fideles think they're going to get?" Christine asked. "The masters are the true threat here. Don't tell me we went to all the trouble to get the cipher for nothing."

"Hardly nothing," Rupert said stiffly. "Even if saving the Endicotts holds no worth to you, Nyarlathotep is no longer a threat. Not having to face it alongside the masters will surely be to our advantage."

Christine colored. "That isn't at all what I meant, and you blasted well know it."

"There is more," Whyborne said hastily, before tempers could flare any further. "As to when the masters will return, I don't know. But according to the fragment, certain events will precede their emergence into our world."

I sat forward. "That could be useful." More than useful—it would give us time to prepare, to plan, to get our forces in order before the final confrontation. "What are they?"

"I'm afraid the first part is rather cryptic once again."

"You didn't write the accursed thing, so there's no reason to apologize." Christine helped herself to Whyborne's untouched toast and began to slather it with more butter. "Out with it, then."

Whyborne didn't object to the theft; he rather seemed to have become accustomed to sharing his meals with Christine now. "There is a great deal of ranting about the return of some king. The 'Lord of All Lands, who shall awaken from his long slumber remade by the masters, and herald the coming of the new world, when all will be purified.' He will walk at the head of an army of the risen dead."

"That sounds like necromancy." Heliabel's remaining tentacles began to lash in agitation.

Whyborne nodded grimly. "Agreed, but who are the Fideles going to resurrect? Who is this Lord of All Lands?"

"We can probably assume it won't be King Arthur," she said with a faint smile.

"*Rex quondam, rexque futurus,*" Rupert murmured.

I arched a brow in Whyborne's direction, who clarified, "*King once, king to be.* And yes, I doubt whatever figure they intend to call up will be half so benign."

"Not much of a sign to look for, then, since we don't know who—or what—they wish to summon." My eggs had gone rubbery, so I pushed them aside, fork scraping against my plate.

Whyborne's mouth flexed down. "Then perhaps you'll prefer this. Once this 'king' has risen, he'll begin the subjugation of humanity. In the meantime, some sort of vanguard will gather to greet the masters and form the foremost of their army."

"So we can expect the Fideles to try for Widdershins shortly before the masters arrive." Finally, something solid, around which we could formulate a plan. When we arrived in Widdershins tonight, I'd go straight to Niles. Between the old families, the police, and the librarians, we had men enough to set a constant watch on land. Heliabel could take word to Persephone before we even touched the dock, ensuring the sea was guarded as well.

There came the sound of running feet overhead. A moment later, the hatch opened, and Basil dropped through. "There's a ketoi here," he said. "One of the Widdershins colony, I think. She wants to come aboard. She says she has a message for Fire in His Blood. That's you, isn't it, Dr. Whyborne?"

Heliabel rose to her frog-like feet, her mouth pressed into a thin line. Rupert, Whyborne, Iskander, and I hurried to rise as well. "The city is still some distance away. Persephone wouldn't have sent a messenger unless something was truly urgent," she said.

I hastened up the ladder behind Rupert and Whyborne, my mind racing. Persephone had no way of knowing we were even returning to Widdershins, and yet something so urgent had happened that she'd sent a messenger to look for us anyway. Would the messenger have swum all the way to the city of the Cornish ketoi, if need be? Surely that would be a long journey to make in haste for even the strongest swimmer among their people.

The ketoi clambered over the railing as we reached the deck. The dark swirls and markings covered more of her skin than the average ketoi, leaving behind only a small amount of pearlescent white. Her golden jewelry stood out all the brighter—as did the blood seeping from her wounds.

"Longfin!" Heliabel exclaimed. She rushed to support the other ketoi, who leaned heavily on a spear tipped with a swordfish bill.

"There's no time." Longfin's eyes were bright and wild in her dark face. "They're following me! Get ready to fight!"

The Endicotts didn't have to be told twice. The words were barely out, before they were rushing to the railings. Sorcery flared in my shadowsight, and one of them sent up a flare to warn the other ships of the flotilla.

"Who is following?" Rupert demanded. "Or should I ask: what?"

"Sings Above the Waves called them nereids." Longfin gripped Heliabel's arm in one clawed hand. "They came in overwhelming force, from every direction at once. We had no warning—sorcery must have hidden them until they were at the very boundaries of the city."

I felt as though the ship had dropped away from beneath me. The plans I'd already begun to formulate dissolved like foam. The masters' vanguard had already arrived.

"No." Whyborne swayed, his lips parted in horror.

"Other creatures attacked on the land." Longfin's dark eyes turned to his. "I'm sorry, Fire in His Blood. Widdershins has fallen."

CHAPTER THREE

hyborne

BANDS TIGHTENED around my chest until I couldn't breathe, could barely think. Longfin's words hung in the air, stealing the moisture from my mouth, the breath from my lungs, the blood from my extremities.

All the months of study, of striving; the late nights, the early mornings, the missed dinners. All the blood we'd spilled to keep Widdershins safe.

All for nothing.

"Something in the water, starboard side!" shouted an Endicott from the crow's nest above.

Griffin ran to the railing, where Hattie, Basil, Christine, and Iskander had already gathered. The salty wind blew his overlong hair back from his face, and he gripped his sword cane in one hand. "There!" he called, pointing.

"Nereids," Longfin said, readying her spear.

I could just make out three lights beneath the water, moving fast—

and heading straight for us. They broke the surface just before they struck the side of the ship, and Basil gasped.

The nereids were like ketoi in some ways, and in others utterly different. Their bodies glowed from within with a sickly green luminescence. Rather than the coiling tendrils of anemones, their heads were adorned with the stiff spines of sea urchins. Their eyes were inhumanly large, their skin uniformly pale, and their bodies pared down to move like bullets through the water.

One sank her claws into the side of the ship, beginning to tear at the wooden hull with startling strength. The other two climbed toward the railing, their mouths gaping open to reveal a forest of needle teeth, like those of a moray eel. The gills in their neck flared, then sealed away. Unlike the ketoi, they wore no decorations, no armbands or skirts of gold, and carried no weapons. Nothing existed to mark them apart from one another.

Mother's eyes widened in shock at the sight of them. Then her expression firmed. "Longfin, with me," she ordered—and launched herself over the side, at the nereid attempting to open a hole in the hull.

Longfin followed her without question or hesitation, despite her obvious exhaustion. I wanted to call out, to warn Mother to be careful, to do something—but there was nothing to be done. Mother was a sorceress in her own right; I had to trust she and Longfin would keep the nereid from sinking the ship.

The other two nereids reached the railing. Griffin lunged forward with his sword cane, but the point skittered off the creature's hide. Hattie's witch hunter's daggers whistled as they cut through the air toward the nereid's arm. Their keen edges bit deeper than Griffin's sword cane, slicing the nereid's rubbery skin and letting out a trickle of blood.

It wasn't enough.

Griffin and Hattie both dropped back as the nereid slashed at them with wicked claws. Meanwhile, the other had clambered over the railing and leapt to the deck. One of the sailors rushed it, swinging a boathook. It ducked, fast as a striking snake. Its mouth gaped wide, jaw unhinging farther than what seemed possible.

The forest of needle teeth sank into the sailor's arm, tearing away a hunk of flesh. He screamed and stumbled back. Then his screams choked off, and his body stiffened. A series of convulsions sent him to the deck, heels drumming and back arching. Basil ran to him, even as green foam formed on the unfortunate man's lips.

"Their bite is poison!" Basil shouted.

A gunshot rang out, and the nereid jerked back before it could turn its attention to Basil. Christine strode toward the nereid, rifle drawn as she chambered a second shot and emptied it into its skull. It took two tottering steps toward her—then collapsed.

The other nereid charged forward, even as Griffin, Hattie, and Iskander closed with it. My heart pounded—I had to do something before one of them was bitten or killed. They were too close to call down the lightning, and a fire on the ship might reduce us to ashes alongside the nereid. There was nothing to funnel the wind; I'd only capsize the entire flotilla if I called up a gale.

"Whyborne!" Griffin called. "Fire!"

I channeled power into the sword cane, and its blade flashed red-hot a second before he thrust it at the nereid again. With a horrible sizzle, the point penetrated the tough hide. Its jaws gaped, as though it meant to scream, but no sound issued forth.

Iskander and Hattie closed from either side, their blades flashing in tandem. Within seconds, it dropped dead to the deck.

I ran to the railing and leaned over, searching the water. Blood stained the waves, and for a terrible moment I imagined it belonged to Mother. Then she surfaced through the red cloud, blinking seawater and blood from her eyes. Longfin emerged beside her.

Thank heavens.

"The nereid fled," Mother called. "We wounded her, but not badly enough. I didn't want to risk following her into an ambush."

The other ships in the flotilla made their way across the waves, shouts ringing out as they tried to discover what assistance we needed. Rupert called back, but his words seemed to float past me, meaningless.

I turned slowly from the sea and back to the deck. The two dead nereids sprawled silent, their bodies rocking slightly along with the ship.

One by one, all eyes turned to me. Expecting answers. Or direction. Or...something.

But I had nothing to offer.

CHAPTER FOUR

riffin

"THESE...NEREIDS...AREN'T of the Outside," said the flotilla's doctor an hour later. I'd never been introduced to the man, though I'd seen him among the Endicotts on the Isles of Scilly. At Rupert's instruction, he'd conducted a hasty autopsy on the two nereids we'd slain on deck.

"We already knew that," Hattie remarked. She sat on a coil of rope, sharpening her knives. "They ain't turned to green slime, have they?"

She had a point. Creatures of the Outside, from the yayhos to the rat-things, tended to disintegrate shortly after dying in our world.

"Despite their outward differences," the doctor continued, "there are enough structural similarities between ketoi and nereid to suggest they are in fact the same species, or very closely related."

Heliabel watched the doctor with distrust. Or perhaps it was simple dislike; if he'd been dissecting ketoi, it was because they'd been captured and killed. "Then why have we never encountered them before?" she asked.

"That I can't say." He rubbed absently at his thin mustache. "I did make some observations that trouble me. The brains of ketoi have a sort of gland or organ not found in pure humans, which I theorize is what allows them to hear the dwellers in the deeps, as well as the song of the summoning stones."

Whyborne hadn't spoken since the battle, merely sat in one of the deck chairs and stared at his hands. Now he frowned and rubbed at his forehead, as though he might feel it through his skull.

"In these nereids, the gland is much enlarged. In compensation, perhaps, the areas believed to be involved with decision making and emotion are smaller than usual."

"Which implies what, exactly?" Rupert asked.

The doctor spread his hands apart. "That they could be more easily controlled by outside forces? That they hear their god more clearly? I could theorize all day, but I can't say anything for certain."

"I see." Rupert folded his arms with a sigh. "Thank you, Huang. If you could take a look at poor Donal below, I would appreciate it."

The sailor bitten by the nereid had succumbed to its poison with shocking quickness. According to Longfin, the ketoi were immune to the venom, so at least they had some advantage. But if the nereids were as numerous as Longfin had implied, Persephone's forces would have a fight on their hands no matter what.

I did my best to put aside my worries for now. The doctor took his leave, and silence settled over the deck, broken only by the creak of rope and the endless whisper of the sea against the hull. Eventually, however, Whyborne stirred.

"I'm sorry," he said. "This is my fault."

Christine perched on one of the deck chairs, enjoying a post-battle snack of toast and jam. At Whyborne's declaration, she lowered her toast to her plate. "Don't be absurd."

"I'm not." He looked up at last, but his gaze went to me rather than to Christine. "Griffin told me not to come. Father did as well. I let myself be guided by my own pride rather than their good sense. I left Widdershins undefended, at the very moment I was most needed."

The misery in his voice wrung my heart. "If you hadn't come, we would all be dead. Nyarlathotep would be alive and free to use Morgen's Needle for whatever mischief it had planned."

"And you wouldn't have the key to the Codex," Iskander added.

"For all the good it's done!" Whyborne rose to his feet, fingers curling at his sides. "Without the full manuscript, we're no better off than we were before."

I silently damned Justinian Endicott once again. If he hadn't practically handed over Balefire to Nyarlathotep, if he'd not been ruled by fear, we wouldn't have been forced to leave Widdershins. Perhaps we might have negotiated for the key months ago, and been prepared when the vanguard arrived.

But he had, and we weren't.

"We would have had no forewarning of the attacks even if you'd stayed," I said, as calmly as I could. "Persephone was there, and if she and her forces couldn't turn back the nereids, there's no reason to believe you would have had better luck on the land."

"Griffin's right," Christine put in. "On the other hand, you did leave, and we *do* have the key. We just need to get to the museum and give you time to translate the full Codex. Then we'll kick the masters back to whatever hell they crawled out of, and *finally* get back to the important things in life. By which I mean my next dig site."

A reluctant smile twitched one corner of Whyborne's mouth. "Obviously. I'm so sorry saving the world has interfered with your work."

"It has been a trial," she agreed.

I turned to Longfin. "You said other creatures attacked on the land. Do you know what they are? Or what's happening in the town itself?"

"No." Longfin crouched on the deck, her arms wrapped around her knees, her fins jutting out awkwardly. "I understand you wish to return as quickly as possible. But I have to warn you, there's some sort of difficulty with ships entering Widdershins waters. Something has caused them all to turn back."

"Magic?" Rupert speculated.

"Blast." Whyborne began to pace. "The nereid that escaped will surely alert the rest of her kind to our presence. If we counter whatever spell is keeping ships from entering Widdershins, they'll be waiting to meet us in force. Unless Persephone keeps them distracted."

The tendrils of Longfin's hair coiled restlessly. "I must return to Sings Above the Waves. Perhaps I can carry messages back and forth…?"

"That sounds risky," I said. "And not just to you. If you or another messenger was caught or killed, any plan we made would likely fall apart." I turned to Whyborne as he paced. "I think our only choice is to go overland."

Hattie cocked her head. The patch over her ruined eye gave her a piratical look. "If I was the Fideles, I'd have lookouts in neighboring towns, waiting for us to put in. The *Melusine* ain't exactly inconspicuous."

She had a good point. I considered the tactics we used back in my Pinkerton days, when much of my work consisted of tracking fugitives. "We must assume they're watching the docks and the hotels. The roads into Widdershins as well."

Whyborne stopped his pacing. "Then what are we to do?"

Rupert folded his hands behind his back. "We split up. The ships of the flotilla carrying noncombatants will turn south and seek refuge elsewhere."

It seemed we were thinking along similar lines. "I don't know how much help she can offer, but my cousin Ruth lives in Baltimore. If your people tell her I sent them, she'll do what she can."

"Thank you," Rupert said, inclining his head to me. "Some of the other ships can go north to Salem. If the Fideles are watching the docks there, they'll have a fight on their hands. Similarly, the *Melusine* will put in at Boston." He paused. "But not until after Dr. Whyborne and a few others take our remaining lifeboat and land on a stretch of coastline outside the city."

I would have preferred the Endicotts enter Widdershins with us. But so long as I was wishing, I would have preferred for none of this to have happened at all. "A sound suggestion. We can slip into Boston and go to the Pinkerton office. I have friends there, who will let me use their phone to call Whyborne House. Once we talk to Niles, we'll have a better idea of what to do next."

"Agreed." Rupert's lips thinned. "I'll call a meeting of all the captains. The *Thessalonike* is larger than the *Melusine,* so we'll gather there. In the meantime, Dr. Whyborne, choose who will go ashore with you."

"I'm going, of course," Christine said as Rupert departed. "And Kander."

"And I," I said. "Heliabel?"

She looked to her son…then shook her head. "I'm made for the sea. My place is with Persephone now."

Whyborne didn't say anything, only nodded. His gaze fixed on the waves, hiding his thoughts from me.

"I think the four of us will suffice," I said. "Iskander and I will gather what we need for the journey up the coast to Widdershins. Christine, Whyborne, I suggest you take the opportunity to rest."

Christine looked as though she wished to argue, but couldn't. "Oh, very well. Kander is much better at organizing than I am anyway."

Whyborne remained staring out at the waves as the three of us started below. "My dear? Are you coming?"

"In a bit."

I hesitated. We didn't have a great deal of time, but… "Do you want to talk?"

"Not really."

I longed to have the words to lift the unhappiness from his shoulders. "I know what I said before we left Widdershins. I argued for you to stay. But I didn't know we were going to encounter Nyarlathotep. If you hadn't gone, if it controlled the Needle still, there's no telling what damage it might do. Reweave the arcane lines to starve the maelstrom of power, or flood it to scour earth and sea of life, or something I can't guess at. You made the right choice." I paused, then added. "None of this is your fault."

He didn't answer. The wind ruffled his hair, and the sunlight shaped his beloved features. His hand rested on the rail, the black pearl of his wedding ring gleaming. I watched him for a long moment, then turned and went below, leaving him to his thoughts.

CHAPTER FIVE

hyborne

I STOOD ALONE for a long time, watching the heaving waves. Salt spray coated my lips, and the endless sea wind relieved the growing heat of the day. There came a splash as the lifeboat lowered to take Rupert to the *Thessalonike*, where he would meet with the other captains and give them their orders. The flotilla bunched together, at least for the moment, the other sailors and passengers visible as they moved about on the decks.

My heart lay so heavy in my chest, if I jumped overboard I'd surely sink straight to the bottom. There was one thing I was meant to do—that I'd been *created* to do—and I'd still managed to fail the task. None of Griffin's reassurances changed the fact that I should have been in Widdershins when the masters' vanguard attacked.

I had my army of the land, such as it was: the old families, the police, the librarians, the umbrae. But I hadn't been there to lead them. Or at least, to unite them while Father did the actual leading.

Father. He'd told me not to leave, and I'd reacted in anger. Blinded by old hurts, I'd assumed he thought me a coward, eager to remain behind while my husband and friends went into danger. I'd called him my general, then ignored his advice on strategy.

But if I hadn't gone…

Balefire would be under the control of Nyarlathotep. Morgen would be enslaved within the Needle. The Endicotts would be dead or scattered. Christine and her unborn child, Iskander, my Griffin, would all likely have died. Mother, too.

"Percival?"

I turned as Mother approached. Looking at her now, it was hard to recall her as she'd been before she took to the sea. Corseted, clad in expensive gowns on her healthiest days, or else tucked into her bed and wrapped warmly in a dressing gown. Pale and wan, unable even to go up and down the stairs without leaning on Miss Emily's arm.

In some ways, it felt like a lifetime ago. Or a strange dream, unconnected to the strong ketoi woman in front of me, with her body honed from swimming, clad only in gold mesh and jewelry. The claws that tipped her hands, the rows of shark teeth in her mouth, had drawn blood more than once.

Then I saw the fierce look in her dark eyes, and recognized it from the day she'd pressed the money to fund my scholarship into my hands and told me to follow my own path, rather than the one Father selected for me. Perhaps things weren't so different now, after all.

"Will you be going soon?" I asked.

"I fear time is of the essence, and waiting will do no one any good." Mother stopped close to me, her voice pitched to keep our conversation private. "I'm sorry I have to leave you."

My throat tightened. For a moment, I was a boy again, sitting at her side as she read from old tomes in German, Latin, Greek, or French. She was the only safety I had then, her room the only place I could be myself. Selfishly, I wanted to ask her to stay.

"My sister needs you," I said instead. "I understand."

She took my hands in her own, looking up at me. "Be careful. Or as careful as you can."

Nyarlathotep had claimed Persephone and I were fated to die.

Even if it had lied, the situation looked grim at best. There was every chance these would be my final moments with my mother.

I gripped her long fingers. "Thank you. I don't know if I ever said that before, but…thank you. For teaching me any language I wished to learn, for selling your jewelry so I could escape Whyborne House, for loving Griffin, for…well, everything."

She smiled gently up at me. "There's no need to thank me. You're my child. My wonderful, brilliant, brave son."

"I don't feel any of those things."

"I know." Her smile faded, and her look grew fierce, as if she wished me to feel as she did with all her heart. "I am so proud of you, Percival. I always believed you would do great things, and you have. And you will."

My eyes burned, and I embraced her. "I love you."

"I love you, too."

Then we parted. She stepped back, and Longfin rose to her feet. They went to the rail near the bow of the ship. Longfin leapt over the side, like an arrow fired into the water. But Mother paused, one foot on the rail, and looked back at me.

"Farewell, my knight," she said. "I believe in you."

Then she was gone.

CHAPTER SIX

riffin

As the sun sank below the horizon, we put into a salt marsh just south of Boston.

The *Melusine*'s sails had already filled with wind, thanks to Basil, and the schooner veered north and away from the coast. Making for the harbor at Boston, where they would hopefully draw the attention of the Fideles. If not, or if they defeated any cultists waiting for them, they would then turn north to Widdershins.

Whyborne stared at the retreating ship as Iskander and I rowed for shore. Christine opened the basket of food Rupert had given us and took out a wedge of cheese. "Do stop moping, Whyborne," she told him before taking a bite.

"I'm not moping." He turned toward shore, his mouth set in a pensive line.

"Worrying, then."

"I'm not worrying, either."

It was a blatant lie, and we all knew it. Iskander and I exchanged a glance, but before I could think of anything tactful to interject, Christine said, "Don't be ridiculous, man. Heliabel just swam away into danger. Of course you're worried about her." She considered a moment. "I suppose the Endicotts just sailed away into danger, but after everything they put us through, I don't imagine you're terribly concerned about them."

"Perhaps I'm concerned about *everyone*," Whyborne shot back.

"It's out of our control at the moment," Christine replied, finishing off the cheese. "Fretting won't help matters."

A small creek made its way through the marsh grass, a sandy bank beside it. It seemed as good a place as any to put in, and the bottom of the boat scraped on sand as we slid into the shallows. As I peered across the marsh, I spotted the muted glow of an arcane line stretching across it. Not an uncommon sight; though Widdershins was well on the other side of Boston, the many lines that fed into the maelstrom stretched across the landscape of New England.

I hopped out and steadied the boat. Iskander helped Christine out. Whyborne followed, still glaring at Christine. "Not all of us can simply switch off our—blast!"

He stepped back onto the narrow sandy bank, shaking the foot he'd set in the marsh. His shoe was covered from sole to ankle in unpleasant gray muck.

I winced. "Perhaps we should go barefoot and roll up our trousers."

"Thank you for the suggestion, Griffin," Whyborne snapped. He shook his shoe, trying to get the mud off, but only succeeded in flinging it onto his clothing. "Curse this place! Why did I ever leave Widdershins?"

After our years together, I'd learned when to be silent when my husband was of a mind to argue. Christine took the opposite approach.

"Don't take your foul mood out on the rest of us," she said, as she went about binding up her skirt up so it fell only to her knees. Whyborne might have kept arguing under normal circumstances, but at the sight of her calves he turned hastily away. She smirked at his back.

We tied our shoes together by the laces and slung them around our necks, to leave our hands free as we navigated the marsh. The light faded from the sky above, and fireflies appeared, bobbing over the tangled grass. A few lonely birds called, but most had bedded down in the tall grass for the night. Frogs sang stridently, falling silent at our approach, then resuming the chorus once we were past.

I lit our lantern. Even though the stretch of marsh was fairly narrow, it was hard going. The mud squelched under my toes, and dried grass stems stabbed my feet. Iskander tripped over a tussock and nearly fell. A bird flushed almost from under our feet, and Whyborne did fall over backwards in an effort not to step on it.

Christine burst out laughing, which caused Whyborne to flush scarlet. I winced. His trousers would never survive the reeking mud now smeared over them.

"Let me help you, my dear," I said, holding out my hand.

"No, thank you. I can manage myself," he muttered, determined to be churlish.

The frogs abruptly fell silent, not just around us, but all across the marsh. The hair rose on my neck, and I looked around, scanning for some sign of danger.

But this danger came from beneath.

Whyborne had only half-risen to his feet, when a tentacle burst forth from the thick mud and wrapped around his ankle, yanking him down.

CHAPTER SEVEN

hyborne

I LET OUT A STARTLED SQUAWK, and nearly swallowed a mouthful of marsh water as I was dragged rapidly backward through the grass. Griffin managed to get a grip on my wrist, but only momentarily; the thing was far too powerful.

More tentacles rose from the marsh around us, punching up through grass and watery mud. Christine ducked as one grabbed for her. Iskander's knives flashed as he sliced through it—only to be seized himself by another rubbery arm. Was each one a separate entity, or did they all belong to some terrible creature burrowed down into the mud?

I felt the arcane line as the thing dragged me over it. Was it in some fashion like the rust, a parasite that fed on magic?

I didn't know, and it didn't matter. I reached for the power flowing through the line, and it answered me like an old friend. Arcane fire flowed through me; rather than shape it into a spell, I turned myself into a conduit.

Few things could withstand the touch of raw magic. The tentacle wrapped around my ankle let go, whipping back as though burned, and the ground trembled beneath me.

My lips drew back in a snarl, and the scars on my right arm ached. Every second I wasted on this hidden thing, this lurking predator, delayed my return to Widdershins. It was keeping me from my town, it was assaulting my friends, and thanks to it, my coat and vest were ruined along with my trousers.

I lurched to my feet and flung myself on the nearest tentacle, digging my nails into its tough hide. In that moment, it seemed to stand for everything that had gone so horribly wrong, and I wanted it dead. Blind fury roared through me, accompanied by the power of the arcane line, and a distant howling filled my ears.

It tore itself away from me, ripping one of my nails. A stench like burning rubber filled the air. I tried to grab it again, but the tentacle vanished into the mud. I turned, intending to continue my assault, only to find it had given up on its attack altogether.

"Come back out, you damned coward!" I shouted. "Come back! *Come to me!*"

"*Come to me,*" something else whispered in my mind.

It shocked me back to myself. I blinked, and realized my friends were staring at me with varying levels of concern.

"Oh good," Christine said, slinging her rifle back over her shoulder. "I thought I was going to have to slap you."

I put my fingers to my temple. My head ached, and the smell of scorched cotton rose from underneath my suit coat, where my shirt had begun to char above my scars. "Please don't," I said. "I…sorry. I got carried away."

Griffin rubbed my back with one hand. "It's all right, my dear. Whatever that thing was, it's in hiding for now."

"I suggest we depart before it decides to come back out," Iskander suggested. "I hate to just leave it here, but I'm not certain we're in any position to kill it at the moment."

"Agreed." Griffin dropped his hand. "Our focus has to be Widdershins. Once all of this is over…well, I'm sure some of the Endicotts would be thrilled to dispatch it for us."

We resumed our tedious hike through the muck. "Do you think that creature was waiting here for us?" Christine asked.

"I don't see how anyone could have guessed we'd put in at this exact section of coastline." Iskander had put away one of his knives, but kept the other drawn. "Even we didn't know we were coming this way until a few hours ago."

"So it was just a coincidence?" Christine frowned. "Surely someone would have noticed a tentacle-monster living in a marsh so close to Boston, if it had been here long."

"It hasn't been." Dreadful certainty settled over my heart. "It's part of the Restoration. We stopped the rust, and the Endicotts put a halt to some other manifestations. But who knows what else the Fideles awakened to greet the return of the masters?" Miss Parkhurst had combed the newspapers daily for any hint of Fideles activities. But it seemed they'd been too good at keeping their secrets hidden. "Who knows what else we missed?"

We reached the edge of the marsh at last. Christine untied her skirt and let the hem drop to her ankles. "Nothing to be done about it now, old thing," she said. "Let's put this wretched place behind us and find a hotel. I'd say we all could use a bath."

CHAPTER EIGHT

riffin

UNFORTUNATELY, getting to Boston proper was easier said than done. We were a rather disreputable looking bunch, with our clothes covered in reeking mud. A coach and a wagon alike passed us by, the drivers giving us suspicious looks. But eventually a wagon driven by an old man nearly as filthy as ourselves halted.

"Want to ride?" he asked. "I'm on the way to Boston and could use the company, if you don't mind sharing with a few bags of potatoes. The young lady can sit up by me."

Iskander helped Christine into the front of the wagon, while Whyborne and I scrambled into the back. The burlap sacks of potatoes didn't make the most comfortable seat, but I'd endured far worse. As soon as Iskander climbed in with us, the old man clicked his tongue at the mules, and we set off.

"What happened to you, then?" he asked.

"An accident," I said before anyone else could answer. "We were boating and overturned near the marsh."

The old man shook his head. "You're lucky, young fellow. I wouldn't go into the marsh for all the money in Boston. These are strange days. Strange days, indeed."

My ears perked at his cryptic comment. "Strange in what way?"

"People disappear. People always have, I guess, but more than usual." He spat casually in the direction of the road. "Folks've seen strange lights in the sky north of Boston, along the coast. It's in all the papers; I'm surprised you haven't seen it. And Zeke's cow just gave birth to a two-headed calf. Signs of the End Times, I say."

I doubted the masters had any interest in calves, no matter their number of heads. The disappearances and lights in the sky, though...

"We've been traveling," I said, to explain our ignorance. "The lights are north of Boston, you say? What are their nature?"

"I ain't seen them myself. You'll have to read the paper." The old man glanced back at us, then turned to Christine. "Do you live in Boston, missy?"

She bridled at being called 'missy.' "Certainly not. We're from Widdershins, and—"

"What?" The old man's eyes widened, and he jerked on the reins. The mules slowed, grumbling as they did so. No doubt they wanted a comfortable stable just as badly as we wanted a hotel. "Widdershins?"

A scowl began to form on Whyborne's face, and he opened his mouth, no doubt to demand what our driver found wrong with the town. I cut him off hastily. "Not at all," I said. "You must have misheard—we were on our way to Widdershins for business. We hail from Philadelphia."

"I'm from England," Iskander added.

The old man glanced at us uncertainly, then nodded. "Aye, my hearing ain't what it used to be. But I hope you'll lend a keen ear and take my advice: don't go to Widdershins."

"Why ever not?" Whyborne demanded.

"It's always been a strange place, filled with strange people. Not an honest, God-fearing man among them, I reckon."

I stiffened, and had to force my expression to remain one of neutral curiosity. I longed to snap at him, to tell him he hadn't the slightest idea of what he spoke.

To my surprise, Whyborne's expression turned rueful. "I hear it's a horrible murder town."

Christine let out a snort of laughter, quickly covered. Our driver nodded sagely. "That it is, and always has been. Cursed since the day it was founded, if you want my opinion. But now it's gone even stranger. Some kind of electrical storm or something has settled over it. Fog so thick you can't see anything, just sitting atop the town day and night. I heard ships' compasses go crazy when they enter it, and they find themselves sailing back out to sea no matter what course they set." He spat again into the road. "The newspapers say it's just peculiar weather, but I think it's some deviltry. You should stay far away from that place if you value your souls."

The old man seemed to have exhausted the subject, and began instead to talk about potato farming. As he droned on, I leaned close to Whyborne. "It sounds as though getting back to Widdershins might be more difficult than we thought."

His mouth pressed into a tight line. "Yes. More difficult—and more urgent. We have to find out what's happening as soon as we possibly can."

"We'll go straight to the Pinkerton office." I brushed ineffectually at the mud caked on my vest. "And hope they don't throw us out on our ears."

CHAPTER NINE

hyborne

WE RODE in the potato wagon all the way into the city. I'd been to Boston, but only while passing through on the way to Threshold or Fallow, and so had experienced nothing but the train stations. The city itself proved to be as large and unpleasant as I'd expected. Even at this hour, far too many motor cars navigated the streets, vying with carriages and cabs. Music spilled from saloons, people shouted greetings at one another, and there wasn't a single cloaked figure scurrying from shadow to shadow.

I didn't want to stay here, not even for the night. I wanted to go home.

Only I was no longer certain I had a home to return to.

"What do you think is happening?" I asked, as soon as the old man rolled away.

The affable expression Griffin had worn vanished, like a mask being dropped. "I don't know. I would have preferred the chance to make ourselves more presentable, but time is of the essence. We need to get to the Pinkerton office and place a phone call to Niles."

"I hope it's not far," Christine said. "My ankles are quite swollen, and I should like the chance to put my feet up. And perhaps dinner?"

"Only a few blocks," Griffin assured her. "Though if you'd prefer to go to a hotel, I can join you all once I'm done...?"

"Don't be daft, man. I'm as anxious to learn the situation as you." Christine straightened her shoulders, as though prepared to march across the city if need be.

We walked in silence. Dread crept through my veins: what was happening at home? Had the armies of the masters engaged in wholesale slaughter? Enslaved everyone in the town? Razed Widdershins to the ground?

What had become of my friends? My father? *My cat?*

"I hope Saul is all right," I said.

Griffin started to reach for my hand, then remembered where we were, and instead clapped me on the back. "I'm certain he's fine."

"He'd better be." If anyone had dared touch a whisker on his head, I'd use every sorcerous ability I possessed to make them pay.

"He's a clever fellow," Griffin said, though I suspected he was trying to reassure himself as much as me. "And Jack wouldn't let him come to any harm."

I immediately felt foolish. "I'm sorry, Griffin. You must be terribly worried about your brother."

His green eyes darkened. "I'm doing my best not to think about it. As Christine pointed out earlier, fretting won't accomplish anything. I keep telling myself that Jack is a survivor; he won't endanger his life without need."

"Even so, perhaps you can put in a call to him at our house, once we've spoken with Father?"

"That's assuming he and Saul aren't with Niles already. It would make sense for them to take refuge in Whyborne House."

We arrived at the Pinkerton office soon after. The building was mainly dark, but there was an agent on duty, who gave us a wary look when we stepped inside. "Can I help you folks?"

Griffin approached with his hand out and a cheerful smile on his face. "Griffin Flaherty. I used to work out of the Chicago office. I'm friends with Will Andrews—he's still stationed here, isn't he?"

While Griffin talked to the agent, Christine took the opportunity to find a seat near the window. A folded newspaper had been abandoned on the chair next to her; Iskander picked it up and paged through it. After a moment, he held it out to me. "Look."

A short article near the back bore the headline: STRANGE ELECTRICAL PHENOMENA ISOLATE WIDDERSHINS.

"Our northern neighbors have long had a reputation for oddness," I read aloud, then broke off. "Oh, for heaven's sake, what is *wrong* with these people?"

"Don't mind them, Whyborne." Christine took the paper from me and continued reading: "Now it seems the weather has turned as strange as the citizens. Fog has cut off the harbor, while captains report seeing glowing lights beneath the waves. Glowing lights have also been reported in the sky by travelers along the coast roads. One weather expert says the lights may be ball lightning or Saint Elmo's fire, and that the electrical charge in the air is responsible not only for compasses failing to work near the city, but for the subsequent failure of telegraph lines."

Damn it. If the Fideles had cut the telegraph lines, they might have done the same for the telephones as well.

"Whyborne?" Griffin called from across the room.

I stood up straight and crossed to him. "Any luck?"

"Indeed." Griffin smiled at the fellow at the desk, who smiled back. "Mr. Frye has been most accommodating."

Of course he had. In my experience, Griffin could charm almost anyone when he set his mind to it. "Thank you."

"I'm always willing to help an investigation, even if the agent in question isn't one of ours anymore," Frye said, his eyes fixed on Griffin. Or rather, Griffin's lips. I restrained the urge to put a possessive hand on my husband's arm. "Follow me, and you can use the telephone in private."

Christine and Iskander joined us; I hadn't the slightest idea what excuse Griffin had given Frye for our presence and couldn't ask lest I give us away. I was a bit worried he would try to hang about after showing us the telephone, but true to his word, he excused himself after issuing an invitation to Griffin to join him for a drink as soon as his business was done.

"What a friendly fellow," Iskander said innocently once he'd left.

I frowned, and Christine guffawed. Griffin shot me a wink. "Would you like to place the call, Whyborne?"

As a matter of fact, I wouldn't. If the old farmer who'd let us ride in his wagon wanted to complain of deviltry, he ought to focus his wrath on the heinous contraption that ensured a man could no longer hide away from the rest of the world in his own home. Though I did have to admit, in this case, it was convenient.

"Assuming the telephone lines are up," I said. Iskander showed Griffin the newspaper article, while I put the receiver to my ear and spoke with the operator.

To my surprise, the call seemed to go through. The telephone rang, then rang again, before someone picked up.

"Who is this?" asked a female voice. She sounded familiar, though I couldn't think why. A maid, perhaps?

If so, an impertinent one, to answer in such a way. Fenton would be furious if he found out about her lack of manners. But I had a great deal more to worry about right now than a maid who hadn't been trained in telephone etiquette, so I only said, "This is Dr. Percival Endicott Whyborne, calling for my father, Niles Whyborne. Could you please wake him—this is a matter of urgency."

She laughed, a sound of wicked delight. "Dr. Whyborne! I must say, I wasn't expecting to hear from you. How lovely of you to call."

Recognition snapped into place, and I felt all the blood drain from my face. I'd last heard this voice on the high plains of Kansas, while we fought against the very monsters she had unleashed. "Mrs. Creigh?"

Griffin's eyes widened in horror. Iskander blanched, and Christine swore.

"Indeed," Cordelia Creigh said through the receiver. "I told you we'd meet again."

I GRIPPED the phone receiver so hard my hand ached. Cordelia Creigh was a sorceress, and a member of the Fideles. She'd unleashed the rust on Fallow, corrupting first the unfortunate inhabitants of the poor farm, and later most of the town. She'd infected Iskander and made him her slave, and used Griffin as bait in a trap meant for me.

If the rust itself hadn't turned against her, she would have happily killed us all. Instead, she'd been practical enough to form a temporary alliance, then absconded before the end of the fight, leaving behind only a note promising to see me again.

In Fallow, she'd witnessed me drawing on the arcane line and realized I was even less human than the Fideles knew. Thanks to her, Nyarlathotep had recognized the truth—that I was part of the maelstrom, a spark detached from the whole and set in flesh. If not for that, the Fideles would have had no reason to get Stanford away from the asylum he'd been locked in, or to murder members of the old families. My brother might be alive and human, instead of the horror that had befallen him.

And now she was answering the telephone in my father's house.

"What are you doing?" I demanded. "Where is Father? What have you done to him?"

She laughed again. "I'm sure you'd love to know, wouldn't you? Let's just say I have him safely tucked away." She paused. "I can make sure he stays safe, if you cooperate."

I gritted my teeth together. Blast her! I should have realized they would strike at my family first, looking for hostages. And since I'd taken most of my family with me to Carn Moreth, that left Father as the obvious target.

Dear lord, I hoped they hadn't realized Miss Parkhurst's connection with my sister. Surely they wouldn't take her if they believed her merely to be my secretary, would they? Unless they thought she might have some knowledge of my dealings.

I couldn't ask Mrs. Creigh, for obvious reasons. So I only said, "I want proof my father is alive and in good health. Put him on the telephone so he can reassure me himself."

I glanced at my companions as I spoke. Christine's eyes widened, and Iskander's face took on an expression of dismay. Griffin's look became even grimmer than before.

"You don't seem to truly appreciate the situation, Dr. Whyborne," Mrs. Creigh replied. "I hold all the cards. I offered you the chance for an alliance when we met in Fallow, and you declined. Now I fear you will pay the price."

Curse the woman. My tongue burned, longing to unleash the dark spells I'd learned from the *Liber Arcanorum*. But I didn't think they would work through the telephone wires. "What do you want?" I asked instead.

"Nothing dire. Though many among the Fideles *are* rather unhappy with you right now. I assume they're right to be? You're the reason Nyarlathotep no longer speaks to us in our dreams?"

My heart beat hard in my chest. "That's right," I said. "It's dead, by my hand." Which wasn't entirely accurate, but close enough.

The line was so silent that for a moment I thought the call had been interrupted. "That's not possible. You can't kill a god."

I grinned savagely, even though she couldn't see me. "You have no idea what I'm capable of, Mrs. Creigh. So I suggest you release my father and any other hostages immediately."

"And you have no idea what we're capable of," she shot back, but her tone was far less confident than before. "The Lord of All Lands has returned, and he is a thousand times the sorcerer you are."

The Lord of All Lands. The one the Wisborg Codex had spoken of, far, far too late.

"So you've raised some ancient necromancer," I said, but now my own voice shook. "Why should he fare any better than Blackbyrne? Than Nitocris? Than Nyarlathotep himself? They all wanted me dead, too, and yet here I stand, while they are dust."

"But we don't want you dead. In fact, we are very, very interested in keeping you alive." She paused, and I caught the faint sound of someone else speaking to her. "I'm done sparring with you," she said to me. "Surrender to us, and your father will be released unharmed. Refuse, and I'll start carving off pieces."

There came a click, and the line went dead.

CHAPTER TEN

riffin

WHYBORNE CAREFULLY REPLACED THE RECEIVER, his face the color of old milk. "They have your father," I said; that much was clear from the side of the conversation we'd heard. "Did she mention Jack?"

Bands of fear tightened my chest. When I'd asked Jack to help relocate the umbrae and join me in Widdershins, it had seemed a good idea. I could work with him, and when the chance offered itself, we could join forces to try to discover what had become of our missing brother.

I'd brought him into danger. And then I'd left him to face that danger alone, while I sailed off to Cornwall.

"No." Whyborne shook his head. "Perhaps the Fideles don't know about him, and his connection with us. She only said she had Father, and that she'd start mutilating him if I didn't surrender."

"I knew I should have shot her when I had the chance," Christine muttered. "Oh well, I packed plenty of ammunition, so better late than never as they say."

"I'm sure you'll have your chance, love." Iskander patted her on the arm. "For now, let's hear what Whyborne has to say."

"There isn't much to tell." He folded his hands behind his back. "The Fideles are in Whyborne House, answering the telephone of all things. They've captured my father and wish to capture me. They've also resurrected the Lord of All Lands the Codex speaks of."

"The one who will command armies of the dead?" Iskander shook his head. "Things are sounding worse by the minute."

"The Fideles are probably using Whyborne House as a base of operations," I said. "If that's the case, it's likely the other old families have either fled or been taken as well."

"At least Mrs. Lester has her tunnels," Whyborne said. "Though I suppose there's no way to know if she managed to reach them in time."

We were all silent for a long moment. Fear curdled my blood. What had become of Jack? Of Maggie Parkhurst? Of Dr. Gerritson and his wife? Of Mr. Quinn? Of Police Chief Tilton? Of Saul?

Whyborne's army of the land had been shattered before we even had the chance to use it.

"We're still here," I said into the silence. "On our feet and fighting. Whyborne, I hate to say it, but you can't exchange yourself for Niles."

Whyborne's lips tightened unhappily. "He'd agree."

"Don't worry, old chap, we'll rescue him." Iskander nodded determinedly. "And we have a much better chance of doing so with you than without you."

"They don't want me dead." Whyborne crossed his arms over his chest, shoulders hunched slightly.

Christine snorted. "And if you believe that, I have some lovely seaside property in Kansas for sale."

Whyborne's gaze dropped to his shoes. Something was wrong. "I'm not so certain."

Worry feathered across my nerves. "What do you mean?"

"It was something Nyarlathotep said to me. Showed me."

I didn't like this at all. But before I could ask what he meant, there came the creak of a floorboard just on the other side of the door.

Someone was listening.

I TOOK a single stride to the door and flung it open, expecting to find Mr. Frye lingering outside. A blistering lecture for allowing curiosity to overcome good sense died on my tongue.

Rather than Frye, two men and a woman stood in the hall, their bodies shining with the light of sorcery.

I stepped back, revolted by them before I even consciously understood why. At a glance, there was nothing wrong with them at all, save for the glow of magic my shadowsight betrayed. Quite the opposite, in fact: their hair gleamed in the electric light, the teeth revealed by their smiles were even and white, and no flaw or blemish touched their skin. Their features were perfectly symmetrical, and no wrinkles creased the corners of the eyes or mouths.

They should have been beautiful, but instead the overall effect was strangely horrifying. Rather than real people, they resembled the wax mannequins at the department store, roused to some mimicry of life.

The one in front smoothly raised his hand and pointed a gun at my head.

Everything happened very fast. Whyborne shouted the secret name of fire, and the gun exploded, even as I dropped to the floor. The man—the creature?—that had held it stumbled, but the expression on its now-bloody face never changed. Neither of its companions seemed at all disturbed by the fact its hand was now a mangled ruin, or that a chunk of metal protruded from one cheek.

"What's wrong with them?" Christine exclaimed.

"Sorcery." I rolled to my feet, my sword cane in my hand as the three charged at us.

The other two were armed with knives. The one that had tried to shoot me swung its bloody fist at my face, and I ducked. "Stop, and we won't kill you!" I ordered.

"Dr. Whyborne, come with us," it said in a flat, emotionless voice.

"Come with us, Dr. Whyborne," repeated the other two, even as they attacked Christine and Iskander.

Whyborne's eyes went wide with revulsion. "Devil take you," he said, and laid frost on their skin.

It must have hurt, but they didn't so much as flinch. Surely they were minions of the Fideles, some new horrors attempting to masquerade as humans. I stabbed my attacker with my sword cane; it made an odd gurgling sound, and blood came out of its mouth before it collapsed. Christine's rifle was of no use at such close quarters, so she drew her cudgel, bashed the knife out of another's hand, then hit it on the head repeatedly, until it fell to the floor and stayed there. The third never stood a chance against Iskander's knives.

It was over very quickly. We stood unmoving for a moment, the only sound that of our breathing. Then I hurried out to the front room, to check on Mr. Frye.

As I'd feared, he was dead, his throat cut so blood covered his desk. I swore. He'd seemed a good man from our brief acquaintance, and he'd still be alive if we hadn't brought trouble to his door.

Curse the Fideles. How many innocent lives had they already ruined? And how many would follow, if the masters returned?

"Griffin." Ival put a hand to my arm. "We need to get out of here. If we're found covered in blood, with a dead Pinkerton…"

"There's nothing we can do for him, old chap," Iskander said gently.

"Except get ourselves arrested for his murder." Christine took out a handkerchief and carefully wiped the blood from her cudgel. "Which won't help anyone."

"You're right." I shook myself. "Let's go."

We stepped out onto the sidewalk and nearly collided with a cloaked figure.

"Widdershins," she said. "I've been waiting for you."

CHAPTER ELEVEN

hyborne

"More Fideles," Christine said, smacking her cudgel against her hand.

"I assure you, I am not." The figure threw back the hood of her cloak, revealing a bony face with strange, silvery eyes. Her black hair was drawn back into a severe bun, and a pair of spectacles perched on her nose. "I'm here to help you, in fact."

There was something naggingly familiar about her. "Who are you?"

"Xanthia Quinn Rodgers." She drew herself up. "My brother is the Head Librarian. I'm here to offer my assistance."

"How did you find us?" Griffin asked suspiciously.

"I've kept an eye on the Pinkerton office, ever since…" She glanced about, nostrils flaring. "Nothing I wish to speak of in the open. Suffice it to say, my brother knew you'd made use of them before, and that you likely would again if you came to Boston. Now, if you have no more foolish questions, follow me."

No one moved, but I felt their eyes on me. I knew Xanthia Quinn —or Mrs. Rodgers, I supposed—had left Widdershins many years ago, and that Mr. Quinn still visited her. As for why she'd left, I couldn't imagine; it wasn't something Widdershins natives did very often.

She would have known about the prophecy and the maelstrom. Perhaps she simply didn't care to be collected, and leaving Widder-shins for Boston had been her way of refusing to participate in the maelstrom's plans. I almost envied her for having the choice.

"Very well," I said. "Lead the way."

THE HOUSE WAS small but neat from the outside. Flowers sprouted in pots on the steps leading up to the front door, and each window box sported a rainbow of blooms. The scent of jasmine perfumed the air.

It was nothing at all like the boarding house Mr. Quinn resided in, or even the simple homes on the street Griffin and I lived on. There, one could count on the privacy of a hedge, or drawn curtains, not this...exposure. The houses to either side were almost identical to Mrs. Rodgers's, with little to set them apart one from the other. It seemed subtly wrong to me in a way I couldn't entirely articulate.

The one or two people we encountered on the street outside were terribly rude, staring with open curiosity at Mrs. Rodgers even though she wore a cloak with the hood pulled up to conceal her face. That sort of behavior would never do in Widdershins; no one wore a cloak in the middle of the summer to be *looked at,* for heaven's sake.

The front door wasn't even locked; she simply opened it and beck-oned us inside. I glanced at Christine, who shook her head. "It reminds me of parts of Philadelphia," she whispered as we made our way up the steps.

No wonder she'd left.

As soon as we were inside, Mrs. Rodgers shut the door behind us and pulled off her cloak. The parlor opened immediately to the right; I glanced inside and started badly.

Two girls, perhaps six or seven years of age, stood in the parlor staring at me unblinkingly. They were absolutely identical and dressed in matching frilly dresses. Each held the hand of a golden-haired doll, which hung between them limply.

"Er," I said. I'd never been certain how to behave around children.

"Hello," one of them said. She had the silvery eyes that seemed to run in the Quinn family; they reminded me uncomfortably of mirrors.

"Rose, Lily, it's past your bedtime," Mrs. Rodgers said.

"We wanted to see Widdershins," the second twin announced. They finally blinked, though in perfect unison, so it wasn't much of an improvement.

I didn't want to imagine what Mr. Quinn might have told them about me. I glanced desperately at Griffin, who bent over and smiled at the girls.

"We met before, do you remember?" he asked.

"We remember," one said.

"It was our birthday," added the other.

"We're twins."

They both looked at me, then. "You're a twin, too. But not like us."

"No," I agreed firmly. "Not like you."

"To bed," Mrs. Rodgers told them. "The rest of you, follow me."

"Are you going to the basement?" one of the girls asked with glee. "We want to go to the basement, too!"

"Bed!"

They both stuck out their lower lips, but obeyed their mother. As Mrs. Rodgers led the way toward the back of the house, Griffin leaned over to Christine and murmured, "Perhaps they can be playmates for your child."

She thumped him hard on the arm.

We reached the kitchen, and Mrs. Rodgers stopped and turned abruptly to me. "I wish to make one thing clear, Widdershins." Her eyes locked with mine. "This wasn't what I wanted for my family. I'm not one of your cultists, so do not think I will obey you blindly the way my brother does."

"I never asked for a cult of book-wielding librarians!" I exclaimed.

Quite the opposite; the only thing I'd really ever wanted was to be left alone and allowed to do my job at the museum. "And it's Dr. Whyborne, not 'Widdershins,' if you please."

Skepticism sharpened her silvery gaze. "I love Xanthius, but he will never understand my decision to leave Widdershins behind."

"Xanthius? Is that Mr. Quinn's first name?" Christine asked, before turning to Iskander. "It's Greek. Do you think…?"

"Good heavens, no!" Iskander exclaimed in horror.

She frowned thoughtfully. "I suppose not. What do you think about Bellerophon?"

"Not now, Christine," I said. "Mrs. Rodgers, I have no desire to impose on you or your family, and I quite understand Widdershins isn't for everyone. You have every right not to be collected by the maelstrom if you don't wish to be."

She seemed surprised by my words. "And my daughters?"

"That's their decision, once they're old enough." I could more easily imagine them skipping through the Draakenwood, picking up skulls, than playing…whatever it was that children played in Boston. It seemed impolitic to say aloud, however, so I kept the opinion to myself.

She didn't look happy at my words, but only said, "The problem is, they have to live long enough to grow up. I may not want to return to Widdershins, but I'm not a fool. Xanthius has sent me any number of hints in his letters, but I only recently found out just how dire the situation is."

Griffin cocked his head. "And how did you learn that?"

Mrs. Rodgers opened the pantry door, shoved aside some sacks of flour—and swung open a trapdoor, presumably leading into the basement. "The answer to your question is down there."

I CAUTIOUSLY DESCENDED the steps into the basement. Spells tingled on my tongue, and I readied myself to either leap forward or sound the retreat. It wasn't that I didn't trust Mrs. Rodgers, but my general experience with underground spaces had been less than ideal, to say the least.

But this time, a sense of odd familiarity swept over me as soon as I glimpsed the room. The warm glow of a lantern greeted us, offsetting the cool air of the stone basement. Rather than the jars of preserves one might expect, these walls were lined with shelves, each one of them packed with books. Some of the tomes had modern bindings, but others were of cracked leather, or aged wood, or bound with iron hinges. We might have been in one of the Ladysmith library's more distant chambers, the air full of muted whisperings whose origins could never be traced.

The space was provided with a desk and chair; a flask sat on the desk, beside the remains of someone's dinner. There was also a small pallet against one wall, a bundle of blankets and pillows that looked hastily put together.

A young man propped himself up on the pallet, blinking owlishly as he fumbled on his silver-rimmed spectacles. His golden hair was in disarray, his clothing stained with dust, ink, and blood. A crude splint encased the lower part of his right leg. When he caught sight of me, he let out a gasp. "Widdershins! You're here."

I was truly weary of being called that. "It's Dr. Whyborne, please," I said. "And you are...?"

A light blush spread over his face. "Sebastian Rath, Junior Librarian, at your service. Mr. Quinn sent me here. His nieces said you'd come."

Prophetic children. Wonderful. What would we encounter next?

Griffin stepped past me. The lantern light caught on a strand of silver amidst his hair, and the strain of the last weeks showed in the fine lines around his eyes. "What's happening in Widdershins? Why did Mr. Quinn send you here?"

Mr. Rath struggled to sit up, wincing as he did so. "Do you know— but if you're here in Boston, you must know something."

I gestured impatiently. "A ketoi told us Widdershins has fallen to the vanguard of the masters. The Fideles are in control of Whyborne House and have my father hostage."

Father would be fine. He'd survived the War Between the States, he'd survived Blackbyrne, survived being captured and tormented by my brother. Likely, he was even now driving Mrs. Creigh mad with his implacable demeanor and imperious demands.

He'd be fine.

"Oh dear." Rath paled. "I'm terribly sorry, Dr. Whyborne. I didn't know that."

"Then what do you know?" Christine demanded. "Stop dawdling, man!"

"It began at the museum," he said hastily. "Or at least, things went wrong at the Ladysmith very close to the same time as the creatures appeared."

"The nereids?" Iskander asked, at the same moment I said, "The museum?"

My heart twisted at the thought of something befalling the Lady-smith. True, I'd confronted monsters and cultists before in its halls, but it was still far more dear to me than Whyborne House ever could be. Not to mention the irreplaceable collections. "Please tell me none of the artifacts or specimens were damaged."

Christine paled. "My work!"

Rath glanced between us, confused. Griffin held his hand up. "In order, if you please, Mr. Rath. Tell us what you saw and heard. The rest of you, let him speak."

Rath bit his lip. Exhaustion aged his features, but he was likely a decade younger than myself. I strove to recall if I'd noticed him among the librarians, but no memories came.

"I haven't been a librarian—junior librarian—for long," he said. "But I was born and raised in Widdershins, and getting the job was a dream come true."

"Poor fellow," Christine muttered to me. I shushed her.

"I was in one of the more distant rooms, returning books and making certain the shelves were ordered properly, when I heard… no, not heard." His thin lips pressed together. "I *felt* it in my bones. Like thunder so distant it reaches the nerves but not the ear. The air seemed to shift somehow—perhaps a change in pressure, I couldn't say, only that everything felt different somehow. Off."

Griffin's green eyes sought mine, but I had no answers for him. No doubt magic was involved, but that much was obvious.

"I stopped what I was doing and hurried to the more trafficked parts of the library, to see if I was needed. My fellow librarians ran past me—in the opposite direction. I grabbed one and was told Mr. Quinn had ordered them to evacuate to the tunnels."

"The tunnels Blackbyrne used?" I interrupted. "I thought those were sealed off."

Rath's expression grew pained. "Mr. Quinn would never let such a resource go to waste."

"Of course." How could I have imagined the Head Librarian would simply look the other way, when there were tunnels filled with unknown horrors to be explored? He'd probably sent some other hapless junior librarians to do it.

"I probably should have gone with them, but I didn't wish to run away the first time I was asked to confront danger. I missed the action in the Draakenwood, you see." His mouth curved into a rueful smile. "I should have listened more closely to the other librarians' stories. If I had, I would have realized just how bad the situation must be, if Mr. Quinn ordered us to flee rather than fight."

I wasn't certain if Rath was brave, or simply a young fool. "Go on."

"Yes, Wid—Dr. Whyborne." Behind the lenses of his spectacles, Rath's eyes were a murky shade of hazel. "I left the library in search of Mr. Quinn. People were running, some shouting about a fire, others about an earthquake." Christine clutched my arm at the mention of fire, her grip hard enough to bruise. "The guards were busy trying to get the visitors out safely."

"What about Miss Parkhurst?" I asked, a new fear crowding out my worry for the exhibits.

Rath shook his head. "I can't say. I didn't see her, for whatever that might be worth."

Very little, blast it. "She's a sensible woman," Griffin reassured. "I'm sure she left at the first sign of trouble."

I might have believed him, but the very fact she'd taken up with my sister cast doubt on her sensibility. But there was no point saying that, certainly not in front of Rath.

"Dr. Gerritson finally said he'd seen Mr. Quinn near the Isley Wing earlier." Rath went on. I felt Christine tense beside me. The Isley Wing had been built to exhibit a selection of the artifacts from her Nephren-ka excavation, including the ancient pharaoh's mummy. If the Fideles had damaged the collection, she wouldn't rest until every last one of them were dead. "So I made my way there. That's when... when I saw it."

His face took on an ashen hue. Griffin took the flask from the desk and passed it silently to Rath. Rath managed a grateful smile and took a swig from the flask.

"They were at the entrance to the Isley Wing," he said, his voice rough from the alcohol. Or from remembered fear. "Dr. Hart. Some of the guards. Men and women in horrible masks."

"The Fideles," Griffin murmured. "We've seen them."

"And *he* was there, too." Rath swallowed, Adam's apple jumping in his throat. "His flesh stained by ancient resin, desiccated by natron, the skin cracking as he moved. His face...he *had* no face that I could see. Only the featureless funerary mask, fused to the skull."

All the hair on my arms stood up, but it was Christine who spoke. "What...what are you saying?"

Rath bowed his head. "Nephren-ka, the Sorcerer-Pharaoh, has risen from the dead."

CHAPTER TWELVE

hyborne

"The Lord of All Lands, who shall awaken from his long slumber remade by the masters, and herald the coming of the new world, when all will be purified," I quoted through numb lips. "It was Nephren-ka the Codex referred to."

"No." Christine straightened her back, her eyes blazing. "No, you're quite wrong. Mr. Rath is confused by what he saw."

"I assure you, I'm not," Rath protested.

"You have to admit, Christine, it does make sense." I turned to her. "Nephren-ka worshipped Nyarlathotep as a god. And remember what you always said—his tomb was designed as though to keep something *in*, rather than tomb robbers out."

"I know what I said," she snapped. "But you're wrong. We'll get back to the Ladysmith and find him lying peacefully under glass, just as he has been ever since he went on exhibit. It was some other mummy Mr. Rath saw."

The librarian's brows drew together. "I've viewed the funerary mask, and I'm certain I recognized it."

"Exactly." For once, all the hours Christine spent in my office were paying off. "Remember, Christine, how you always said it was incredibly unusual for the period? Other Sixth Dynasty mummies only have a plaster covering, whereas Nephren-ka had an actual gold mask, if a simple one. And—"

Christine rounded on me, one hand on her belly, the other curled into a fist. "I know what I said! But you're wrong. It can't be Nephren-ka, because I brought him to Widdershins. I didn't invite some unholy monster into the heart of the museum I love! I didn't fight my way through university, didn't climb over every barrier men placed in my path, didn't leave my family and abandon Daphne, only to unleash something that will kill us all!"

Oh. I fell silent, unsure how to respond. Because it sounded as though that's exactly what had happened.

"Christine, love," Iskander said softly. He put his hand on her shoulder, but she shook it brusquely off. Her eyes glittered with tears of fury, or anguish, or both.

"This is all your fault, Whyborne." Her voice cracked, but she soldiered on. "Your precious maelstrom *collected* me, after all. If it had just…had just left everything alone, Nephren-ka would still be in Egypt."

"That isn't fair," Griffin objected.

Iskander glared at him. "Nor is it fair to blame my wife."

"No one is blaming her."

"As though none of you are thinking it," she snapped at Griffin. "'Look at the woman, who should have stayed out of a man's field, and left well enough alone!'"

I couldn't take it anymore. The arguing sawed at my nerves, even as Griffin replied, and Iskander shot back something angry drowned out by the blood rushing in my ears. "Stop this!" When no one so much as looked at me, I gave up all pretense at decorum. "I said, *stop this!*"

The house above us creaked and groaned, and wind suddenly

gusted from nowhere, scattering the papers from the desk across the floor. The flame in the lantern flared, the glass cracking from the sudden heat.

Silence fell. I'd gotten their attention, at least.

"Now isn't the time to turn against one another." I folded my arms across my chest. "Iskander, Griffin, there's no need to lash out. We aren't enemies. And Christine, be reasonable: no one is blaming you for any of this. None of us are even thinking it."

She lowered her eyes. "Perhaps I am," she said in a small voice.

My heart contracted painfully. "Then continue to blame me instead." I'd rather she turn her anger on me than herself.

"Don't be ridiculous." She wiped angrily at her eyes. "Finding the tomb of Nephren-ka was my greatest triumph. I thought I'd showed everyone who doubted me that they'd been wrong. I wanted to wipe the sneers off the faces of the men who told me I didn't belong in archaeology. And I did, at least for a while. To find my victory led to this…how can I ever be proud of anything again?"

"If I hadn't insisted on going to Balefire, the Fideles might never have dared approach the museum and raise the pharaoh," I replied. "There's plenty of blame and guilt to go around. Let's just…just concentrate on what we can do now to fix things."

She nodded miserably. Iskander wore a stricken look on his face, as though he wanted very badly to make her feel better, but had no idea how to do so. When no one said anything further, I turned back to Rath, who sat quietly on his makeshift bed. "What happened then?"

Rath had kept politely silent during our conversation. He tensed at my question, then shook his head slowly. "Dr. Hart had brought some guards to try and stop Nephren-ka and the Fideles. One of the guards was dead—there was too much blood for him to have survived—but even as I watched, he got to his feet and attacked the man next to him."

"The Codex said Nephren-ka would walk at the head of an army of the dead," I murmured. "For every one of our people he kills, he gains a new soldier."

Rath looked ill. "So it would seem. From the shadows of the Isley

Wing, behind Nephren-ka, I saw...things moving. A creature that was nothing more than a mismatch of disparate parts—crocodile and lion and I don't even know what else. And things that had to be dead, because surely nothing could survive with so much dissected from it. Let alone walk, though walk they did."

God. "And Mr. Quinn?"

The corner of Rath's mouth lifted slightly. "He saved my life, I think. I would probably have stood there, frozen like a fool, until they noticed me. Mr. Quinn grabbed me from behind—one hand over my mouth, thank heavens, or I would have screamed my lungs out. We fled, back to the staff areas. Once there, he told me he meant to escape into the tunnels, with the Codex. But he wanted me to come here, to his sister's house. To carry word outside of Widdershins."

And to do the bidding of the prophetic children, no doubt. "I see."

"He asked me to remind Mrs. Rodgers of her heritage. I believe he hoped his sister would help me get word to you."

"What happened to your leg?" Griffin asked.

Rath's lips thinned with remembered pain. "Mr. Quinn and I parted near the library. I made for the staff exit near the rear of the museum. I was shocked to find the streets outside were as chaotic as the interior of the Ladysmith. Fideles were everywhere, and there were terrible creatures in the sky. They reminded me of drawings I've seen of the umbrae, except these glowed from within with light."

Iskander glanced at me. "The nereids are like warped ketoi. Could these creatures be some mockery of umbrae?"

"Lumina," Christine suggested. "Lights rather than shadows."

"I tried to blend in," Rath said. "The police were trying to get people inside, to safety. I don't know if the old families rallied, or if the attack was too unexpected. I stole a horse and almost made it to the coast road, when a cultist shot at me." He reached toward his leg, as if to rub it, then caught himself. "Thank God he didn't hit the horse, or I'd be dead. It took off at a gallop, and I clung to its back until it ran itself out. By the time I made it here, I'd taken a fever. Mrs. Rodgers hid me down here, and, well, here I am." He hesitated, his eyes canting toward me, then away. "I executed the Head Librarian's orders to the best of my abilities, Dr. Whyborne."

I rubbed at my eyes. I wanted to collapse into sleep. To wake up at home, in Griffin's arms, to find this had all been a dream.

"You did well, Mr. Rath," I assured him.

"I'll come with you to Widdershins, though with my leg in a splint, I don't know how much good I'll do."

I dropped my hands. Rath's eyes were wide behind the reflection of the lantern in his spectacles. Broken leg or not, he'd come with me if I asked it.

"Why?" I asked abruptly.

He frowned a little. "Why…?"

"Any of this!" I gestured vaguely to myself. "You sound as though you knew the librarians were some kind of-of cult devoted to the maelstrom, but you still wished to join their ranks. You saw horrors unleashed in the museum, in the very streets of our home, but you still offer to go back on nothing more than my say-so. *Why?*"

Why me? was what I really wanted to say. As I'd told Mrs. Rodgers, I'd never asked for an army of librarians. I'd never asked for any of this.

Confusion drew Rath's brows together. "*Widdershins always knows its own,*" he quoted. "*In blood and spirit, breath and bone.*" He shrugged uncomfortably. "Widdershins is my *home.* My family. That I'm there… that I'm a librarian…it isn't a mistake."

As an answer, it was spectacularly unsatisfying. But it was probably the best I'd get from him. "Very well, Mr. Rath," I said resignedly. "You should get some rest. As for us, I suppose we'll retire back upstairs and find our dinner."

I glanced at Christine as I spoke. But for the first time in a while, the prospect of food didn't seem to cheer her. I longed to say something to lift her spirits, but I couldn't find the words. Instead, I trailed after her up the stairs and back into the house above.

CHAPTER THIRTEEN

riffin

"You're fortunate my husband is out of town for the night," Mrs. Rodgers said as she bustled about the table. "Otherwise, you'd have to stay in the basement with Mr. Rath."

"Thank you for your hospitality," I said, taking the bowl of stew she ladled out for me. "I'm afraid we've put you to quite a bit of trouble."

"Not as much trouble as the end of the world will put me to," she replied grimly. "Now, if I'm not needed at the moment, I'm off to bed. After I make sure Lily and Rose have stayed put in theirs, of course."

"We'll wash up when we're done," Iskander offered.

She nodded and retreated up the stairs. "A fascinating woman," I remarked when she was gone. "Though I suppose I would have expected nothing less of Mr. Quinn's sister."

Whyborne only grunted in response. No one else spoke, either, which made supper into a gloomy affair.

God knew, we had enough to be gloomy about. Niles captured; monsters openly roaming the streets of Widdershins; nereids battling ketoi; Nephren-ka risen from the dead.

When we'd stood together on the sands of Egypt, Christine had spoken of the curses inscribed on the tomb of Nephren-ka, threatening him should he dare to return to the land of the living. At the time, I'd questioned the wisdom of having removed him from their safeguards, but that seemingly small worry had been buried beneath so many more immediate concerns. I'd not thought of it in years, and I'd wager none of the others had, either.

Christine's usual determination seemed to have faltered, and she ate mechanically. Whyborne stared at his stew, absently poking at it with his spoon without actually sampling it. Even Iskander was withdrawn, his brown eyes troubled. His family were monster-hunters, slayers of ghūls, and yet he'd helped Christine excavate Nephren-ka's tomb. Did he feel he'd betrayed his legacy?

Enough wallowing. It was time to plan.

"We must leave for Widdershins as soon as possible." I took a roll from the basket Mrs. Rodgers had left and began to butter it briskly. "The Fideles will certainly be keeping a watch on the roads and rail lines for Whyborne's return. Therefore, I suggest we hire horses from the local livery stable and go cross-country, where we're less likely to be spotted."

"Must we?" Whyborne asked. He wasn't much of a rider.

"At least it's horses and not camels, my dear."

Iskander roused himself. "A good suggestion. Mr. Rath said Mr. Quinn meant to take the Wisborg Codex into the tunnels. Does anyone know where these tunnels lead to?"

"They could join to the ones beneath Miss Lester's house," Whyborne suggested.

"Let's hope not," I said. "Miss Lester isn't just one of the old families; she's ghūl-blooded. Recall that Nephren-ka was none too fond of their kind. One way or another, she'll surely be high on the Fideles' list of people to capture or kill."

Iskander looked faintly pained—it wasn't easy for him to ally with the sort of creature his family had fought for centuries—but said, "Miss Lester is no fool. Likely she'll have taken to the tunnels herself, when the attack began."

"Possibly." I toyed with my bread roll, ripping it into chunks rather than eating it. "I suggest we make for the Draakenwood. The umbrae won't have surrendered it to the forces of the masters, no matter what. They can fit through tiny cracks and see—well, sense—in the dark. They could be our best bet when it comes to finding the librarians."

"Assuming the Fideles haven't discovered them already," Whyborne said glumly. He buttered his own roll, then handed it to Christine without bothering to take a bite. "Mr. Quinn could be a prisoner alongside Father. Or dead, since I doubt Mrs. Creigh thinks he has much value as a hostage."

"I have a question," Christine said. "Mrs. Creigh originally tried to strike an alliance with Whyborne, but when he wouldn't comply, she was more than happy to leave him for Marion to kill. Stanford and his Fideles allies certainly intended to murder both Whyborne and Persephone. So why are they, and Mrs. Creigh, suddenly so concerned about taking him captive instead?"

I nodded slowly. "You'd think they'd do the opposite. Trapping a powerful sorcerer must surely be dangerous in and of itself. Trapping a fragment of the maelstrom, created to thwart their plans, seems like self-defeating madness." I turned to my husband. "Ival? Do you have any thoughts?"

He drew in a long breath, as though he meant to speak. Then it escaped him in a sigh, and his shoulders slumped. "Nyarlathotep didn't want to kill me, either. Not at first."

This was something I hadn't known. Though it did explain why he'd still been alive for us to rescue atop Balefire. "Why?"

Whyborne bit his lip. Then his dark eyes darted up to meet mine from across the table. "It seemed to believe that, in order for the masters to be defeated...Persephone and I have to die."

~

"RIDICULOUS," I said automatically. "It was lying to you, in order to get you to cooperate with it."

"It certainly lied to Justinian," Whyborne agreed. "It tried to convince me that the maelstrom had created us to be sacrificed in some fashion. It said joining forces with the masters was the only way for us to survive."

My palms went clammy, and my heart pulsed at the base of my throat. "That's absurd. Surely you didn't believe it?"

He lifted one shoulder in a half-shrug. "It didn't matter what I believed. I wasn't going to throw away the entire world just so I could live."

Christine watched him closely. "But you did—you do—believe. Honestly, Whyborne, use your head. Nyarlathotep only wanted you to work with it, so it could use you to control the maelstrom. Just as it meant to use Stanford in the Draakenwood."

"It was quite clear on that point, actually." Whyborne sat back, staring down at his hands. The black pearl on his wedding ring gleamed with hidden color in the light. "But with Nyarlathotep gone, no one remains to use me, or Persephone, to control the maelstrom. The Fideles certainly can't manipulate arcane energy in such a fashion."

I shuddered at the memory of Nyarlathotep's many limbs plucking at the arcane lines themselves. "So we have no need to worry about that, at least."

"And yet the Fideles are still trying to take me alive." He slid his hands back and off the table, into his lap. "Maybe they mean to torture me into working for them, I don't know. But I can't help but think Nyarlathotep wasn't lying, or if it was, it told them the same untruth. They don't want to kill me, because they don't want to risk fulfilling the destiny the maelstrom had planned."

No. No, I would not believe the maelstrom—the entity, the consciousness—that had brought Ival and I together would be so cruel. "It hasn't done all of this work, all of this planning, just to-to throw you away!"

"I'm sure it has no intention of throwing me away," Whyborne replied, an edge to his voice. "It isn't *human*, Griffin. It collected Blackbyrne as much as it collected you. Whatever morality, whatever plans, it has, we can't count on them being kind to us."

"I've heard enough." Christine pushed back from the table. "Whyborne, you are *not* going to die, do you hear me? My child needs its godfather, so you're just going to have to find some other way of defeating the masters, one that doesn't require some absurd sacrifice on your part."

Though her words were bold, I detected in them the same feeling that squeezed my own lungs and thickened the blood in my veins.

Fear.

If winning against the masters came at the price of losing my dear, my love, my husband, my Ival, how could I bear to pay it?

"The Wisborg Codex," Iskander said. "That's where the answers lie. It will tell us how to defeat the masters and keep Whyborne and Persephone safe."

He was right, of course. "We have to focus on getting back to Widdershins and finding Mr. Quinn," I said. "Nyarlathotep's lies, the Fideles' actions, are just a distraction from the only goal that matters."

I spoke with as much certainty as I could, as if my words alone could bend the universe to my will. But I was no sorcerer.

"You're right, all of you. There's no sense in worrying about any of this now," Whyborne said. But the faint smile he gave me failed to reach his eyes.

CHAPTER FOURTEEN

 hyborne

I WAS ALONE.

Utterly alone. Where once there had been voices singing to me, a great bustle of life enveloping me, now there was nothing. Silence. Darkness. Cold.

Flickers traveled to me, borne from distant lands. There was life out there, and the more I became aware of it, the more I ached to be a part of it.

I opened my eyes and found myself in a wild river valley. Dimly, I recognized the river and the coast line where it emptied into the sea. This was the Cranch, which ran through the very heart of Widdershins.

Only there was no Widdershins here. Only trees, and birds, and wind, and silence. Overgrown fields, and empty houses, their inhabitants slain decades ago by the diseases that swept through like wildfire.

I had not really understood loneliness until now. I hadn't understood anything at first, but gradually concepts had built one atop the other. Purpose. Home. Need.

Grief.

Fear.

I didn't want to be alone any more.

Those flickers of life, some almost too distant to feel, drew me. Some of them were cruel and hard, though not all. I sensed their jumbled desires, most of them so very alien to my own, but one I recognized all too well.

They wanted a tool, just as the masters had wanted a tool. I could be that tool. And if I was…

No matter what the outcome, I wouldn't be alone anymore.

"Come to me," I said.

I BLINKED awake and found a pair of identical faces staring down at me.

I let out a muffled shriek, my sleep-fogged mind scrambling to remember where I was and what was happening. An instant later, recall returned: I was lying flat on my back on the couch of Mrs. Rodger's parlor. Only the faintest dawn light showed around the curtains, but it was enough to illuminate Lily and Rose's curious features.

"Uncle Xanthius says you're part of something very old," one said. I hadn't the first clue which was which, and wouldn't have even if both girls hadn't had their hair in braids and worn identical white dresses.

"Er, yes," I said. "Does your mother know you're up at this hour?"

They ignored my question, perhaps considering the answer too obvious to bother verbalizing. "Do you know what I think?" one asked the other.

Her sister nodded. "They didn't know what they were making."

"They didn't know with the ketoi, either. Or the shadows."

"They knew," the other objected. "They merely underestimated."

She peered down at me. "They had no place in their plans for *you*, though. I wonder what they'll do?"

Good heavens. Surely all children weren't this odd, were they? I'd been sickly at their age, my world largely confined to Whyborne House, and my only society with those close to my own age had been with my sibling's friends. Stanford's had joined in his torment of me, and Guinevere's with her mockery, so I'd been more likely to hide than socialize. What if Christine's child proved to be this inscrutable?

"You mean the masters?" I sat up cautiously, and they stepped back in unison. "Not to disparage your mother, but none of this seems at all an appropriate subject for such young children."

"Mother doesn't know how much the bones tell us," the one on the right explained.

I started to ask what she meant, then decided I was likely better off not knowing. "Er, of course." I cast about, looking for rescue, but the chair where Griffin had slept was empty. Christine and Iskander had taken the spare room with its bed. "Even so, perhaps you should concern yourselves with..." I tried to remember what I'd done for pleasure at their age "...translating the classics from Greek? Or building altars in the garden?"

"Oh, that does sound like fun," said the one on my left. "Let's build an altar beneath the roses, where Mother won't see it."

The two girls scampered off, and I relaxed. At least they now had an ordinary, wholesome childhood activity to occupy their minds. Perhaps I'd be a better godfather to Christine's child than I'd thought. Assuming I survived, anyway.

The front door opened, and Griffin entered. "You know," I said, "it seems to me, the key to handling children is to distract them."

He eyed me curiously. "I'm afraid to ask."

"Just thinking about the future." I stood up and retrieved my coat from where it hung over the back of a chair. I'd brushed it before retiring last night, but the stains would likely never come out. "About Christine's baby."

Griffin's expression softened. "How so?"

"What it might be like. Do you imagine it will be similar to Lily and Rose?"

"I doubt anyone is quite like them," Griffin said with a smile.

Perhaps that was for the best. Still, I hadn't given much thought to the fact Christine's offspring would eventually be, well, a person. One who might look to me, as I'd once looked to my own godfather, Addison Somerby.

Of course, Addison had ultimately betrayed us all and almost brought about the end of the world. Even if I died in the upcoming battle, I'd do a better job than him.

My hands tightened on my coat. Last night, everyone had been determined to assure me I'd survive, that Nyarlathotep had been lying.

I hoped they were right. But I'd made my choice atop Carn Moreth, when I realized it wasn't enough anymore to simply fight to keep what I had. The world would go on without me, one way or another. It was my duty to secure the best possible world for Christine's child, and my young nephews, and everyone else who would have to live in it.

"I've hired our horses," Griffin said.

I blinked, realizing I'd been woolgathering. "Thank you."

He cocked his head. "Are you all right? You aren't still thinking about dying, are you?"

"No," I lied. "I just need coffee."

"That can be arranged." He clapped me on the arm. "Come now, I'll rouse Christine and Iskander, while you let Mr. Rath know we're off."

CHAPTER FIFTEEN

riffin

"MUST WE REALLY?" Whyborne asked as he eyed the four horses I'd hired from the livery stable. "Perhaps we should investigate the train as an alternative?"

I suppressed a sigh. I loved my husband, but traveling with him was always a bit of a trial, even under better circumstances than these. "I suppose we could steal a motor car. If I drove it very, very fast, perhaps we could get past the Fideles before one of their sorcerers set fire to the gasoline."

"Never mind," Whyborne said hastily. Then he frowned and turned to Christine. "Is it safe for you to ride in your, er, condition?"

Christine scowled at him, but before she could reply, Iskander said, "Among my mother's people, women often ride until the babe is quite far along. So long as Christine doesn't fall off, she'll be fine."

"Thank you, Kander," she said with a nod to him. She seemed a bit more herself this morning, though I suspected it was something of a brave front. I couldn't imagine how she must feel, to have her greatest professional triumph turn into a source of despair. Especially considering how hard she'd had to fight for it. She'd once told us that the only reason she received the firman to dig at the site of Nephren-ka's tomb was because no one else believed anything was there.

She wasn't the only one putting on a brave front. I didn't believe for a moment that Nyarlathotep had done anything but lie to Whyborne, but if *he* thought himself doomed…

In dangerous circumstances such as ours, such thoughts could too easily become a prophecy of the self-fulfilling sort.

I worried, too, about Maggie Parkhurst, and Jack, and our other friends. If the worst had happened, would we find ourselves facing their resurrected corpses in battle? Whyborne had already endured such an ordeal once, when Stanford called up the dead of the old families, including their own sister. I had no desire to relive the experience.

I patted the neck of one of the horses, a solid beast with a light tan coat. "I'm told this one is quite gentle, though it will quicken its pace to keep up with the others, so there's no fear of falling behind." Since Christine had begun to scowl again, I added, "Whyborne, if you'll get in the saddle, I'll help adjust the stirrups for you."

Christine's scowl turned into a snort. Whyborne glared at her, then at me…but he didn't argue.

"Does it have a name?" he asked as I adjusted the stirrups for his long legs. "No wait, let me guess. Those are War, Pestilence, and Famine, and this pale fellow here is Death."

"Suitable for the apocalypse," Christine said, swinging into the saddle and arranging her skirts. "Though aren't we supposed to be stopping it?" Then she brightened. "Iskander, what about Thanatos if the babe is a boy?"

Whyborne's horse began to turn in a slow circle. He tugged at the reins, but it ignored him. "Honestly, Christine, you can't name a baby after my horse."

"I don't see why not. Besides, that's not even the horse's name."

"It is now."

I met Iskander's gaze ruefully. "Perhaps you should keep hold of this," I said, passing him a basket. "I took the liberty of obtaining supplies, since we don't wish to draw attention to ourselves by stopping at a saloon or hotel."

"Brilliant," Christine declared. "A picnic lunch it is. If that's all, then let us be off, gentlemen."

WE SLIPPED OUT of the city as quietly as we could, though it was impossible to say what spies the Fideles might have searching for us. Rat-things, cultists, some sorcerous spell I knew nothing of, all might carry the tale of our departure to their ears. At least my shadowsight detected no magic, aside from the arcane lines bending across the countryside, drawn into the mighty vortex beneath Widdershins.

What would have been a quick journey by motor car or train became a frustrating trek on horseback, especially given the need to stay off the main roads. We stuck to the countryside as much as possible, but I soon realized our options were limited. Marshland claimed the coast, the ground too treacherous to keep anything resembling a steady pace on horseback. Further inland, fields bounded by rock walls made up much of the landscape, interspersed with clusters of forest.

In the end, we kept to the smaller roads, occasionally cutting across fields when there was no sign of anyone working them at the moment. The farmer in me winced at every plant crushed beneath the hooves, though we went in single file to keep the damage to a minimum.

The day grew hot, the sun glaring down until my hatband was damp with sweat. We ate and drank in the saddle, Whyborne wincing with every step of his horse. Despite all my encouragement to move with the gait of his mount, he still bumped along like a sack of laundry.

"How much longer before we reach Widdershins?" he asked eventually. His horse dawdled at the back, keeping pace with the rest of us but clearly unhappy about it.

I took off my hat and fanned myself. "Our route has been circuitous, but we've made decent time nonetheless. Given our early start, I'd say we'll arrive on the outskirts of the Draakenwood by sundown."

Assuming we met no opposition. Assuming the umbrae hadn't been overwhelmed. With Jack's help, we'd brought them to Widdershins after defeating Stanford, so in theory their presence in the wood should have been a nasty surprise for the Fideles.

Since Whyborne House had fallen, had Jack thought to take refuge with them? Or had the Fideles burst in on him, looking for us? Dragged him away, or cut him down on the doorstep?

I forced my thoughts away from such speculation. I couldn't know, could only hope and pray that he still lived. That he and Saul were safe somewhere together.

The closer we drew to Widdershins, the more wild and empty the landscape grew. And not simply because the ground became rockier and the farmsteads farther apart. "I haven't seen anyone working in a field for the last hour."

Iskander's brow creased in a frown. "I've noticed that as well. I know the growing season is somewhat different here than in England, but shouldn't some of these crops need tending to, let alone harvesting?"

"Yes."

"Longfin and Rath both said the attack came from outside Widdershins," Christine said. "The Fideles would have needed time to gather their forces with no one noticing."

My blood chilled at the thought. "If they slipped into the countryside a handful at a time, took over the remote farmhouses one by one..."

Whyborne blanched white. "We were so worried about the Restoration, about Widdershins..."

Miss Parkhurst had been searching the papers for months, looking for any sign of Fideles activity. But the newspapers would only report the grand acts: entire towns gone missing, or ships vanishing in large numbers, or something strange enough to be noteworthy. This had been quiet. Slow and steady. Outside of Widdershins and beneath our view.

Damn them.

"Hello!" called a voice from a neighboring field.

I turned in the saddle, reaching for my revolver even as I did so. A woman stood on the porch of a house I'd at first taken to be abandoned, given the tomatoes that had been left to ripen unpicked on the vines out front.

She waved at us. "Hello, travelers! Come and rest a moment. I've a fresh pot of coffee boiling on the stove. And I'd bet your horses could use a drink on a hot day like this."

We exchanged glances. "I don't trust this," Whyborne murmured. "Does your shadowsight show anything amiss, Griffin?"

A bit too much, unfortunately. We weren't far from the southernmost cluster of standing stones ringing Widdershins, and an arcane line bisected the field, magic flowing across the earth and ultimately into the great maelstrom. Its glare might mask things hiding near it.

I could get a good look at the woman herself, though it didn't help as much as I would have liked. She wore a simple dress, its sleeves buttoned to the wrist despite the heat or any work she might have been doing. Her left hand was gloved, though her right was not.

"There's something about her," I said, casting my voice low. "But I'm not sure what, exactly. I don't think she's a sorceress, if that's worth anything."

"So what do we do?" Christine asked. "Keep riding?"

"We need information," Whyborne said. His dark eyes were fixed on the woman, his mouth set in a firm line. "Let's talk to her, but be careful."

"And if it's a trap?"

He glanced at Christine. "You still have your cudgel, don't you?"

She nodded. "An excellent point."

We turned our horses toward the farmhouse. Sensing the opportunity for rest, Whyborne's horse finally showed some life and shoved its way to the front. Iskander kept an eye on our surroundings, and I remained on guard for the first flicker of the arcane.

"The pump and bucket are there," the woman said, pointing. "Fill the trough and come on inside."

She shuffled into the house. Though her hospitality wasn't particularly unusual, in the circumstances it set my teeth on edge. I worked the pump, keeping a close eye on the water. Perhaps it was simply that the farmhouse reminded me of Fallow, but I half-expected to see spores of the rust come gushing out. But the water was just that—water. Nothing arcane showed to my sight, and even the taste was sweet.

"Should we pretend everything is normal?" Christine asked, her words concealed by the splash of water into the trough. "Or just get right to the matter and ask her where everyone is?"

"Right to the matter." Whyborne absently patted his horse on the withers. It ignored him in favor of the water in the trough. "We can't waste time doing anything else." He perked up slightly. "At least the farm doesn't seem to have any chickens."

The interior of the farmhouse bore evidence of a family. Men's boots lined up near the door, and a photograph on the wall showed a younger version of the woman who had greeted us, alongside what I assumed were her husband and four sons. A pipe sat abandoned on a rocking chair, reminding me of Pa sitting in his chair near the fire, smoking while Ma sewed.

But the house smelled curiously unused, as if none of these people had lived here in a long time. The silence gripping it was broken only by our steps on the floorboards.

The woman waited for us in the kitchen, a smile on her face. There was no evidence of the coffee she'd promised.

We stopped just inside. Christine stepped to one side, her hand dropping casually to her skirts, where she had her cudgel concealed. Iskander moved to the opposite side of the room, and Whyborne faced her directly.

"I can't help but notice your farm seems neglected," I said. "Where's your husband? Your neighbors?"

She blinked at me, and my sense of something very, very wrong strengthened. Out of the sunlight, it was easier to see a faint glow about her exposed skin. Some sort of magic had been done by or to her, that much seemed clear.

"He's gone to Widdershins." I hadn't expected an answer, or not a real one, so her words caught me by surprise. "My boys have, too. I'm going to join them soon."

Whyborne took a small step toward her, and I had to resist the urge to haul him back. "Why have they gone there?"

"To serve," she said, as though it was the only possible answer. "They've been Perfected."

I didn't like the sound of that at all. "Perfected?"

"Yes." Her smile grew wider and wider. "I'm becoming Perfect as well."

Iskander's nostrils flared in alarm. "What the devil have the Fideles done to her?"

Her grin had become a rictus. "They came in the night. I was the only one who woke up. I don't like needles, so I struggled." She *laughed*, a horrid, tinkling sound. "How foolish of me. I see that now. It doesn't matter, though. Soon I'll be Perfect enough to serve."

She lunged forward, gloved hand wrapping around Whyborne's wrist. "Soon we *all* will."

CHAPTER SIXTEEN

hyborne

I TRIED TO PULL FREE, but the woman clung to me, her eyes wide and burning with a strange euphoria. "Let go of me!"

Christine struck her a glancing blow on the shoulder with the cudgel, hard enough to loosen her grip. As I pulled away, Griffin said, "Iskander, help me hold her!"

They grabbed her by the upper arms. She fought them, but was no match for their strength.

"Whyborne, take her glove off," Griffin ordered.

I felt a twinge at assaulting the poor woman, but there didn't seem to be much of a choice. It took both Christine and I to get her glove off, since she tried to stop us by making a fist, but we succeeded. Her right hand seemed perfectly ordinary, complete with all the expected calluses, bumps, pores, and hairs. Her left, on the other hand, had none of those. The skin was perfectly smooth, with only the slightest creases at the joints, the lightest line across the palm. It might have been a wax model, rather than a real human hand.

"I don't understand," I said, very much afraid that I did.

The woman stilled. "I'm becoming Perfect." She looked at me with a zealot's gaze. "Everyone always said I was too loud. Too rambunctious. Too much. I had thoughts about other women, the sort of things I should only think about my husband. I tried to be smaller, to make the thoughts go away, but I couldn't." Her mouth curved in a beatific smile. "But soon all of that will be gone."

Christine stared at her in dismay. Griffin's brows drew together. "You spoke of a needle," he said.

"They came in the night. The people in masks. I fought them." She shook her head, as if in disbelief at her own actions. "I think that must be why it's taking so long. I didn't get enough. My boys did, though." She frowned slightly. "Did I have sons? Or was that a dream?"

All the hair stood up on my neck. "The Fideles injected her with something that's physically transforming her. Do you think it could be something like the rust? Only administered through the blood instead of through water?"

"If so, maybe we can free her from it." Hope took some of the worry from Iskander's features. "Just as you freed me from the rust."

"Perhaps?" I said uncertainly. "This seems very different from the rust, though."

"There's an arcane line outside," Griffin said. "Do you think it worth a try?"

Did I? Exposing an ordinary person to the arcane fire was painful at best, deadly at worst. I'd done it often enough to judge when to stop, before causing any sort of permanent damage, but it still wasn't an experience she would enjoy.

But if it worked…the woman couldn't even remember her own children. Surely she would prefer to be free of the infection, no matter the pain.

If so, her current state didn't allow her to come to the same conclusion. "No!" The woman's eyes widened. "No, what are you doing?"

"It's for your own good," Iskander said soothingly. "Just come with us—"

She began to scream and fight, her entire body twisting and bucking like an animal in a trap. "We're going to have to bind her," I said. "If you're touching her while I channel the arcane fire through her, it will spill over into you as well."

"Not an experience I'd care to repeat without necessity," Iskander said ruefully.

Christine tore a curtain into strips, and we used them to bind the woman's hands and ankles. She struggled the entire time, and even though I knew she wasn't in her right mind, that we were in fact trying to help her, I felt like a cur to treat her so.

We carried her between us, following Griffin's direction to the line, which lay close by. She tried to roll away when we put her down, so I was forced to kneel beside her and pin down her shoulders. "I'm sorry," I said desperately. "I don't want to hurt you."

"Let me be Perfect!" she screamed at me. "I don't want to be flawed anymore!"

"It's all right," I said. "It's going to be all right."

"Get it over with, Whyborne," Christine said. "Before her shrieking brings something down on us."

I drew on the power of the line, making myself a conduit. But, as in the marsh, something had changed. I heard the howling again, the cry of rage or pain, but far louder than before. I didn't know what it meant, and tried to ignore it, funneling raw magic directly into the woman's body.

She screamed. Flesh wasn't meant to contain such power; most sorcerers used wands when tapping into arcane lines to spare themselves. I'd been shaped by the maelstrom, my ancestors nudged onto just the right course to create a hybrid of ketoi and human, sorcerer and old family, able to use my own body as a wand. I'd been called abomination for it, an affront to the natural order of things.

The woman beneath my hands was no abomination. She was human, under attack by whatever sorcerous infection the Fideles had forced on her. Touching the arcane fire hurt even me; it was agony for her.

"I think it's working!" Griffin called. "The skin on her hand isn't as waxy!"

Her eyes rolled back in her head, the capillaries bursting and staining the whites red. Her body began to shake, then to seize.

It was too much.

I let go of her. My scars burned, and my fingers ached where I'd clutched her. "It's killing her."

Her body arched, then went limp. Griffin dropped beside her, fingers pressed to her neck. "She's still alive," he said after a moment. "But her hand is back to what it was when you started." He tugged at the neck of her dress, revealing waxen skin. "And it looks like the infection is still spreading."

"Should we try again?" Iskander asked.

I shook my head wearily. "No. Whatever this is, it's more resistant than the rust. Possibly it can't be burned out at all, and we'll succeed only in killing her."

"Then what should we do?" Christine sounded uncharacteristically tentative. "If we just leave her, she'll transform and be one more enemy to fight."

I stood up and dusted off my trousers. I'd brushed them as best I could last night at Mrs. Rodgers' house, but they were still a disaster, and the gesture did no good. "We certainly can't murder her in cold blood. And we can't leave her tied up to starve to death. There's nothing to do but untie her, put her back in her house, and leave before she wakes up."

We carried her back inside, settling her as carefully as possible on her couch, before cutting her bindings. As we departed, I paused in front of the mantel, staring at the photograph and tasting acid in my throat.

"Does it ever end?" I asked.

Griffin paused beside me. "What?"

"Do you remember Philip Rice?"

He cocked his head in confusion. "The murder case that brought me to you? Of course."

"What about the Kincaid brothers in Threshold? Allan Tambling's uncle? Guinevere and Miss Emily. The cinereous of Fallow, and the murdered heads of the old families, and the transformed Endicotts." My throat tightened around the words, but I forced them out. "Families torn apart by greed, or hate, or the need for power. And now here we stand yet again, in a house where a woman's husband and children were ripped from her in the night, while magic we can't fight slowly subjugates her, body and mind."

I turned away from the mantle and found my friends watching me. "Does it ever end?" I asked again.

Iskander's dark eyes lowered. "No. I don't think it does. Ghūls killed my mother. But it was disease that carried off Griffin's parents and the orphan train that separated him from his brothers."

"Daphne married a terrible man, but an ordinary one," Christine added with an unhappy twist of her mouth. "Our parents were pleased because he had a title, and the rest didn't matter."

Griffin stepped closer to me. "The important thing is, we try to do something about it. In whatever fashion we can."

"Did you ever get discouraged, when you were in the Pinkertons?"

"Yes, of course." Griffin's eyes shadowed with memories. "There were days when it seemed the tide of human misery never ended. But I always reminded myself that the tide of human joy likewise is unending. Think of those we've saved, as often as those we've lost."

I couldn't share his optimism. I was weary to the bone of grief, of struggle. "If we don't stop the masters, nothing we've done will have been to any purpose."

Griffin's fingers tightened. "That isn't true. If the world ends tomorrow, it will still have mattered."

Christine put her hand to her belly. "Sometimes I wonder what I'm thinking, bringing a child into all this."

I gaped at her, astonished. Christine was seldom one to be vulnerable; it wasn't part of her nature.

"What if it becomes one of those broken orphans?" she went on. "Or I one of those grieving mothers? And Iskander is right, in one way or another, it doesn't ever end. But what can we do, except live as best we can? Wallowing in despair certainly won't solve anything." Her chin firmed. "If our choices are to throw up our hands and walk away, or to fight and keep fighting, even if there is no end to the struggle, then I know which I'll choose."

I nodded mutely, uncertain what to say. We left the house and returned to our steeds. After I mounted, though, I sat staring at the empty windows, the cold chimney, the walls in which laughter might never ring again.

"I'm sorry I failed you," I said to the woman, too quietly for my companions to hear. Then my horse fell in behind the others, and the farmhouse grew ever more distant, until it was lost behind the trees.

CHAPTER SEVENTEEN

riffin

"I THINK the maelstrom is trying to communicate with me," Whyborne said.

I slowed my horse to drop back closer to his. Thanatos hadn't wanted to leave the comfort of the farmyard, and expressed its displeasure by dallying even farther behind than before. "How so?"

"The dream I told you about aboard the *Melusine*. I had another last night." He shaded his eyes against the setting sun. "And when I touched the arcane line in the marsh, I heard a-a voice, I suppose. Mostly just howling, but it also said *come to me*, which is the same phrase I heard in the dreams. And earlier, when we were trying to cure the woman in the farmhouse, I perceived the cries again."

Unease touched me. The maelstrom might weight the dice of fate, might nudge certain outcomes into being more likely than they other-wise would have, but it didn't directly interact. That was presumably what Whyborne and Persephone were for. "It's never spoken to you prior to this, has it?"

"I'm not sure it's speaking to me now." Whyborne ran his fingers through the strands of his horse's mane. "The sounds might just be how a human-ish brain interprets it. The maelstrom is…I don't know if *angry* is a word one can use for such an entity. But I do think it understands what's happening in Widdershins. That the town is under assault and the masters are returning soon."

"But it's telling you to come home," I said. "Unless I'm misunderstanding something?"

"Presumably." He sighed. "You're right, it's strange. Either something has changed, or else it always had this ability and just…didn't use it. You'd think it would have spoken to me as a child, or at least let me know as an adult that I ought to be studying magic. Not that I believed in magic at the time, but still, I might have majored in any number of useful subjects while at Miskatonic."

"Perhaps it didn't wish to influence you until it had to." I tried to imagine how Niles would have reacted if his youngest son told him he was an eldritch being of vast power. I generally got along with Niles better than Whyborne did, but I couldn't forget the things he'd done as part of the Brotherhood. He might not have killed anyone directly since the end of the war, but there was blood on his hands nonetheless.

If he'd guessed Whyborne's true potential, Ival rather than Stanford would have become the apple of his eye: encouraged and groomed, inducted into the Brotherhood at first opportunity. At a young enough age, Whyborne might not even have realized what they were doing was wrong, not until it was too late.

The world was likely a much better place, thanks to that decision —assuming it had been a decision—on the maelstrom's part. Not to suggest that Whyborne's childhood misery had in any way been for the greater good. Niles might have been kinder to his youngest son, while still not realizing Whyborne's true potential. But the thought of some other version of Whyborne, taught to believe as Stanford had been that he was always right, to take whatever he wanted by any means necessary, was enough to make my blood run cold.

"Or perhaps it simply wanted to make my life difficult," Whyborne muttered.

"That I doubt." I leaned over in my saddle to put a hand to his leg.

"What the devil is that?" Christine exclaimed.

My attention snapped back to the road before us. Streamers of fog rolled across the road ahead, which bent sharply to the north to avoid the Draakenwood. An abandoned field lay on the other side of the road; the fog thickened until I couldn't see the forest which must lurk beyond it. To my shadowsight, the fog glowed with sorcery.

My horse snorted and tossed its head, disturbed. Thanatos came to a dead stop and simply refused to take another step, no matter how much Whyborne alternately cursed and cajoled it. Christine's mount danced skittishly to one side, before she brought it firmly back under control.

"I don't think we're going to be able to ride any farther," Iskander said, patting his steed on the neck. Its nostrils were flared, ears swiveling back and forth to catch the slightest sound.

"The umbrae would likely have viewed the horses as food, anyway." I swung down and gathered my things from the panniers.

We left the horses to their own devices. With luck, they would return on their own to their stable. If not, someone would come across them soon enough. The livery stable would probably go to the police when we failed to return the horses, but right now a warrant for my arrest seemed a minor worry at best.

I led the way into the fog, sword cane unsheathed and at the ready. Whyborne came after me, then Christine, while Iskander acted as rear guard, his knives in his hands. The farm field looked to have been deserted longer than a season, and I couldn't help but wonder what had become of whoever had once worked the land, whose hands had built the low stone walls bounding it. Even before the umbrae came, the Draakenwood had an evil reputation as a haunt of sorcerers and nightmares, and few who stepped within ever returned to tell the tale.

The fog thickened as we entered the wood's edge. "Is this some spell of the Fideles?" Whyborne wondered aloud. "Or Nephren-ka's work?"

"He was from the desert," I pointed out.

"There are fogs on the Nile from time to time," Iskander said. Our voices fell flat on the heavy air, as though it sought to stifle them. "He wouldn't have been unaware of the phenomenon."

"Then I stand corrected." A shiver ran through me. "It would surely take a great deal of sorcerous power to do this, whoever is at the root."

"They have the maelstrom to draw from," Whyborne said softly. "So long as they have a good wand and the spell doesn't need constant upkeep, power isn't a limiting factor."

The trees closed around us, the forest growing darker and wilder with every step we took. Moisture dripped from the leaves, and the branches seemed to form almost human figures, writhing in agony. The sense of being watched pressed down on me, and a chill ran up my back.

"Do we know we aren't just going in circles?" Whyborne whispered. There was no reason to whisper, but I shared the impulse, as if something might overhear us and be displeased.

"We're not," I replied. "I'm not the most accomplished woodsman, but even in the fog, I can keep us going in a more-or-less straight line. Hopefully the umbrae will find us soon."

We came upon evidence they'd been there recently, in the form of a skeleton denuded of flesh. The bones had an almost melted appearance, and lay in a heap with a tattered robe and a mask such as the Fideles often wore.

"A soldier umbra has been here." The work of a soldier's acid feelers was unmistakable. I bore the scar from one of them on my left thigh, made by the broken captive of a sorcerer. It had eaten my partner Glenn, digesting him alive before my eyes, until a bullet put an end to his suffering.

"And where are they now?" Christine wondered, looking about the trees. Not that it was possible to see far in the dense fog.

"Close by, I hope." I started forward again.

We hadn't gone far, when there came a sudden rustling in the canopy. Water cascaded down, dislodged by...something...moving above and in front of us.

Something touched my mind, feather-light and reaching. I'd never before tested how far away I could be and still communicate with the Queen of Shadows without the Lapidem's help. An oversight on our part, but it seemed she could at least find me so long as I was within the confines of the Draakenwood.

The rustling must have come from a soldier umbra in the canopy. Unlike the workers, they could fly. It would be able to communicate with the Queen of Shadows far more easily than I, so I turned in anticipation of using it to speak with her.

"I'm glad to see you," I began to say.

The thing that dropped down from the tree was no umbra. Its bat-like wings were tattered and slimy, its skin furred with mold. Its jaws gaped to bite, and a blast of fetid breath nearly had me retching.

Whyborne's hand closed on my collar, and he yanked me back. The teeth snapped closed where my head had been only moments before. All around us, Hounds of Tindalos bloomed in my shadowsight, darting back and forth through the Veil as they traveled.

"Run!" Whyborne shouted, and hauled me after him.

CHAPTER EIGHTEEN

hyborne

MY HEART thudded and a stitch formed in my side almost immediately. I ignored it in favor of not being eaten.

The thick trees would foil any attempts by the byakhee to follow us directly; it would have to get above the canopy to fly. Unfortunately, they also made running difficult.

My foot caught on a root, and I measured my length on the ground. My chin clipped the earth hard, and lights flashed behind my eyes. An instant later, a heavy weight landed on my back as a Hound emerged directly on top of me.

I didn't have enough time to even react. Griffin skewered it with his sword cane as it came into our world. It howled, and sickly ichor splashed from its wounds, to add to the utter ruin of my clothing.

Christine's rifle barked as she dispatched another Hound. Had the cultist whose bones we'd found summoned them before his death, and now they wandered the woods on their own volition? Or were there more Fideles somewhere nearby?

Griffin hauled me to my feet. "Follow me!" he exclaimed. "Quickly!"

None of us questioned him, only pelted after as fast as we could. Eerie howls echoed through the trees all around us now. "How many of the bloody things are there?" Iskander panted.

"Not far," Griffin said. "We're almost—"

The byakhee crashed down through the canopy, so close to Christine its claws tore a hank of hair from her scalp. She let out a startled cry and ducked instinctively. Iskander shoved her out of the way, only to be thrown off his feet from a blow from one of its rotting wings.

I wanted to call down the lightning, but I hesitated. My target was too close to my friends; what if it hit them as well as the byakhee?

Christine rose to her full height, aimed her rifle, and shot the byakhee square in the eye. It let out a horrible screech and flinched back—but now the Hounds were closing in all around us.

I took a deep breath, centering myself. I wasn't on an arcane line, but I'd burn through what magic I had inside me if that's what it took.

Griffin put out a hand to stop me. Startled, I turned to look at him.

The smile on Griffin's face wasn't his own. His pupils had shrunk to mere pinpoints, the irises around them illuminated from within, so they appeared more like green ice than emeralds.

"The Draakenwood is ours," he said in a voice like a thousand whispers, echoing through cavernous depths. "And you will regret coming here, creatures of the Outside."

Then the soft earth gave way beneath us, and we plummeted into darkness.

MY FALL WAS A SHORT ONE, broken by something soft and coated in slime. A chemical stink flooded my lungs, strong enough to choke me. Dark, billowy forms rushed past, folding themselves through the hole in the tunnel ceiling above us. A moment later, the death shrieks of Hounds and byakhee echoed down.

The squirming mass beneath me heaved, then slid away in a

manner that brought bile to my throat. I swallowed it down, and found myself deposited on the bare rock of the tunnel floor. Umbrae workers scuttled around us like gelatinous pill bugs, feelers protruding and shrinking from their mass according to their needs.

Iskander and Christine sat up, their clothing slick with slime and reeking of the umbrae's acidic stench. Griffin, however, lay on his side, his eyes closed and a line of blood seeping from his nostril. One of the workers slithered over him, cleaning the blood away.

I hastened to his side. "Griffin?"

He blinked slowly at the touch of my hand on his cheek. His eyes had resumed their normal color once again. "You were possessed by the Queen of Shadows," I said.

"Yes." He pinched the bridge of his nose, as I helped him to sit. "She reached out to me just before we were attacked, and told me where to run to find help."

The sound of running footsteps—unexpected in the tunnels of the umbrae—echoed from nearby. A moment later, a light appeared around a bend, revealing the face of Griffin's brother, Jack. In one hand he held a lantern; the other arm cradled a familiar orange body.

"Griffin!" Jack exclaimed, at the same moment I said, "Saul!"

Iskander helped Griffin to his feet. Jack set the lantern down, shoved Saul at me, and then flung his arms around Griffin in a tight embrace. "God! I wasn't sure if I'd ever see you again. There was no way to know if you were still in Cornwall, or if the Fideles had killed or captured you."

"I had much the same fears for you," Griffin assured him.

As for me, I looked Saul over carefully. There was no sign of any harm to him—indeed, his fur didn't bear so much as a smear of dirt. He purred happily, butting his hard little head into my chin in greeting. Since I'd recently hit said chin on the ground when I tripped, the gesture hurt rather more than usual.

Christine came over and scratched Saul behind the ears. "One of the librarians told us some of what happened in Widdershins," she said to Jack, "but he only saw the thing at the museum." I couldn't help but notice she couldn't bring herself to speak Nephren-ka's name. "I assume you had a different vantage during the attack?"

"Yes." Jack hesitated. "Before I speak, was your journey successful? You received the key to the Codex?"

"Yes," I confirmed. "And the Endicotts returned with us, though they're currently at sea. It's a long story," I added at his surprised look.

"I imagine so." Jack shook himself. "A client had just contacted me about missing relatives past the outskirts of Widdershins. Her suspicions were aroused by a lack of letters, so she went to the house. The blinds were drawn, the door locked, and no one could be found. She said there was something unsettling in the air, and explained to me as a lifelong resident of Widdershins, she knew better than to ask the police to investigate something they probably weren't prepared to face."

Griffin swore softly. "Blast. If only this had happened before we left, or at least with enough time for someone to act."

"I take it this means something to you?" Jack asked. "I never had the chance to investigate."

Griffin told him about our encounter with the Perfected woman. Now it was Jack's turn to loose an oath. "Damn it all. If I'd been faster—"

"You'd probably be dead. Or one of them."

Jack paled. "Not a fate I'd wish on anybody. Well, then. As it was, I was at home—your home, I mean—when they came. I heard shouting in the streets, and ran out to see a force of black-robed figures with faceless masks descending on me. I assume they were either after the two of you, or anything you had hidden in the house, depending on whether or not they realized you were gone to Cornwall."

Or they'd come for Jack, intending to use him as a hostage against Griffin, the same way Mrs. Creigh was using Father against me. I didn't see any point in saying that aloud, though.

"At any rate," Jack continued, "I'm not an idiot, so I knew I didn't have a chance against them. I threw Saul in his basket, grabbed the Lapidem, got us to the motor car, and took off as fast as I could in the opposite direction."

"You were lucky no one set fire to the gasoline," Christine put in.

"I hoped they needed some sort of line of sight, so I kept swerving and taking corners as fast as I could." Jack shrugged. "Saul didn't like that part at all. Neither did I, come to think of it. There were masked cultists all over, and these things...the Perfected, I suppose. I thought maybe they were some sort of particularly awful wax mannequins come to life. To think they used to be ordinary people..." He shuddered. "And glowing things in the sky, like the umbrae but not."

"We're calling them lumina," Christine put in.

"I made for the Draakenwood," Jack went on. "As soon as I reached the eaves, I abandoned the car, grabbed Saul's basket and the Lapidem, and ran. Some of them followed me, but the umbrae took care of them." Jack lowered his eyes. "We've been here ever since. I've felt like I ought to go and, I don't know, *do something*. But I can't communicate with the Queen of Shadows, at least not beyond a handful of gestures. She isn't sending the umbrae outside the wood, and I didn't dare go back to town alone." He absently swept the lock of hair that had tumbled over his forehead out of the way. "I feel like a coward."

"Dying with no purpose wouldn't help anything," I pointed out. Saul squirmed, wanting down, and I put him on the tunnel floor. He rubbed against my legs, then did the same for the rest of my human companions, before butting his head affectionately against one of the worker umbrae. It flicked away a bit of dirt that had transferred from my coat to Saul's.

"I suppose." Jack lifted his gaze with what seemed like effort. "I'm just so very glad to see all of you."

"And I, you." Griffin clasped his brother's arm. "The Queen of Shadows would like us to come to her, as soon as we can."

Jack nodded. "I'll show you the way."

CHAPTER NINETEEN

riffin

AT ONE TIME, the umbrae nest would have been my greatest night-mares come true. Their tunnels were dark, claustrophobic, the weight of earth and stone pressing down as we went ever deeper. The same species as the creatures who had killed my partner Glenn and later hunted me through the Egyptian desert squirmed all around us. Worker umbrae scuttled along walls and support pillars, cleaning or excavating or securing food. A larger soldier drifted before us, its stingray-like body held aloft by some power native to its species. The close air reeked, the same way the basement where Glenn died had reeked.

But I felt only calm. Safe, or at least, safer than we'd been since leaving Widdershins for Balefire. Saul trotted alongside us, doing his best to trip everyone. My husband's hand was warm in mine, and my brother was unharmed. It would take a great force indeed to invade the tunnels of the umbrae, so I could let go of any lingering fear of attack for the moment. I wanted to find a cozy side chamber and curl up, my head pillowed on one of the workers, or cradled in the coils of the Queen of Shadows.

Sometimes it occurred to me that I might have gone mad. Certainly I'd been accused of it, locked away in an asylum and all but forgotten until Pa saved me. If the me of then could see the me of now, he'd be horrified. Repulsed. I'd gone from blending in with unsavory characters of the criminal underworld in order to investigate them, to voluntarily consorting with actual inhuman monsters. Surely some sliver of me should be aghast by my behavior.

But it wasn't. Quite the contrary. I was at home among the umbrae, in Widdershins, with my strange family, in a way I'd never been before. If that meant there was something wrong with me, I had no desire at all to have it fixed.

The Queen of Shadows had mostly withdrawn from my mind, but not entirely. Human brains weren't meant for such telepathic communication, and even I, marked by the umbrae as I was, could only bear it for a short time without injury. But I could feel her hovering at the very edge of my perception, fierce and welcoming.

It took some time to reach her chamber—the burrow of the umbrae beneath the Draakenwood was far more extensive than I'd realized. Some of the reason was no doubt due to the fact that many of the tunnels had been already in place, rather than needing to be dug out. Theron Blackbyrne, necromancer, sorcerer, and founder of Widdershins, had once lived in the wood. He'd consorted here with Nyarlathotep, and hidden tunnels both beneath his home and his town, though for what purposes I couldn't guess. Nothing good, for certain.

The Queen coiled in the darkness of an enormous chamber beneath the ruins of Blackbyrne's manor. Someday, if the world didn't end, she'd grow to the length of a freight train. For now, she was only the size of one of the cars. As we entered, she lifted her head, her huge orange eye like a flame punctured with a tripartite pupil. In the coils of her segmented body rested the Lapidem her mother had given to me, which Jack had rescued from our house. Our lantern light flashed off its strange angles, and something seemed to move deep within its faceted depths. Did the Mother of Shadows even now watch us from Alaska?

"*Yes, my brother,*" the Queen of Shadows whispered from the edges of my mind.

I went to her, placing my hand on her head. A feeler curled around my wrist, cool against my skin. "Do you wish to speak through me again?"

"*If you will allow it.*"

I closed my eyes and let out a breath. Then she was there, behind my eyes, a vast, indescribable pressure. My skull ached, as though asked to contain more than it could hold, and I tasted the tang of blood in the back of my throat.

We turned to the others. I forced myself to relax, as though I leaned back into the arms of a friend, trusting her not to let me fall.

"Welcome," she said through me. My tongue felt alien in my mouth.

Iskander gave a courteous bow, and Christine nodded. Whyborne stepped forward, a concerned frown on his lips. "Thank you for the assistance earlier," he said, ever polite. "How are you faring against the vanguard?"

The Queen shifted behind me, her coils whispering against stone. "Some of us have died. But some of us have been lost. Taken by the enemy." Grief coated her words, her thoughts.

"I don't understand. What do you mean, lost?"

She passed through my mind like a whisper, finding the words she needed. "Those you call the lumina were once us. Umbrae."

Dread filled me. Whyborne's eyes widened. "Like the woman in the farmhouse. Dear God. The Fideles have done something to the umbrae to change them, just as they've changed humans into the Perfected."

Just like the cinereous in Fallow.

"Yes," she agreed with us both. My throat ached, the pressure in my skull grew more intense, and the taste of blood became stronger. "The first ones, the vanguard, were not of our nest. They were not of our mother." Sorcerers would sometimes steal umbrae eggs if they could find a nest. The hatched umbrae inevitably went mad, cut off from others of their kind. Was that how the lumina had begun?

"Their minds are unreachable by me," the Queen said. Something warm and wet trickled over my lips. "Even those who were once mine." Grief whipsawed through us. "They are lost, deaf, alone in light."

The image she put into my mind was as clear as my own memories. I swooped down at a band of Fideles who had dared set foot in the Draakenwood. Two died screaming as I lashed them with acidic tendrils, but a third drove a strange, round blade into my surface. The wound sealed instantly, and I left his bones on the leaves.

But then everything went hazy. The place where I'd been stabbed felt cold. And the cold began to spread, even as the vision faded to white.

I STUMBLED FORWARD, my mouth thick with blood but the pressure in my head gone. Whyborne caught me before my knee hit the floor, and I leaned gratefully against him.

"Are you all right?" he asked.

I swallowed. "Yes. Though I could use a drink."

Iskander passed me his canteen. "It's only water, but perhaps it will help."

It sluiced my mouth clean, at least. Whyborne took out his handkerchief, dampened it with the canteen, and carefully applied it to the space between my nose and upper lip. "There." He stepped back, handkerchief rusty-red now. "I know I've already asked, but…"

"I'm fine." A worker trundled over as if to inspect me, then went on its way. "But let me tell you what I saw."

While I spoke, Christine chewed absently on one of the sausages I'd bought back in Boston. "So as I understand it, the lumina are transformed umbrae, presumably now mind-controlled by the agents of the masters, yes? And whatever alters them is delivered through a round knife in the case of the umbrae, and a needle for humans?"

"I image the knife is hollow and packed with some arcane substance," Iskander said. He took out a second sausage and passed it to his wife as she finished the first. "Do you think the situation is the same with the nereids?"

"I don't see why it wouldn't be." Whyborne ran a hand through his disordered hair, making it stand even further on end than usual. "They aren't creatures of the Outside, and the Endicott doctor remarked on their similarity to the ketoi."

"So they can turn our own people against us." I shook my head. "And for every one we lose in such a way, they gain a new soldier."

"Just as with Nephren-ka." Whyborne's shoulders slumped. "Living or dead, we add to their armies."

Christine swore at length in Arabic. "We have to find Mr. Quinn and the Codex, and put an end to this before things get even worse."

The Queen of Shadows touched my mind as lightly as she could, though it still felt like the scrape of a finger over a raw nerve. *"If the librarian is beneath the ground, we will find him."* The impression of a network of tunnels flashed across my thoughts, an image that likely made sense from the perspective of a burrowing species, but little to me.

I longed for a headache powder. "The umbrae will find Mr. Quinn," I related. "Assuming he made it to the tunnels."

Whyborne nodded. "Then our task is to save Father from Mrs. Creigh's clutches."

I exchanged a glance with Iskander. "I'm not certain walking into an obvious trap is the best choice, my dear," I said as diplomatically as I could.

"On the other hand, we would get to finally kill her." Christine patted her rifle. "I've had a bullet with her name on it since Fallow."

"She's a powerful sorceress," Iskander reminded her. "If you bring a firearm near her, she'll set a spark to the powder and kill you instead."

Christine flung up her hands. "Don't be so literal. I'll brain her with my cudgel if it comes to it. My point is, she tried to turn you into a fungus-person, succeeded in doing so with far too many others, and I'll be glad to see the end of her by whatever means necessary."

My heart sank to see Whyborne nodding along with her. "Niles himself would condemn this as poor strategy," I said.

"Since when have my father and I agreed on anything in our lives?" Whyborne's mouth flattened into a grim line. "As long as Mrs. Creigh has Father, she has a hold over Persephone and me. I won't have her threatening to cut his throat in front of our eyes, causing us to hesitate at some critical juncture later on. Powerful sorceress or not, we're no longer in Fallow. We're in *my* home now. My place of power, as the Endicotts would say."

A breeze stirred through the chamber where no breeze should be, ruffling Whyborne's spiky hair with arcane power only I could see. My heart beat faster, and my blood quickened at the sight of him, his chin tilted up, his eyes narrowed with purpose. I'd wanted him from the first moment I laid my eyes on him, and loved him for almost as long, and yet beholding him come into his own had been—was yet—the greatest pleasure of my life. He was still the quiet scholar he'd been when I met him, and yet so much more. The confidence he spoke with now had been hard earned, not given, and I adored him more than I would have believed possible.

"We'll get Niles back," I agreed, in lieu of flinging myself on him in front of everyone.

"Indeed," he said. "Taking Father, holding him hostage against me, is the last mistake Mrs. Creigh will ever make."

CHAPTER TWENTY

hyborne

I SPRAWLED flat on the back of one of the soldier umbrae, clinging to the stubby feelers it had extruded from its upper surface for me to hold onto. The Draakenwood spread beneath us, lost in the unnatural fog blanketing the city. Five other soldiers glided on the night wind alongside mine, three of them carrying similar burdens, the other two on guard.

"This is wonderful!" Christine shouted over the rush of wind. "We're flying, Kander! *Flying!*"

"Yes, dearest," he replied, far more subdued than she. As for myself, I couldn't wait to get my feet back onto solid ground.

The fog thinned as we drew closer to the city. No doubt the Fideles wished to confuse any intruders, but leave the city clear for themselves. The Draakenwood gave way to the cemetery on Kings Hill, and the wide bowl of the Cranch River Valley stretched out before us. As the last of the fog shredded away, I saw for myself what the vanguard had done to Widdershins. To my home.

Unnatural stillness gripped a town cloaked mostly in shadow. The cannery lay dark and silent. No electric lights illuminated River Street, and no hooded figures slipped from the pools of light cast by the few streets lamps still fueled by gas. No friendly candles or lamps showed from the windows of the houses, the people within either asleep or afraid to attract any sort of attention.

Or Perfected. Could they see in the dark? Or did they lie unmoving on their beds, laid out like waxen figures, waiting for dawn?

The wrongness of it gripped me, and anger tinged with despair flooded my veins. It seemed I could once again hear a distant howling, and I wanted to howl along with it. Widdershins, my home, my town, had been transformed from the place I knew to this...empty facsimile. I felt as though I looked upon a sickbed, the patient already going cold as life drained away.

The Fideles had done this. Invaded my home. Imprisoned my Father. Done God-knew-what to my friends.

Anger burned along my nerves, and the umbra hastily adjusted its wings as the wind rose. The howling grew clearer, louder, the maelstrom turning widdershins beneath me.

"Come to me."

THE VOICE SHOCKED me out of myself. The wind died away, and the umbra steadied. The distant howl fell to a murmur that might have been nothing but the pounding of my own blood in my ears.

A sickly, greenish glow, similar to the radiance of the nereids caught my eye. It emanated from the bell tower of First Esoteric Church. Then the glow peeled away and spread out, and I realized just what had spotted our approach.

Lumina.

They were indeed much like the umbrae they'd once been. Light shone from within their gelatinous forms, giving them an almost crystalline appearance. Their single eyes were blue ice rather than yellow fire, the tripartite pupil reformed into a cat-like slit. Their feelers were symmetrical, as opposed to the shifting extrusions of the umbrae, but they still dripped with acid that could strip flesh from bone.

Three emerged from the bell tower and made straight for us. As our two guards diverted toward them, I cast my gaze over the town, looking for landmarks. If that was First Esoteric, then the Marsh manor should be just to the west, and from there...

Whyborne House blazed with light, a beacon amidst the darkness. Either the mansions that stood shoulder-to-shoulder with it along High Street were deserted, or the occupants dead or Perfected.

I took the lights to mean Mrs. Creigh was at home. Probably torturing Father in the wine cellar for a bit of recreation, or else scheming other ways to destroy us all. With any luck, she wouldn't expect us to approach from the air.

But we had to make it there first.

The lumina were fast and sleek, not to mention unburdened with riders who could fall to their deaths. They were also larger than the umbrae closing with them.

"Look!" Iskander shouted, pointing east.

More lumina rose from their roosts about the town, shedding their eerie radiance on the roofs below. We had to get to Whyborne House before they reached us, or they'd tear both us and the umbrae to shreds.

I'd told Griffin I was in my place of power. Time to act like it.

I stretched my right arm out, pointing at one of the oncoming lumina. My sense of the maelstrom below us surged, even though I rode the air high above it. The scars on my arm ached as I used my very flesh like a sorcerer's wand. My focus, honed for so long, settled on the lumina. Clouds scudded across the sky above, and the earth turned below, and I shouted a word of command as I built a bridge between.

A titanic lightning bolt cracked from the sky, so near and loud I was all but deafened. The lumina that had the misfortune to be between it and the ground exploded into charred goo, bits tumbling from the sky to the roofs below.

Even though the two foremost lumina were now too close to strike without risking the umbrae and us, the second wave was still a good distance away. I turned my attention to them, summoning and directing the wind so it sent them tumbling. Another lightning strike, and more wind, and my shirt sleeve smoked as pain hollowed my bones. The Fideles had done this, had made monsters of umbrae, and I howled my rage in time with something ancient.

Then the umbra shifted beneath me, heading rapidly down. I cried out in shock and narrowly grabbed hold of the extruded handholds before I tumbled off. My head ached and my arm hurt from channeling so much arcane energy, but elation thrummed through me. I would destroy them—I would take back my town—I would slam the gates closed before the masters and make their servants pay.

No. I had to think clearly. Storming into Whyborne House while ranting like a badly written stage villain would surely get Father killed.

By the time we reached the small attic windows, I'd managed to calm myself. I looked down, expecting to see cultists rushing outside in response to the obvious display of magic in the heavens. But the streets remained as empty and silent as before.

Griffin slipped open one of the windows and entered the darkened attic. Christine and Iskander followed, and then my umbra took its place by the window. I felt rather unsteady, sliding over its jelly-like flesh to reach the opening. Fortunately, Griffin leaned out, caught my hand, and helped me inside.

The attic was ferociously hot from the long summer day, and sweat instantly dampened my shirt and hair. Griffin took the small lamp from the bag he carried, and I lit the wick with a word. Excess furniture, draped in sheets to keep off the dust, occupied most of the space. We had a mansion crammed with expensive furnishings of every kind, and yet managed to have more than we could ever use. It summed up my family, or at least the Whyborne side, perfectly. *Too much is never enough* could have been our motto.

Flawed as he might be, Father needed my help at the moment, not my condemnation. I silently pointed in the direction of the attic door, and Griffin made for it, the rest of us following carefully after. Or as carefully as I was capable of. I winced every time the floor creaked beneath my weight and nearly tripped over a covered ottoman.

Christine steadied me. "Honestly, Whyborne," she whispered, "you can summon lightning to smite your enemies, but you can't manage to walk in a straight line."

"It isn't my fault! It's dark!"

Griffin shushed us with a glare. The attic door opened onto a steep, narrow staircase, which I knew let out in the servants' hall. Griffin cracked the lower door open, a thin sliver of light spilling inside, then froze. The rest of us froze along with him. There came the sound of another door opening and shutting, and Griffin relaxed.

"I just glimpsed a maid going along the hall," he whispered. "There are servants here."

"The Fideles must have brought their own," I said. Father had demanded complete loyalty from those who worked in Whyborne House. Most of them had lived in Widdershins for generations and served our family for just as long. "Or perhaps some were captured along with Father and agreed to continue working, so long as he's being held hostage. If so, and Mrs. Creigh trusts them, she's a bigger fool than I believed."

"Should we follow the maid?" Iskander asked. "Anyone working here would know where Niles is being held, most likely."

Griffin nodded. "Whyborne, what's through that door? The last one before the stairs?"

I peered past him. I hadn't set foot in the back halls in years, but I'd occasionally been allowed to play in the attic as a child, and old memories struggled to the surface. There were three doors; I didn't know what the first opened onto, but the second led to Miss Emily's quarters, so she could come and go without disturbing Mother. Or, rather, it had led to her rooms before my brother Stanford murdered her.

God, my family was terrible.

"It led into Mother's room, when she was sick," I said. "After she went to the sea, Father turned it into a gathering place for the old families to confer. Probably any contacts he retained among the Brotherhood as well. Meetings he didn't want to take in his study, at any rate."

"What would a maid be doing in there this time of night?" Christine wondered.

I shook my head. "Tidying up, if Mrs. Creigh is using it for the same thing Father did?" Unless Father was being held there, but that seemed unlikely. The wine cellar would be far more secure.

Griffin took his revolver from inside his coat. "I don't mean to harm her, but if she's loyal to Mrs. Creigh, hopefully this will keep her from screaming long enough for us to get some answers."

We followed him down the hall to the door. "We'll need to move quickly," he whispered. "I'll go in first. Whyborne, after me—if she's one of Niles's servants, she'll likely recognize you."

Griffin flung open the door and stepped inside in a single, fluid move. "Don't make a—" he began, then fell silent.

I stepped in after him, then froze as well.

Mrs. Creigh sat at the head of the long table that dominated the room. The maid stopped in the process of opening the curtains to let in the night breeze and turned to us, her face the waxen mask of the Perfected.

A third figure stood at the head of the table, in the act of pouring wine for Mrs. Creigh. He finished, apparently undisturbed by our appearance, then stepped back. At the sight of his familiar features, my heart sank.

It was Fenton, Father's butler, driver, and confidante. But the years had been wiped from his face, the wrinkles about his eyes and mouth erased, the liver spots removed, the sagging cheeks lifted. Every scar, every imperfection was gone, and his eyes were as bright and empty as glass facsimiles.

As a child, I'd been terrified of Fenton. As a man, I'd never particularly cared for him. But I couldn't suppress the gasp of horror that escaped my lips at the sight of someone I'd known for my entire life, his humanity removed and something horrible put in its place.

"Hello, Dr. Whyborne." Mrs. Creigh took a sip from her wine, a gleeful smile on her face. "Welcome home."

CHAPTER TWENTY-ONE

hyborne

"Welcome our guests, won't you?" Mrs. Creigh said to Fenton and the maid.

The two Perfected moved toward us. Griffin dropped his revolver with an oath and snatched out his sword cane. Christine and Iskander had crowded in after us, and she readied her cudgel as his knives gleamed in the candlelight.

It would be a bloodbath. Even if Fenton and the maid grabbed up makeshift weapons, they had no chance against us.

"Stop!" I cried. "We can't hurt them!"

Griffin shook his head. "Look at them, Whyborne. They've been completely turned. Just as with the cinereous in Fallow, they're too far gone to save."

Rather than attack us, however, the Perfected merely pulled out four chairs, two on either side of the long table. The maid then retreated, while Fenton fetched wine glasses from a cabinet and put them one at each seat.

"Join me," Mrs. Creigh said. "I have no interest in fighting you, Dr. Whyborne. I will if I must, of course, but our previous alliance proved you can be reasoned with."

My hands shook, but I forced myself to walk across the thick rugs and take one of the proffered chairs. Fenton filled my glass, but I couldn't bring myself to touch it. My companions silently took their seats; out of the corner of my eye, I could tell Griffin and Iskander were both on high alert. Waiting for the inevitable treachery to come.

"What have you done to them?" I nodded at Fenton, who had taken up position against the wall behind Mrs. Creigh's chair. "This is an infection like the rust, is it not?"

"I told you when we met in Fallow that the rust was but one tool of the masters." Mrs. Creigh took a sip of her wine and smiled at me. "This, however, was a gift directly from them, passed to us by Nyarlathotep itself, after you destroyed the rust. It's much improved, don't you think? The avatar was a weak point in the design of the rust, just as the queens were in the umbrae, and the dwellers with the ketoi. Now, each individual is under *our* direct control, not ordered through an intermediary."

Bile rose to my throat. "It's monstrous."

She shrugged. "I tried doing this the easy way. The rust would have been so much simpler for us all. But you forced us to do things the hard way, and, well, here we are."

Christine sat across from me, her face white with fury. "Oh yes, it would have been so much easier to let you turn us all into terrifying fungus creatures."

"Compared to what will befall you when the masters return, yes." Her glance flicked to Iskander. "I'd heard Dr. Whyborne succeeded in freeing you. Pity."

"Shut up," Christine snarled.

I didn't trust Mrs. Creigh's motivations for talking to us. Were there other Fideles on the way? Perhaps Nephren-ka himself? "Enough of this. Where is my father?"

"He's here," Mrs. Creigh said. "Cooperate, and I might even let you see him."

From behind her chair, Fenton gave a slight shake of his head.

My heart beat faster. Was he trying to warn us? *Could* he try to warn us? Or had it merely been some spasm as the last of his nervous system was overtaken by the infection?

If it was a deliberate signal, it surely meant that Mrs. Creigh was lying. About letting me see Father if I cooperated?

Or was Father not here at all?

My face remained the neutral mask I'd spent so much of my early life hiding behind. "I'm going to require some proof Father's still alive and whole."

She leaned forward, staring at me as if fascinated. "Do you really think you can still win this? We've taken your town. Your place of power belongs to us now."

The distant howling trembled on the edge of my hearing. I balled my hands up to keep my fingertips from scorching the table. "Widdershins belongs only to itself."

"Even now, the maelstrom's power fuels our magic. Nephren-ka's original purpose may have been thwarted, but now he has the bottomless power of the arcane vortex to draw upon."

The howling I'd been hearing was a cry of impotent fury, the maelstrom's rage at being used to feed the machinations of the Fideles and ultimately the masters.

Christine perked up at the mention of Nephren-ka, but she knew enough to stay silent and not betray our ignorance. Griffin sat tense at my side, alert for whatever trap was set to spring around us. Iskander remained as impassive as a bronze statue.

"We haven't been idle since taking your father's house." Mrs. Creigh waved vaguely. "All of his notes, his plans to raise your so-called 'army of the land' against us, are in our hands. The homes of your precious old families have been likewise raided, with the exception of the ghūl, of course. Trapping some of the Fideles in her own house, then burning it to the ground, was a bold move. And one she'll regret, once we catch her."

Miss Lester was free, at least, but it was small comfort. All the planning Father had done was for nothing. The Fideles had the names of everyone in his confidence, from Police Chief Tilton to the agents of the Brotherhood who still remained loyal even after its dissolution. The secrets hoarded by the old families were laid bare, to be used against them.

"You cannot win," Mrs. Creigh went on. "You must see that now. Be reasonable, as you were in Fallow. Death is not—has never been— my goal. Wholesale slaughter is abhorrent to me. I want to help you save as many people as possible. Your friends. Your family. Yourself. But the only way to do that is to join us."

"And become like Fenton?" Griffin asked. "Is he one of the ones you've *saved?*"

She frowned. "Who?"

Of course she didn't know the names of those she'd harmed. She likely hadn't known the names of the cinereous in Fallow, either.

"So the offer is join you or die." I took a deep breath and met her gaze squarely. "You're not the first to make such an offer. I believe you were familiar with the last person to do so. Its name was Nyarlathotep, and things ended very, very badly for it."

I spoke with a confidence I didn't actually feel. We'd barely survived the encounter. We'd barely survived *so many* encounters, and our luck was bound to run out eventually. Especially if Nyarlathotep had spoken truly, and Persephone and I were doomed by the maelstrom's own plan.

"So you claimed when we spoke on the telephone." Doubt flickered in Mrs. Creigh's eyes, and she moistened her lips. "I will admit, Nephren-ka has been…unsettled…at Nyarlathotep's absence. But he believes you're bluffing. The Man in the Woods is simply waiting Outside, to return alongside the masters. You cannot have killed a god."

They didn't know. Which meant they didn't know *how* we'd destroyed it, that our plan would never have worked here in Widdershins. Or anywhere save for Carn Moreth, for that matter.

I leaned forward, resting my hands gently on the table. Lying about my own prowess didn't come easily to me, and I half-wished I had the power of the maelstrom surging through me, that I might deliver an unhinged rant to convince her. "I am the fire that burns in the veins of the world," I said, trying not to cringe as I did so. "I bested Nyarlathotep, and I'll best the masters as well."

The color had drained from Mrs. Creigh's face. "Nyarlathotep created you at the behest of the masters. You can't be greater than them."

"Morgen created me." As I'd guessed, the unfamiliar name caused another line of worry to appear on her brow. "And if I'm lying, then where is Nyarlathotep now? Why doesn't it answer the call of Nephren-ka, the pharaoh who enshrined it as a god and opened the path for four-thousand years of human sorcerers to summon it into our world?" When she made no answer, I nodded and sat back. "You proved yourself reasonable in Fallow, Mrs. Creigh. We can save humanity without bending knee to the masters. We can fight. Help us to do so."

Silence. No one spoke or moved. The maid and Fenton might truly have been the wax statues they appeared. And for a moment, I let myself hope my words had convinced her.

Then she sat back, and I thought her eyes held regret. "You are a monster the likes of which the world has never seen, Dr. Whyborne," she said, almost gently. "As is your sister. In any other circumstances, you might prevail. But the masters are coming, and there is only death awaiting you on this path. I fear I must decline your most generous offer."

The discreet servants' door swung open behind us. On the other side stood footmen, maids, the cook who had created so many of the meals that sustained me as a youth. When I was a child, Miss Emily would invite me to eat at the servants' table whenever Father was away on business, and I'd stuffed my belly there as I'd never been able to do under his disapproving gaze. Some of the faces were new, but so many had sat there with me, no doubt later whispering amongst themselves about poor Master Percival. Father would never have approved, but none of them had betrayed me to him.

And now all were waxen, perfect. The burn scars on Cook's hands had vanished, the elderly laundress sported no limp or wrinkle. No expression of joy or sorrow distorted their smooth faces. In their hands they carried kitchen knives, fireplace pokers, irons, and more. The tools they'd once wielded with pride to keep Whyborne House functioning smoothly, now turned into weapons.

Griffin and Iskander snapped to their feet instantly, Christine not far behind. But I sat paralyzed, my heart pounding, my lips numb. "No. Don't hurt them!" I cried, though I didn't know whom I begged.

One of the footmen took a savage swipe at Griffin with a poker. He barely parried it with his sword cane. "We have no choice!"

Iskander's knives ran red with blood. Christine wielded her cudgel with grim determination. But most of the Perfected were through the door now, and we'd soon be overwhelmed if I didn't do something.

Mrs. Creigh began to chant in Aklo.

I surged up, chair flying to the floor behind me. She'd risen as well, her eyes locked on me, focusing her spell—

Tears stinging my eyes, I spoke the true name of fire, and the curtains behind her erupted into a blaze.

THE CURTAINS WENT UP in flames, far faster than I'd anticipated. Within seconds, tongues of fire licked the ceiling, and sparks fell to the carpet where they began to smolder.

It was enough to break Mrs. Creigh's concentration. With a cry of dismay, she turned to the fire, no doubt intending to use sorcery to smother it before it could spread.

Fenton's arm went around her throat, dragging her against him. A screech of rage escaped her, and she clawed at his waxen skin, blemishing the unnatural smoothness of his face. He said nothing, but his eyes darted in my direction.

Then he hurled them both into the flames.

Mrs. Creigh's dress went up like a torch. She screamed and struggled, but Fenton held fast, even as his own clothing began to catch.

Horror swamped me. I took a step toward them, but Griffin's hand closed around my arm. "Ival! We have to get out of here!"

Something snapped within me. Fenton, the other servants, they were beyond my help. But my friends weren't.

I turned to the main door, leading to the grand staircase. Some servants had moved to block it, but I cleared them out of the way with a blast of wind. Christine and Iskander darted through instantly. Even as the heat of the fire began to scorch me, Griffin dragged me through the door and out.

Smoke stung my eyes and set me to coughing. Sparks and flames followed us, carried by the swirling currents of air. We raced to the head of the stairs, then Christine stopped and turned to me. "We have to find Niles before the whole place burns down around us. Where could they be holding him?"

I remembered Fenton's subtle shake of the head. "I don't think they are. I believe she was lying."

"The devil?" Iskander exclaimed. "We came here for nothing?"

I didn't know. I didn't know *anything*, except Fenton had thrown himself into the fire to save us. He'd overcome the compulsion to obey, held onto some fragment of himself, even when no one else seemed able to do so.

Smoke billowed from the room and crawled along the ceiling. A burning shape stumbled out of the flames, and I caught sight of the charred remains of an apron around her waist before she flailed into the wall. Her hand struck one of the paintings hanging along the wall, oil and canvas igniting even as it tumbled to the floor.

"We can't stay here," Christine said, and punctuated her words with a bout of coughing. She started down the marble staircase, and the rest of us followed.

"If Niles *is* here, where would he be?" Griffin demanded. "Ival, think!"

"The wine cellar."

"Then take us there, and hurry!"

We ran down the stairs to the ground floor. What sounded like fighting came from the street outside, but I had no time to wonder about it. Though there were servants' entrances to the basement, the quickest way to the wine cellar lay through a door near the dining hall. A flight of marble steps led down to a wooden door banded in iron.

And locked. "Only Fenton has the keys." Or had, rather, and there was certainly no recovering them now.

"There's no time to pick it," Griffin said. "Whyborne, you're going to have to break it down."

Summoning the wind might fan the flames even now devouring the house, but I didn't know what else I could do. I'd interpreted Fenton's signal as meaning Father wasn't in the house, but what if I was wrong? If he was here, and Fenton had meant to indicate something else, my father would die here as his own mansion burned down above him.

At my nod, Griffin pounded on the door with his fist. "Stand back!" he yelled through the keyhole.

I tried not to think of the flames, instead centering myself and focusing my will. My companions flattened themselves against the walls, well back. The scars on my arm hurt now with a constant, sharp pain; I'd channeled too much power through myself in too short a time. I ignored it as best I could as I called upon the arcane forces once again.

It felt as though someone had taken a knife to my arm, but the roar of the gale howled from above, twisting through open windows and funneling down the staircase. It ripped at my hair and clothing, nearly knocking me from my feet as it tore past. Smoke and sparks came with it, stinging my skin, my throat.

The lock creaked and groaned—then burst open, the heavy weight of the door shearing off the bolt as it flew back.

I let the wind die away, but the stench of burning was all around us now. As I lowered my hand, Griffin peered into the lightless cellar. "Hello? Is—"

To my utter shock, a figure appeared from the shadows. She held a wine bottle in her hand as if she intended to use it as a weapon. Her skirts were gathered in such a fashion as to allow her freedom of movement, though it also exposed such a scandalous stretch of calf that heat rose to my face. Dirt and grime clung to her, and her hair looked not to have seen a comb recently, but her features were unmistakably those of my secretary Miss Parkhurst.

CHAPTER TWENTY-TWO

hyborne

"Dr. Whyborne!" she exclaimed, at the same moment as I said, "Miss Parkhurst? What on earth are you doing here?"

"It doesn't matter now," Christine said curtly. "Are there any more captives in there?"

"No." Miss Parkhurst shook her head. "Is that smoke?"

"Whyborne House is on fire," Griffin said. Her eyes widened in fear.

Iskander tugged Christine in the direction of the exit. "And we'd best leave now before it gets worse."

It wasn't until we'd reached the foyer that I remembered the sound of fighting I'd thought I heard outside. "The side door," I began to suggest.

Before I could continue any farther, the front door burst inward. A man in the blank mask and robe of the Fideles stumbled inside. Griffin whipped his sword cane about, but the cultist simply dropped to his knees—then pitched forward, face-down on the marble tiles. The back of his robes was soaked in blood.

Father stepped into view. In his hand he held the saber he'd carried during the War Between the States, its blade now stained with blood. Behind him crowded men I thought I recognized from the Widdershins police force, though Chief Tilton wasn't among them. Members of the old families mingled with them: Waites and Marshes, though again I saw neither Orion nor Fred.

Father's eyes widened in shock at the sight of me. "Percival? What are you doing here? Did you set the house on fire?"

Miss Parkhurst peered out from behind Christine. "Mr. Whyborne!"

Father blinked, before firming his expression. "At least you found Miss Parkhurst. Let's hurry, then, before more of those blasted Fideles appear. Put out any lanterns and follow me. Night and shadow are our friends now."

He turned and strode away, and we hurried after him. Some of the men touched their caps to me as they fell in around us. High Street led directly to the river, and we followed it down, past mansions gone dark and cold. An alarm of some sort must have spread, because a glance back showed more Fideles silhouetted against the blaze. None of them gave chase; perhaps the brightness of the fire blinded them to our movement in the shadows.

The mansions fell behind, the area becoming rapidly more humble until we reached the river. "There are smugglers' tunnels all along here," Miss Parkhurst explained in a whisper.

Dear heavens, the ground Widdershins sat upon was so riddled with secret underground passages, it was a wonder the entire town hadn't collapsed into a pit by now.

"We've been hiding in them ever since it all began," she went on. "But they aren't directly connected to the tunnels beneath the museum. I was trying to get a message to the librarians when I was captured."

"And Father came to save you?" I could scarcely believe it.

"Miss Parkhurst has been one of our best messengers," Father said gruffly. "She's quick, small enough to hide, and appears harmless enough we didn't expect the Fideles to pay her much attention. It seems we were wrong on that last assumption."

"One of the security guards from the museum recognized me." Miss Parkhurst's mouth turned down unhappily. "He'd been Perfected. Since I'm Dr. Whyborne's secretary, that horrible woman at Whyborne House thought I might know something to use against him."

It said a great deal about Mrs. Creigh's character that she hadn't thought I'd care whether she had my secretary held hostage. For all her grand talk about saving humanity, she hadn't seemed to care much at all about *people.*

We stopped at a house alongside the river, and one of the Marshes opened the door, before she and several others slipped inside. Making sure it was safe to go in, I assumed. When she reappeared and beckoned to us, the others entered.

I paused just outside and looked back. It was too far to make out details, but the fire consuming Whyborne House was yet visible. Flames leapt high, endangering the homes to either side. A huge column of smoke rose into the night sky, lit from below with a hellish orange glow.

God.

I'd hated the place with every fiber of my being. Beneath its roof, which now looked to have collapsed into the lower stories, I'd known little save for misery. I'd walked out the door the first chance I had, and would never have returned if Mother hadn't still been there.

But it was also where I'd first discovered my love of languages. The joy of translation. Where my mother had read me tales of Achilles and Patroclus, Alexander and Hephaestion. Of the knight Parzifal, who went into the world dressed as a fool, destined to find both true love and the Holy Grail.

I sensed Father hovering beside me. Taking his own last look at what had been his home for his entire life. "Did anyone escape?" he asked.

My heart felt like a ball of lead weighing down my chest. "I hope so. Some of the servants might have, even though they…they were all Perfected."

"I see."

I swallowed hard. "Fenton…I don't know how, but he managed to hold onto some piece of himself. When the time came, he acted in our defense and killed Mrs. Creigh. But it cost him his own life."

Father's eyes were suspiciously bright, but he straightened his shoulders. "Fenton was the most loyal man I ever met. He could have no more fitting a funeral pyre." Then he stepped past me and into the house. "Come along, son. We must keep moving."

CHAPTER TWENTY-THREE

riffin

THE SMUGGLERS' tunnels led to another basement, where we stopped to regroup. I walked silently beside my husband, hoping my presence offered him some comfort. Though he'd hated Whyborne House, he'd spoken fondly of the servants many times, and I knew their loss hung heavy on him.

Though Niles allowed himself to show no flicker of emotion, I guessed he grieved as well. All of the Whyborne family heirlooms, the portraits of their ancestors, the journals and books stretching back generations: all lost. Not to mention the photographs of Heliabel, Guinevere, and Stanford, or even of Ival as a child.

And I felt certain he grieved for the servants. Niles, was many things, but he wasn't heartless or without loyalty. Many of the servants were the third or more generation of their family to serve the Whybornes, to keep their secrets along with keeping the house. Niles had always made it clear he trusted them, and the loss of people he'd known for his entire life, whom he'd relied upon for decades, must surely weigh on him.

As for Fenton, how long had he been Niles's companion? He'd been the one to drive Niles to his meetings, to let in his guests, to do whatever was required, a staunch shadow at Niles's side.

But I knew from Ival that Niles considered displays of tears "womanish." He hadn't even wept when Guinevere was murdered, at least not where anyone else could see.

Christine broke the silence. "Did you hear what Mrs. Creigh said, about thwarting Nephren-ka's original purpose? Maybe my expedition didn't doom us all."

"What do you think he was meant to do?" Iskander asked.

"The blasted Codex might tell us, if we can only get to it." Ival sounded exhausted. He stank of smoke, as did the rest of us, and his clothing was covered in ash and sported tiny burn marks where sparks had settled. Between the marsh, the umbrae nest, and the fire, none of our attire was fit for anything besides rags. "Miss Parkhurst, you were on your way to the librarians when you were captured?"

She nodded. But before she continued, I held up my hand. "Forgive me, Maggie, but there is a matter of some urgency. Since you were a captive of the Fideles, it would behoove us to make certain you aren't infected."

Niles's gaze sharpened. "Infected?"

"The Perfected are created by injecting something similar to the rust into them."

Maggie's face paled sharply. "She didn't…but, no, you can't take my word for it. I'd probably lie if I was turning into one of them."

"I'll conduct an examination, if there's anywhere private to do so," Christine offered.

In the end, they retreated to the tunnel, which was expected to remain deserted for the time being. And if it didn't, we had bigger problems than modesty. While they were gone, we told Niles all that had happened since we departed Widdershins on the *Melusine*.

Including Stanford's ultimate fate. Niles turned away as Whyborne haltingly described what Nyarlathotep made Stanford into, and Stanford's final attempt at bravery.

"I see," Niles said at last. "He recovered some honor at the last, then. Thank you for telling me, Percival."

Niles had done so many horrible things. If he'd raised Stanford differently...

But his grief was real, and there was no point to rubbing salt in the wound. Nor would Niles thank me for trying to offer him comfort. I picked up the thread of the tale and continued on as matter-of-factly as possible. By the time I finished, he was able to turn around and face us again with a calm expression.

Maggie and Christine returned as I finished. "All clear," Christine announced.

One of the tight bands around my chest loosened. "Thank God."

Niles nodded in Maggie's direction, which was as far as he was likely to go expressing relief. "Miss Parkhurst has been invaluable to our efforts," he said. Ival looked shocked at the sentiment, but I found myself less surprised. Niles hadn't exactly welcomed me into the family with open arms, at least, not the way Heliabel had. But he never tried to remove me from Whyborne's life, either, and over the years his tacit acknowledgement had grown into the sort of acceptance I'd never imagined possible. When he'd shown Persephone the portraits of their ancestors, so she might learn of her human heritage, he'd included me just as he would have any legal spouse of his son's.

Now all of those portraits were ash.

Maggie blushed bright pink. "I'm only a secretary," she mumbled.

"You've heard our story," Whyborne said. "How did Whyborne House fall? And what about the other old families? Mrs. Creigh said Miss Lester escaped, but what about Orion Marsh and Fred Waite?"

"Missing," said one of the Marshes. I struggled to recall his name and failed. "Or at least, we ain't heard from either of them. Maybe they're hidin' in tunnels like we are."

Or maybe they were dead, or Perfected. That didn't need saying, so I only nodded.

Niles's lips formed a tight line. "As you've already heard from others, the attack was sudden and overwhelming. The Waites had set a watch on the Front Street Bridge as both the most likely target of the Fideles and the place where the masters will probably emerge. The police knew to look for any signs of unusual activity. More unusual than normal, of course," he added.

"So basically what you were doing before we left," I confirmed.

He nodded. "They struck from a direction we didn't expect and hit both land and sea simultaneously. The Perfected, the lumina, the nereids, and the cultists, all at the same time as Nephren-ka arose in the museum. The museum guards attempted to stop him, of course, but he slaughtered them. And once they fell, Nephren-ka worked necromancy to raise them, this time as his minions." Niles's expression grew increasingly grim. "Our forces were fragmented from the start. Almost before we knew anything had gone wrong, Mrs. Creigh invaded the house with the other cultists at her back. I knew from the start we had no hope of holding against such a powerful sorceress, so I grabbed my saber and ordered the servants to flee."

Niles stopped and took a deep breath. For a moment, he struggled against emotion he couldn't allow himself to express. "Fenton refused, as did the others. At the time, none of us had even seen the Perfected, let alone knew that they'd once been...well. And we thought they'd be safer if I left. I was the one Mrs. Creigh wanted, after all. I truly believed the Fideles would follow the conventions of war and leave bystanders unharmed."

Grief showed under his voice, no matter how he tried to quell it. "I'm sorry." I put my hand to his shoulder. "What happened to them isn't your fault."

He pulled away, and I let my hand fall. "There are casualties in any war," he said gruffly. "We must be prepared to sacrifice whatever it takes to win. The loss of Whyborne House is a personal blow, but as it took one of the highest ranking Fideles with it, strategically speaking we're in a better position now than we were this morning."

Whyborne gaped at him. "How can you be so callous? Didn't you listen earlier? We thought you were being held captive. I didn't go there to kill Mrs. Creigh; I went to rescue my father!"

"And that's always been your problem, Percival," Niles snapped back. "You want to save people, when what you need to want is to win! During the Overland Campaign, each battle cost the Union enormously. General Grant didn't *want* to send those boys to die, but he knew that was what was needed to win the war. And he was right."

"This isn't the War Between the States!"

"No, this is a war for the very fate of the world!" Niles flung up his arms in despair. "Unless I have badly misunderstood, the maelstrom ensured you and Persephone were born to win it. You're a living weapon, so stop being squeamish and *do your job.*"

I gaped at Niles's harsh words. Iskander and Maggie both looked as though they very badly wanted to be anywhere else. Christine, however, drew herself to her full height, her eyes flashing.

"Now see here," she began.

Ival held his hand up to stop her, before she could start hurling profanity. "You're right. I was made for this. And the maelstrom was created to be a tool of the masters. So maybe it shouldn't be surprised if I don't know my place any better than it does." He met his father's gaze, eyes fierce. "I'll sacrifice whatever I need to, but I won't throw people away and pretend it's a victory."

Pride swelled my heart. At times I might curse my husband's stubbornness, but he'd never let the world make him into something he was not. I'd tried so hard to fit in, to become whatever it was I thought those around me needed, as if love was a thing to be earned rather than given. But his life had been one of quiet defiance, of a refusal to compromise who he was at the center of his being. I loved him, so intensely it seemed it must be written on my skin for the world to see.

Iskander cleared his throat awkwardly. "So, Miss Parkhurst, you've been visiting with the librarians?"

She nodded, eager for any turn in the conversation. "Yes. I know how to find them, though it won't be safe for a large group to move through the streets."

"That's quite all right," I said. "We won't be moving through the streets. We'll be moving under them."

CHAPTER TWENTY-FOUR

 hyborne

EVEN THE UMBRAE could only burrow so fast. Though the existence of the previous network of underground passages aided them greatly, not everything was interconnected. Additionally, collapses had closed off tunnels that had been connected when originally excavated. But thanks to Miss Parkhurst, we at least could now pinpoint precisely what part of the underground maze the librarians were lurking in, which made the task infinitely easier.

Griffin suggested we take the opportunity to catch some sleep, and Father agreed. I ended up propped against the wall, my folded coat behind my head, while Griffin pillowed his head on one thigh and Christine on the other. Iskander started off sitting with Christine's legs in his lap, but soon slumped sideways and was now snoring on my shoulder.

Exhaustion tugged at me, but sleep remained stubbornly elusive. My tired mind returned again and again to Whyborne House. To the fire, and the deaths, and the destruction.

124 JORDAN L. HAWK

How dare Father lecture me about my destiny? He'd thought our enemies would offer to let those not involved in the struggle vacate the city. His presumption led to everything that had happened tonight —or last night, by now.

A few of the police officers who had been hiding with him came up to tell me how Father's leadership had saved their lives more than once. It didn't mean he was right in my case, though.

Was he?

I shifted and tried to find a more comfortable position, without waking any of the sleepers using me as their pillow. The Fideles were clearly willing to do whatever it took to win. They always had been. Stanford and Bradley had wanted power and acknowledgement of their superiority. Mrs. Creigh claimed she wanted to save what of humanity she could, but at the same time treated people as disposable tools, to be transformed into whatever form she needed and then discarded when they no longer served.

Justinian Endicott hadn't been one of the Fideles. He'd wanted to save people. To save his family. Then turned far too many of them into pitiable, though incredibly dangerous, monsters as punishment for what he perceived as betrayal. And though he'd seemed sad when others died as a consequence of his actions, he'd still allowed those deaths to happen, so certain was he that he'd made the right—the only —choice.

Was I making the same mistake as Justinian? Not turning people into monsters, of course, but would my desire to avoid sacrificing my friends, my family, my town, end up costing everything?

Maybe the only way to defeat the masters was to be like them. To sit like a spider in the center of my web, and send out the police, the old families, the umbrae, the librarians, to die in whatever numbers it took to ensure victory.

I was so tired.

There came the scrape of claws somewhere on the outside of the house facing the river. I sat up, heart beating faster. A soft murmur of voices filtered down from above, followed by footsteps on the wooden stair to the basement. Whoever it was, the lookout had let them pass without challenge.

Everyone else awoke as well, Griffin lifting his head in silence, while Christine whispered a curse, and Iskander started off my shoulder.

The door was barred from our side. "Father," said a muffled voice. "I've come to see my brother."

Persephone.

Miss Parkhurst's face lit up, and I almost thought she would shove aside the policeman who unbarred the door. The moment it was open, Persephone stepped in and caught Miss Parkhurst in an embrace.

I turned away, my face heating at the shocking display. I didn't disapprove, but I did wish my sister wouldn't go about kissing my secretary in my view. I certainly didn't go around kissing Griffin in front of her, let alone our father. No one else seemed to agree with my reserve, though, as Griffin gave me an amused grin and clapped me on the shoulder.

"You're safe, cuttlefish?" Persephone asked Miss Parkhurst.

"Yes. Well, I was captured by Mrs. Creigh, but only for a few hours. Dr. Whyborne and the others rescued me."

Persephone growled. "Did she hurt you? I'll bring you her skull—"

"No need," Miss Parkhurst said hastily. "She was caught in the fire when Whyborne House burned. Um, I'm sorry. About the house, I mean."

I chanced turning back around. Persephone stood straight, but her eyes, so similar to my own, betrayed her weariness. "What are you doing here?" I asked. "Surely the ketoi need you."

"You risked yourself coming here," Father added. At least I wasn't the only one he was put out with.

"I didn't come alone. Calls Dolphins diverted the nereids in the river, and Tide Tamer, Coral Teeth, and Plays Among the Kelp accompanied me." She turned from Father to me. "Brother. We must talk."

I nodded. "We'll be more effective if we can coordinate our forces."

"Yes. But there's something I wish to speak to you about." She glanced reluctantly at Miss Parkhurst. "In private."

"Of course." There were things I wanted to say to her, as well, that would be easier alone.

"The tunnel running away from the river should be deserted," one of the men offered. "And if it isn't, anyone in there is someone who shouldn't be there coming up behind us." He lowered his gaze. "I was in the Draakenwood with Chief Tilton, and I'm guessing the two of you can handle most things."

Unless they were people I'd known, Perfected and changed. But I didn't say anything, only took a lantern and slipped through the concealed entrance.

My sister and I walked a short distance away, to avoid being accidentally overheard, then stopped. "Have you been having dreams?" Persephone asked.

She'd never been one to waste words. "Yes. I assume it's the maelstrom, trying to communicate in some fashion."

She nodded. "I dreamed of the empty ocean. Unsettled by ketoi. No city beneath the waves."

Just as I'd seen a vision of the deserted Cranch River Valley. "I felt so alone." I frowned. "But why would it show us something like that? What possible purpose could it have?"

"I don't know." She sighed. "I hoped you might have some better idea, with your books and your knowledge. But it seems we are both swimming blind."

I ran my hand back through my hair in a half-hearted attempt to tame it. The scent of smoke clung to the locks, and some were stuck together from the slime of the worker umbrae that had cushioned our fall in the Draakenwood. I must truly look a fright. "Mother...did she reach you?"

"Yes. She said you found the key to the Codex and defeated Nyarlathotep." She gave me an approving grin, displaying her rows of shark teeth when she did so. "Well done, brother."

"It was a group effort." I hesitated, but it had to be said. "Nyarlathotep claimed the maelstrom created you and me to be sacrificed. That our place in its design was to die. It doesn't really change anything, I suppose, but I wanted you to know."

"Why would you believe such a creature?"

"I don't know that I do." I shrugged. "Its words had the ring of truth...but how many of its previous victims would have said the same?"

"Indeed." She put a clawed hand on my arm. "As you said, it makes no difference. If our deaths are required, we will not hesitate."

I found myself oddly touched that she had such faith in me. I couldn't help but wonder how different things might have been if we'd grown up together.

Startled exclamations came from the other side of the door behind us. We exchanged a glance, then hurried back into the room where the others waited.

The cries had come from some of those who had never seen umbrae before. The workers had burrowed straight through the wall, using some combination of acid and unnatural powers, and immediately scuttled up to cling just below the ceiling. Griffin had put himself in front of one of the police officers who'd drawn a gun.

"Put that down," Father said, grabbing the man's wrist and forcing the barrel away. But I couldn't help but note he was almost as pale as the officer. He'd never viewed our umbrae allies up close, either.

Jack emerged from the tunnel, grinning broadly. "There you are, Griffin. I brought some friends."

Behind him came the librarians. Most of them were dirty and a bit on the ragged side, but they were all armed with books, knives, guns, cudgels, and bookbinding awls. In their midst came Mr. Quinn, his silver eyes burning with fervor. In his hands, he held the complete Wisborg Codex.

He ignored everyone except for Persephone and myself. When he reached us, he bowed low, holding out the Codex like an offering. "Widdershins. I've kept it safe for you."

I took the book from him. Its leather binding bore stains I hoped were merely rust from the heavy iron latch. In between these covers, the key to our salvation might lie.

"Well," I said. "I suppose I should get to work."

CHAPTER TWENTY-FIVE

riffin

WE WAITED for Ival in the chamber of the Queen of Shadows. He'd holed up with Mr. Quinn and another librarian, several lanterns, a few sheaves of paper, and the Codex.

Persephone and the Queen studied one another with open curiosity after I introduced them. Jack chatted with one of the many Waites, whose name I couldn't recall, and Niles discussed ketoi strategy with Tide Tamer. Christine took the opportunity to recline on one of the huge funguses the umbrae farmed, to give her swollen ankles a rest. Though her skirts largely concealed the bulge formed by the baby, none of us forgot it was there. I suspected Iskander wished there was some hope of convincing her to stay behind, or to act in a safer manner, but he knew as well as I that she'd never agree. As she'd pointed out on the way to Balefire, the child would need a world to grow up in, and it was up to us to make certain there was one left.

The hours dragged by while we waited for Whyborne to finish

his translation of the Codex and find whatever answers waited within. We ate, and dozed, and marked time by our pocket-watches, since day and night were the same in the halls of the umbrae. Saul curled up on my chest, his purr thrumming in my lungs.

I awoke once to find Christine and Iskander discussing the fact that the burrow made naturally by the umbrae was quite different from the city in Alaska.

"The city was built for the masters," Iskander said. "Clearly the umbrae have a sense of architecture that differs quite a bit from the race that enslaved them."

Christine chewed thoughtfully on a strip of pemmican; where she'd gotten it, I had no idea. "Does that mean the masters have anything in common with us? With humans, I mean? The architecture of the city was strange, but not entirely alien."

He put a hand to her knee. "I can't imagine, dearest. Perhaps Whyborne will find the answers to your questions."

"He'd better." She huffed. "What the devil is taking so long?"

I slipped back into sleep as Iskander pointed out the undertaking of translating the remaining parts of the Codex was no small thing.

I woke again to the smell of coffee. Such a homely scent was jarringly out of place amidst the acidic stink of the umbrae, the cold wet smell of earth and stone. Jack and one of the detectives had built a small fire with fallen branches scavenged by the umbrae, and were using it to boil campfire coffee. Where the coffee itself had come from, I didn't know.

Saul had abandoned me, so I sat up. As I did so, Persephone stilled and looked up from where she sat talking quietly with Maggie. A moment later, Whyborne emerged into the chamber, Mr. Quinn and the other librarian following.

Mr. Quinn beamed, as if he'd just had the most delightful experience of his entire life. Ival, on the other hand, looked utterly exhausted. Shadows encircled his eyes, and his shoulders sagged. His hair stuck up in every direction, the lantern's light picking out the first silver threads amidst the darkness.

I rose to my feet, my hand outstretched. He offered me a weary smile in return. "Is that coffee I smell?"

Jack and the detective both looked as if they'd meant to have it for themselves, but Jack nodded. "Yes. I think there's a cup somewhere about—let me find it and pour for you. There's no sugar, I'm afraid."

Niles cleared his throat. "I think it best if anyone who doesn't need to be here leaves before Percival tells us what he's found."

Some of the members of the old families frowned. Mr. Quinn clapped his hands sharply, and the librarians quickly followed him out, deeper into the burrow. Persephone's entourage slipped out at her nod. Jack beckoned to the detective he'd been making coffee with. "Come on, lads."

"Jack," I began, but he shook his head.

"Tell me only what you think I need to know." His green eyes met mine. "That way, if I end up Perfected, I won't be able to tell them anything."

His words got the stragglers moving, but they also chilled my heart. The thought of losing Jack bit deep. We'd not yet found our other brother, assuming he was even still alive. The rest of our family had died in New York. He was the only connection I had left to the family of my birth. The only member of my current family related to me by blood.

But this was war. We all stood to lose everything we cared about. Every one.

Maggie looked uncertainly at Persephone. "I should probably leave."

Ival winced as he took a sip of the campfire coffee. "You've been a part of this from the first, Miss Parkhurst. Maybe not directly, but still. I'd like for you to see it to the end."

We arranged ourselves in what comfort we could. Ival drank down the rest of his coffee, swallowing even the bitter grounds. "I want to begin with a caveat."

"Of course you do," Christine said with a roll of her eyes.

Ival glared at her. "To put it in archaeological terms, the provenance of this information is suspect. We have no idea what older sources the author of the Codex might have been drawing on, or even when it was first written, only that all the copies we've seen date from the fifteenth century. As there's no way to verify any of it, it could all be unhinged ranting."

"Except the Fideles used it to send the Beacon and begin the Restoration," I pointed out. "Clearly that part was correct."

"Yes." Ival's shoulders slumped. "The Codex is in part bestiary, showing the many servants of the masters. Ketoi, umbrae, rat-things. The artist also had an obsession with flora, but that seems to have been more decorative than anything else. There are also star-charts, which...well, one thing at a time." Whyborne lifted his cup to his lips, discovered it empty, and lowered it again. "The rest of the Codex is no less than a history of the masters in this world...and a history of this world, in part. There are no dates, but it must have been a very long time ago, for both humans and ketoi to have forgotten them, and the umbrae to remember only fragments. If we consider the stele from Alaska..."

"Stay on topic, my dear," I reminded him gently.

"Er, yes." He paced a few steps away, then back to us, gathering his thoughts. "According to the author of the Codex, the masters come from a species which travels from dimension to dimension, conquering those they find suitable for their occupation. They enslave what useful species they find there, and in turn use them to conquer the next world, if it's a dimension in which their slaves can survive. Initially, six masters ruled the Earth."

"That's all?" Christine exclaimed.

Whyborne frowned at her. "Christine, these are beings of immense power, who commanded entire armies of creatures of the Outside. Hounds, byakhee, yayhos—"

"Yayhos?" I asked in surprise.

"Yes, yayhos. I suppose we should have known they'd be tangled up in all this." Whyborne opened the Codex to a page he'd marked with a scrap of paper, and read, *They have lost many of their skills over the eons since, and now skulk in the empty places of the earth, plying their petty surgeries as they seek to recover some shadow of their former glory.* He looked up. "I don't know if that means the masters discarded them, or if something else went wrong. But at the beginning, they were a slave species the masters brought to our world. The yayhos had great skill in biology and medicine—even greater than what we saw in Threshold, when they wished to put my brain in a jar."

I pursed my lips in thought. "Do you think they sensed your connection with the maelstrom? Not clearly enough to be certain, but they did have a marked interest in you."

"Who knows? At any rate, with the aid of both science and magic, the yayhos created the ketoi from humankind at the behest of the masters. Which explains why we can, er, interbreed." The tips of Whyborne's ears flushed pink. "And why those of us who are hybrids can be transformed. Whatever the yayhos did, it still lies within us, dormant until some echo of the magics they used awakens it. The umbrae were similarly created from earthly life, though the author doesn't seem to know what creature or creatures they were originally."

Iskander nodded. "It makes a great deal of sense, especially in the case of the ketoi. I wonder what the basis was for the dwellers in the deep?"

"The six masters ruled their global empire in sets of two," Whyborne went on. "Why, the Codex doesn't say. They don't seem to have reproduced, though there's no knowing what sort of life cycle such beings have. Though they had smaller enclaves scattered across the earth, where their servants and slaves lived, each pair had its own great city to call home. One in Alaska, one in Australia, and one in Antarctica."

Christine's eyes lit up. "Do you think the other two still exist? We could mount an expedition to Australia—"

"Now is not the time, dearest," Iskander said with a pained look.

"Bah." She settled back. "I suppose it will have to wait. Do go on, Whyborne."

"It's unknown how long the reign of the masters lasted. The author says 'eons,' but that's hardly reliable. He might be referring to hundreds of years, or thousands. Or tens of thousands, as unthinkable as that might seem." Whyborne shrugged. "Eventually, two things happened that ended their rule. One is that some of their creations began to develop the inconvenient habit of acting on free will."

The Queen of Shadows loomed in the back of my mind. "The umbrae," I said for her. "And the ketoi."

"Yes." Whyborne nodded in my direction. "The second problem was that strife broke out amongst the masters themselves. One of the pair in Australia murdered the other."

"Why?" Could such creatures have knowable passions, similar to our own? Greed, rage, envy, lust? Or had the killing been done for reasons we could never hope to comprehend?

"It doesn't say. But, as you can imagine, the act shook the empire to its core. The masters from the city in Antarctica took the side of the slain, while those in Alaska decreed the killer in the right. As they fought one another, the ketoi and the umbrae rose up, and everything descended into chaos." He paused. "The author implies that the lone master, which had slain its partner, was weakened in some fashion from the loss. The ketoi managed to destroy it with the artifacts we encountered at Balefire."

"If only the Source hadn't been lost," I said. But we'd had no other choice.

"The masters from the city in Alaska eventually triumphed over the other two and killed them as well. But in the meantime, their empire had fallen into chaos and ruin. The umbrae and ketoi no longer responded to their control. In the midst of confusion and madness, they withdrew from our world, planning to return some day in the far future, when they might resume control." Whyborne took a deep breath and let it out as a sigh. "And so things remained, until Nephren-ka found the Occultum Lapidem."

Christine scowled. "Blast him. Why couldn't he have stayed dead?"

"Or not murdered his way to power in the first place," Iskander said.

Whyborne ignored them both. "He was the first to call Nyarlathotep back into this world. To let something of the Outside return, for the first time since the masters had been banished. It gave them the foothold to begin the long work of preparing to reconquer this world."

"Do you mean to say the same masters are alive today?" I interrupted.

"Nyarlathotep survived through the eons." Whyborne shrugged. "There's no reason to think its creators couldn't have as well."

It was nearly incomprehensible. I recalled the weight of time that had lain over the city in Alaska, how dwarfed I had felt compared to the massive architecture, the endless silence. And again in the bowels of Balefire, where Nyarlathotep had perhaps made its own home.

I still held faith in God, but Whyborne's talk made me wonder about His role in this. I'd never asked myself whether He created what lay beyond the Veil, in the Outside, and to what purpose. Certainly nothing I was learning today meshed with any Biblical story I knew.

Humans were fallible, and I knew from Whyborne that what I'd learned as unalterable truth as a child, had in fact been altered many times with every translation. Perhaps I'd be better served by simply trusting some divine providence had brought us to this moment.

"I do have some good news for Christine," Whyborne went on.

She perked up. "Oh? Don't make me wait!"

"The Codex is quite clear that, heralding the return of the masters, Nephren-ka will rise in Egypt. He will then go to the fane and use its power to raise a vast army of the dead. Not only the restless mummies we encountered, but some untold number buried in the Red Lands from time immemorial. Thousands of years of withered husks returned to unlife by his hand. His great army will then sweep across Africa and Europe, obliterating all before it, and adding the dead of those who oppose them to its ranks." A small smile curled up one corner of his lips. "I imagine Nephren-ka was quite put out to discover himself in a museum in Massachusetts when he woke up."

Christine hugged Iskander joyfully. "I knew it! Whyborne might not have any sense to speak of, but the maelstrom made its best decision when it called me."

"Excuse me!" Whyborne exclaimed. "I have plenty of sense, as you put it. I'll have you know—"

"Later, Percival," Niles interrupted. "This has all been fascinating, and entirely useless! The point of translating the Codex wasn't to retrieve a history lesson. It was to find a way of defeating the masters. Is there or isn't there anything of use within its pages?"

"Er." Whyborne deflated slightly. "There is, but I'm not quite sure what it means. The Codex claims the priests who opposed Nephren-ka, and who buried him after his death, knew some great secret. Something with the power to bind not only Nephren-ka, but those he served. There's a copy of some Egyptian artwork—how the author obtained it, I've no idea. Perhaps they were a necromancer who called up one of the priests. But I'm not certain as to what it could mean."

Niles frowned. "I thought that was your specialty."

"It is," Whyborne snapped. "But this isn't a phrase to translate, it's more a pair of images."

"Let me take a look," Christine said.

Whyborne passed her the book. "It's the symbol for *ka*, repeated."

She nodded. "Yes. And this is clearly the heart being weighed in the afterlife." A slow grin spread over her face, and she exchanged a look with Iskander. "Good news, Whyborne. We've seen this before."

He frowned. "Where?"

"Inscribed on the seal holding the doors of Nephren-ka's tomb shut." Her dark eyes gleamed with excitement. "The seal was meant to keep him inside. And I bet it has some magical property that would enable it to keep the masters Outside."

I STRAIGHTENED, heart pounding. "And where is it?"

Christine's grin didn't falter. "In one of the storerooms at the Ladysmith. It's not much to look at—just a bronze bar, really—so it was never put on display or closely studied."

Whyborne sagged back. "Well done, Christine."

Persephone's tentacle hair lashed. "What does 'ka' mean?"

"The ancient Egyptians believed there were multiple parts of the soul," Whyborne explained. "The ka was one such part, and a focus on it dominated in the Old Kingdom, when Nephren-ka lived. Later—"

"Ival," I said. "Concentrate, my dear."

"Er, yes." He shot his sister an apologetic glance. "The ka was the part of you that, well, distinguishes something alive from something dead. The part that has earthly relationships and is a member of the community, which is why offerings from family members were made to it at tombs, rather than to the other parts of the soul. As for the weighing of the heart, the heart was thought to be the center of the self. Of consciousness, personality, emotion, everything."

"It was the only major organ retained in the body of the mummy for that reason," Iskander put in.

"I bet if we stabbed Nephren-ka through it, it would be enough to kill him a second time," Christine said excitedly.

"You could very well be right," Whyborne agreed. "As for the ceremony of weighing the heart, it was believed that before the soul could take its place in the afterlife, the heart would have to be balanced against ma'at—truth, represented by a feather. Evil deeds would weigh the heart down, whereas a life of good deeds would lighten it. So the inscription is…"

"Two ka on one side, and the weight of the heart on the reverse." Christine shrugged. "Perhaps it's judgment against the two remaining masters? Or it could mean something special to the priests who ordered it made, which we can't guess at. Either way, I'm certain the seal could be used, much the same way you used the bronze wand in Egypt." Her smile returned. "And just think—if I hadn't excavated the tomb, it would be sitting beyond our reach, while Nephren-ka raised an army of the dead."

"Wouldn't it have kept him in?" Niles asked.

Christine looked annoyed. "Presumably the Fideles could have moved it as easily as I did. It isn't meant to bind ordinary people."

I held my hands up. "I think we can all agree we owe any chance of victory to Christine, and move on."

"No wonder Nephren-ka and Nitocris didn't get along," Iskander mused. "Her ghūls would have eaten his army of the dead before he had the chance to call them up."

Maggie looked uncertain. "So we need to retrieve the seal from the museum somehow. Which means facing Nephren-ka."

"It won't be an easy fight," I said. "Not that any of this has been easy. But if we can prevail at the museum and retrieve the seal, we'll avoid an even worse battle against the masters."

"Er, there is one more thing." Whyborne shifted uncomfortably. "The star charts I mentioned...once I deciphered the labels and accompanying texts, the meaning became clear. The masters will return when the star Sirius reappears in the night sky."

A line sprang up between Iskander's brows. "The appearance of Sirius marked the yearly inundation of the Nile. In July, or there-abouts, if I recall."

"Yes. But in these more northerly latitudes, it rises later in the year." Whyborne's lips flattened. "Specifically, it will first appear on the horizon about an hour before dawn tomorrow."

CHAPTER TWENTY-SIX

hyborne

FOR A LONG MOMENT, no one answered my pronouncement. Predictably, it was Christine who broke the silence with a long string of curses, first in Arabic, then in English. Father and Miss Parkhurst both looked shocked at her more colorful turns of phrase, though Miss Parkhurst much less so.

When Christine finally wound down, Persephone turned to me. "Very well, brother. We know what must be done. There's only the question of how to do it."

"The Veil will open where the Beacon did—above the eye of the maelstrom, on the Front Street Bridge," I said. "That's where we'll have to activate the seal. At a guess, it might take both of us to channel enough magic into it to hold them back."

It made sense. The maelstrom couldn't act directly; it had no hands, no eyes, but ours. We'd hold the seal for as long as need be, the power raging through us...

How long could we withstand it? Was this how we'd die, burned away from the inside by the very force that had created us?

That didn't matter. It couldn't. I had to focus on getting us to that point, not on what might come after we arrived. "Christine knows where the seal is, and she and Iskander can both identify it quickly, as they've seen it before. But before we can even hope to find it, there's the problem of Nephren-ka. He won't just let us stroll in and take it."

"This is what your army of the land is for," Father said. "In the absence of Police Chief Tilton, the officers will continue to follow me. The same can be said of the old families whose heads of house are missing. The librarians will fight, of that I've no doubt." He turned to the Queen of Shadows, and though he paled at the sight of her, he remained courteous. "Will your umbrae join with us, my lady?"

Griffin shut his eyes briefly, then opened them again. "Yes. A few soldiers will remain behind to guard the Draakenwood, but the rest will go into Widdershins with us."

"You concentrate on the museum," Persephone said. "I'll return to the ketoi, and we and the Endicotts will do everything in our power to distract their forces away from you." She rose to her feet. "I'll see you on the Front Street Bridge, brother."

I nodded. As she stepped away, Miss Parkhurst caught her hand. "I want to come with you."

A shadow touched Persephone's face. "I wish you could, cuttlefish. But we have to swim too far. I couldn't even leave you at one of the Endicott's ships. Not to mention the bites of the nereids are poison to your kind. I'd rather have you facing foes on land you have a better chance of defeating."

Miss Parkhurst's eyes gleamed, but she forced her shoulders back. "Then...then let me walk with you as far as I may."

"Yes." Persephone's expression gentled. "I would like that."

Persephone didn't look back at me as she left. There was no need. Either we'd both survive to meet up again on the bridge...or we wouldn't.

"It will take time to get our forces gathered, especially the remnants of the old families," Father said when she was gone.

I swallowed against the dryness in my throat. "Don't take too long."

"We'll gather what strength we can in the time allowed." He turned to me, his brows beetling over his nose. "Do try to have some faith in me, Percival."

I could have asked the same of him. But he was trying. We both were. "Forgive me."

"In the meantime," he said, "I advise everyone to rest. You especially, Percival. If I learned anything during my time on the battlefield, it's to snatch whatever sleep you can, whenever you can."

I wanted to ask if he meant to take his own advice. But the impulse was unworthy; he'd sleep if he had the chance. Otherwise, he'd do what I'd asked of him and be my general. Gather my troops, help plan my assault.

"There are numerous small chambers we can bed down in," Griffin said, no doubt relaying the thoughts of the Queen of Shadows. "Jack taught them what we need for comfort, so the workers have lined the rooms with moss and soft branches."

While Father hurried off in the other direction, we four ducked down a side tunnel. "I can't believe we're about to attack the museum," Christine said before we'd gone very far.

Neither could I. "Take it as revenge for all the awful galas and donor events we had to suffer through."

It made her laugh, as I'd hoped it would. "Perhaps we should dress for the occasion. I don't suppose the umbrae can fashion a gown, or white tie and tails? Do you remember the time—it must have only been a month or two after I was hired on—when that one young idiot got drunk and tried to ride the hadrosaur? What the devil was his name? He was a friend of Mathison's daughter, if I recall."

"Lee Dachsel," I said. I'd almost forgotten the incident. Like so many other times, I'd spent the evening tucked into a corner, watching everyone else socialize. He'd been one of a contingent of rich, careless young men, and I'd observed him with a longing I could barely admit to myself. At least, until he'd shown complete disregard for a valuable scientific specimen, at which point any appeal instantly evaporated. "I believe that was the same evening Mr. Farr threw a glass of champagne in Mr. Durfree's face. Or was it the other way around?"

"God knows." She sobered. "I wonder if they're still alive. Any of them."

"So do I." I stopped and looked down at her. We'd been together the longest, first as a pair of misfits who found refuge in each other's company, then as friends, and finally as family. "Christine, I want to say that...that it was my greatest fortune to have met you. I'm honored beyond words to have been your friend."

"Really, Whyborne, don't talk like that." She blinked rapidly. "We're going to get through this together, do you hear me? And then you and Persephone will seal off our world from the masters, and I'll have my baby, and you'll be the best godfather any child ever had."

She finished by throwing her arms around me. I hugged her back; in such a position, it was far easier to feel the bulge of new life in her belly. There was so much I wanted to say to her: how she'd been a true sister to me, my best friend, the one who was always ready to fight our way out of any situation.

But she already knew it. I'd made many mistakes in my life, but I'd at least learned to tell my little family that I loved them.

"You'll feel less morose after some sleep," she finished, patting me on the arm. "Now, Kander, which nest would you prefer?"

As she wandered away, Iskander shook my hand. "We have a plan, Whyborne," he said seriously. "After all we've experienced together, I truly believe that, if anyone can get us through this, it's you. So buck up, old chap, and get some rest."

"I will. Thank you."

Griffin took my hand without speaking and drew me farther along into the warren, until we came to a side room with a narrow entrance, but larger interior. Workers wandered the hall outside, perhaps at Griffin's request to protect our privacy.

A deep bed of moss and ferns from the forest floor filled a bowl-like depression in the center of the room. I wondered what the umbrae normally used the chamber for, or if it was some sort of guest room they'd devised should humans or ketoi have reason to visit. Maybe if we'd been ketoi, the depression would have been filled with water instead.

Griffin set the lantern well away from the bedding. We stripped off our filthy coats and spread them over the makeshift mattress. Not the best accommodations, but I was long past complaining. At least it would be soft and shared with no one except my husband.

Griffin came up behind me and slid his arms around my waist. "My dear," he murmured. "What can I do for you?"

I closed my eyes and leaned back against him. His familiar scent rose up around me, and I breathed deep.

Tomorrow, we'd be going into terrible danger. But at least this time we had an army. It wasn't just the four of us against the world.

And yet I was afraid. Afraid Nyarlathotep had been right, and Persephone and I were somehow doomed. It was foolish—the seal would work. Nyarlathotep was a monster, a thing of the masters, and it lied as easily as I drew breath.

Still, so many things could go wrong. It was practically a miracle we were both alive and breathing, after all we'd been through. If luck ran out, if something happened to me—or, God forbid, to Griffin—

This might be our last night together.

"Make love to me," I whispered.

His lips pressed into my neck, curling into a smile. "Of course."

I TURNED around in my husband's arms, reaching for the buttons on his vest. He kissed me softly, fingers threading through my hair. We both smelled of the umbrae's slime, and of smoke from the fire that had consumed Whyborne House. "I love you," I whispered against his mouth.

"And I love you, Ival."

We undressed one another, lingering over each inch of exposed skin. I kissed the freckle on his shoulder, then went lower to lick first one nipple, then the other. He ran his hands over my shoulders, tracing the scars that laced my right arm like frost branching across a windowpane.

When all of our clothing was in a pile on the floor, I tugged him down into our makeshift bed. The moss let out an earthy fragrance, as though we made love on the forest floor. I took my time, exploring his body leisurely, mapping out the skin I knew so well.

Before we'd met, I'd never imagined having anything remotely like what I shared with him. I'd resigned myself to a lonely life, telling myself I was content to watch, as if through a window. My world had been so drab, as though I lived inside a photograph, without color or sound.

Then he'd come to the museum, and nothing had ever been the same. From the beginning, he'd seen something in me that no one ever had. The maelstrom had collected him, and no matter what else it had planned for me, for that I would be eternally grateful.

I worked my way down his body, all the way to the scar wrapped around his thigh, left by the acid touch of a captive umbra in a basement below Chicago. Then back up, to the juncture of his legs, pausing to nuzzle and lick. His familiar scent fired my blood, and I tasted salt as I ran my tongue up the length of his cock.

"Ival," he whispered, and reached for me.

I slid up to kiss him. We wrapped our arms and legs around each other, tight. I delighted in the flex of muscle beneath his skin, in his warmth, his solidity. I wanted to commit every freckle, every scar, to memory.

We moved together, our bodies intertwined. "My husband," I said into his ear. "My love."

"All yours," he murmured back. "Only ever yours."

I closed my eyes and gave myself over to the building sensation. The taste of salt, of his body flexing against mine, of the exquisite friction of skin against skin. He cried out softly, shuddering, and his spend slicked my own member. I bit his shoulder, and he cried out again, even as my own climax rushed over me.

We were sticky and damp with sweat, but I didn't care. I held him close for a long time, before reluctantly shifting off of him. He curled against me, head on my shoulder. His hand traced idle patterns on my chest, the light of the lantern gleaming from the white pearl in his wedding ring.

"You're everything to me," he said quietly. "None of this means anything, if you're not with me."

I ran my fingers through his overlong hair. He was the center of my world, and always would be. "I want to grow old with you," I whispered, and my throat tightened with emotion. "I want to see what you'll look like with silver hair and laugh lines around your eyes. I want to hobble down the street together when we're eighty, or sit on the lawn and watch you tend our garden. I want to wake up in your arms for every single day of the next fifty years, until I take my last breath."

"So do I." He shifted position to kiss me, with such tenderness it made my heart ache. "Don't leave me, Ival. Please."

It wasn't a promise I could make. "I won't, not if I have any choice at all."

It seemed to satisfy him. We curled up together in our little nest. A short time later, Saul wandered in and lay across our feet, and I fell asleep to the comforting rumble of his purr.

CHAPTER TWENTY-SEVEN

 riffin

WE RECONVENED HOURS LATER, in the great chamber of the Queen of Shadows. I stood in front of her, her presence close in my mind, her huge orange eye watching over us all. As many members of our gathered forces as could fit crowded into the chamber with us. Niles waited in front of the assembly, and Jack, Maggie, Christine, and Iskander gathered by me.

We had laid our plans. While the ketoi created a distraction, we'd mount a multi-pronged attack on the museum. The police and the old families would attempt to go in through the staff doors, or at least occupy anyone inside in keeping them out. The librarians and most of the umbrae would come through the secret tunnels into the library. As the entrance to the tunnels had likely been discovered, we expected they would meet heavy resistance.

While the obvious attacks went on, some of the worker umbrae would burrow directly into the steam tunnels beneath the museum.

Whyborne, Christine, Iskander, and I would slip in, find the correct storage room on the lower levels, and then retreat the way we'd come once we had the seal. From there, we'd make our way to the Front Street Bridge and rendezvous with Persephone.

As plans went, I had to admit it was one of our best.

Whyborne emerged from one of the side tunnels, where he'd freshened up in a pool formed by an underground spring. We had no oil to tame his hair, but at least the wild spikes were clean of umbrae slime. When he saw the crowd awaiting him, his step hitched.

The man I'd first met would have hunched his shoulders and fled such scrutiny. Now, I could only marvel in admiration as he took a deep breath and straightened his back. "Centuries ago, Theron Black-byrne founded our town, alongside the ancestors of some of us here today. He inscribed his symbol on the very streets, believing he would set its destiny in stone."

Whyborne clasped his hands behind his back and paced to one side, though his attention remained on his audience. "Together, we have the power to overwrite that destiny. Blackbyrne, Nyarlathotep, my own brother Stanford, all believed we should follow *their* plans, live the lives *they* wanted for us. None of them succeeded." He stopped walking. "Now, we face an even greater threat. But the masters will fare no better than the rest. Because we have something they will never have, something Nephren-ka and the Fideles will never have. We have each other."

My heart swelled with pride, and I touched the ring on my left hand.

"Widdershins might be a horrible murder town," Whyborne went on, "but it's *our* horrible murder town. Only we can decide its fate, and we can only do that if we embrace one another." He looked up at the Queen of Shadows, then at Mr. Quinn. "Some of us aren't human. Some are. But our differences vanish when we understand we all want the same thing. Home. Safety. Family." He swallowed. "Our past looms over us, but we don't owe it fealty. We deserve the chance to make a better world than we've been told we can have. When you go forth from here, remember it's up to us to choose our future. Fight for that future with all you have. And remember, always, that Widdershins knows its own."

Mr. Quinn let out a rousing cry, quickly taken up. I added my own voice. The tips of Whyborne's ears turned bright red, and he no doubt would have hidden behind a rock if he could have.

"All right," Niles called, "You all have your orders."

As the crowd broke up, Whyborne joined us. "Well done, my dear," I said.

"That was excruciating," he replied. "Of all the terrible things the masters have done, forcing me to speak in front of people is the worst."

"Their reign of terror knows no bounds," I agreed. "Is everyone ready?"

Christine tapped her cudgel against her palm. "Ready." Iskander nodded, silent but determined. Whyborne looked over us and offered a faint smile.

"All right," he said. "Let's see this through together."

CHAPTER TWENTY-EIGHT

hyborne

"Percival, a moment," Father said as I made my way toward the burrows that would ultimately lead us to the tunnels beneath Widdershins.

I stopped and turned to him. Had he come to berate me? No doubt my silly speech wasn't up to his standards. Possibly he meant to tell me how much better General Grant would have done.

Instead, he stood silent in front of me for a long moment, his hands clasped behind him. Then he cleared his throat. "We haven't always seen eye-to-eye," he began. I refrained from rolling mine at the understatement, but only just. "I admit, when you were younger, I despaired of the direction you were so intent on taking. I perceived what I believed to be weakness and failed to recognize the strength it took for you to walk your own path."

"If you're attempting to boost my morale, you're doing a very poor job," I said.

He started to glare, then cut himself off with a chuckle. "No. You're right. I only meant to say that I'm proud of you. You've grown into as fine a son as any father could ask for. Though we might not agree on some things, that doesn't mean it isn't an honor to fight beside you today."

I gaped at him. Even in the wildest of my childhood imaginings, I'd never thought to hear such words of praise from my father's mouth.

Our relationship had never been an easy one, but to have him here, at my back in these dark hours, softened the edges of my memories. He had made a true effort to do better, and though that didn't mean I owed him forgiveness, I found myself moved to look upon him with a more charitable gaze. His own younger life had likely not been easy, certainly not his experiences in the war and the loss of his brother, and he had done what he thought best. To admit he'd been wrong about what the best had been, both for me and for Stanford, took courage on his part.

I'd been thinking of my own mortality, and worrying about Mother, yet I'd somehow taken it on faith that Father was invincible. But he was a man like any other. If he fell to our enemy...

I would miss his presence in my life. Perhaps it reflected poorly on us both, that the thought came as a revelation.

I extended my hand. "Thank you, sir. It means a great deal to hear you say that."

He clasped my hand—then pulled me into an embrace. Startled, I returned it. Then he stepped back and clapped me awkwardly on the arm. "Good luck, son."

"And to you."

Father led his forces into the burrows first. They would emerge onto the streets near the museum and attack from there. As we would be using the same tunnels as the librarians, at least until we were beneath the museum, we fell in with them. Most of the librarians looked grimly ready for battle, but Mr. Quinn wore a delighted grin, as though he couldn't think of anything better than the chance to save the town from otherworldly invasion. He clutched an enormous dictionary to his chest, clearly ready to brain the first Fideles he came across.

We hadn't gone far, when Griffin abruptly stiffened. "What's wrong?" I asked in alarm.

His features settled into a dark look. "The Queen of Shadows spoke to me. The guardian umbra at the edge of the Draakenwood overlooking the cemetery showed her an image. The dead of Widdershins have clawed their way out of their graves en masse."

"No." The horrifying memory of my dead sister Guinevere, raised by Stanford's necromancy, struck me forcefully.

Christine swore. "It seems Nephren-ka wants his army of the dead, no matter where he has to look for it."

"They're marching on the town," Griffin went on. A small trickle of blood leaked from his nose, and he wiped it off.

"Probably making for the museum and Nephren-ka." Blast. "We need to warn Father they're coming up behind him."

"Go," Mr. Quinn said to one of the librarians. The man nodded and trotted back the way we'd come.

Our mission was more urgent than ever. We had to get the seal and then to the Front Street Bridge as quickly as possible, before our losses grew too high. We went as swiftly as we could, until we reached the umbrae's side excavation into the steam tunnels. We paused at the raw juncture, and Mr. Quinn bowed to me. "We won't let you down, Widdershins," he vowed. "We'll fight to the last man."

"I hope it doesn't come to that. Don't sacrifice yourself needlessly." Feeling a bit uncertain, I awkwardly patted his shoulder.

He gasped at my touch, his eyes widening. For a moment, I was afraid he was going to burst into happy tears. "Of course, Widdershins. Thank you. But don't worry. The library is thoroughly trapped, and of course I began concealing weapons in the stacks the day I was hired."

"I'd expect nothing less," I said, though in truth I was rather taken aback. "Good luck."

"That man is odd, even for this town," Christine remarked as he scurried away. "What on earth has he been *doing* down there in the library all these years?"

Iskander winced. "Some things are better left a mystery."

The umbrae's new excavation was narrow and hasty, and we had to crawl to get through, though fortunately not very far. They'd neatly stacked up the bricks they'd removed from the steam tunnel floor to one side, and two worker umbrae sat guard, waiting for us to emerge. As soon as we did so, they slipped back down into their digging, leaving us alone.

"Do you know where we are?" Griffin asked.

The light from the lantern I carried revealed plain brick walls lined with pipes. Moisture beaded on the pipes, and humidity thickened the air. "I've never been in the steam tunnels before."

"I have." Christine plucked the lantern from my hand. "I explored them on a lark, shortly after I was hired."

"Of course you did," I muttered.

Christine ignored me, lifting the lantern and illuminating wires and a naked bulb hanging from the ceiling. She tugged on the pull chain dangling from it, but nothing happened. "The electricity seems to be out."

She shrugged and led the way. The only sounds consisted of the scrape of our shoes on brick, accompanied by our breath and the occasional drip of water. What had become of the janitorial staff, I couldn't guess. Hopefully most had escaped. At any rate, we neither saw nor heard anyone as we made our way to one end of the hall and up a short flight of stairs.

The door let out on the lowest level of the museum proper, not far from the storerooms we sought. We paused for a long moment, listening intently, but heard nothing. Hopefully, that meant our ruse had worked, and any defenders had been drawn away to fight off the various attacks.

"This way," Christine said. Within a few moments, we were at what I assumed to be the correct storeroom.

"I'll stand guard, since I don't know what to look for," Griffin said in a low murmur.

As with most of the storerooms at the Ladysmith, it was packed nearly to the rafters, in this case with wooden crates, mummified crocodiles, and a disassembled boat retrieved from Nephren-ka's tomb. One crate, however, had been dragged free from the mess and its lid pried off.

Christine's eyes narrowed in fury. "The devil? When I find out who's been rummaging about in my crates..." She trailed off as she inspected the remaining contents. "Blast it, no."

Iskander joined her, then swore. "This was the crate we packed the seal into, wasn't it?"

She nodded. "Yes. It was just beneath the cosmetic pallet, which has been moved aside."

My heart sped. Our plan depended on getting the seal and reaching the Front Street Bridge before Sirius rose. "Are you certain? Perhaps it's in another box?"

Christine turned a withering glare on me. "I oversaw the packing and inventory of every single artifact we retrieved from the dig. I can tell you the contents of any crate at a glance. The seal was in here. And now it isn't."

"Nephren-ka must have realized it was important," I said, my lips going numb with dread. "He took it."

One of the mummified crocodiles turned its head.

CHAPTER TWENTY-NINE

riffin

WHYBORNE'S startled shout echoed out of the storeroom. I spun, in time to see a mummified crocodile lunge at Iskander, its bandages shredding so its withered jaws gaped open. Its teeth closed on his sleeve, but missed the flesh beneath. Before I could move to stab it with my sword cane, Iskander whipped out his knife in his free hand and skewered it through the torso, piercing the heart. It thrashed, shuddered, and stilled.

From the hall behind me, I heard a strange scraping and shuffling that caused every hair on my arms to stand straight up. My heart raced and my hands went cold, and for a moment I wanted nothing more than to slam the door to the storeroom shut and not face whatever came for us in the hall.

But that wasn't a choice. I firmed my grip on my sword cane and stepped out. "We have a problem," I said, and my voice remained surprisingly steady.

Until that moment, I'd never quite appreciated just how full of dead things the museum was. Those of most interest to the public were displayed above, but down here, every storeroom, cabinet, and drawer contained ten times the number specimens, meant only for research.

Crumbling mummies, far too damaged for display, shuffled down the hall toward us. One held a shrunken head by its hair; the sewn-shut mouth tugged futilely against its bindings. Dozens of birds, from jewel-like hummingbirds to an enormous swan, dragged themselves across the floor with their wings. Preserved for science rather than taxidermied for the public, only sunken holes remained where there should have been eyes, and their boneless necks twisted impossibly in an attempt to see.

Cabinets lining the hall suddenly swung open, revealing row upon row of specimen jars, the pickled things within twisting in a manner that brought bile to my mouth. They slammed against their glass prisons, until the jars began to topple from the shelves, exploding onto the floor in a bright shower of glass and formaldehyde. Eyeless worms, amphibians, fetal things I couldn't name, began to crawl and flop and squirm toward us.

"Don't just stand there, Whyborne!" Christine shouted as she crowded behind us. "Set them on fire!"

He shook his head, his hand snagging my elbow as he backed away. "The formaldehyde—that much will go up like a bomb. It will kill them, but possibly us, too."

Christine swore. "Then run."

We ran. The dead, thankfully, didn't move quickly. But even as we left the initial group behind, more doors opened to disgorge skeletons on wire, or flopping bags of skin uncovered from bogs. More cabinets opened as we dashed past, showering us with fragments of glass and formaldehyde.

A storm of butterflies, some still with pins sticking through their bodies, exploded through a door and instantly blanketed us. Their dry wings beat against my skin and covered my eyes. I felt their tiny feet prodding at my nostrils, my lips, and tore them off with both hands.

Whyborne shouted and cursed, then went into a fit of coughing as one took advantage and crawled into his mouth.

The madness of butterflies slowed us. A sharp, stinging pain started in my ankle. Dashing butterflies aside, I looked down to see one of the preserved specimens, a thing like a rat but blind and hairless, its formidable teeth sunk in my flesh. With an exclamation of disgust, I kicked it aside.

The dead closed around us from every side, leaving only one route forward. Slipping in formaldehyde, covered in shards of glass and crushed butterflies, we fled blindly. The things that issued from the taxidermy room overwhelmed my ability to hold back my gorge, and I vomited on the floor even as Whyborne tried to pull me along. Iskander gagged, and even Christine turned green.

Some of the half-finished things were faster, still having bone and muscle even if most of their skin dragged behind them, or was gone altogether. At first, I thought it was sheer luck that we managed to outpace them, until Whyborne said, "We're being herded."

Of course we were. That was why we'd always had one stairway, one hall, left unblocked for us to escape through. "Where?"

"The front of the museum," Christine answered. "The grand foyer."

"Then we can escape out the doors," Iskander panted. His brown skin had taken on a greenish hue, and sweat stood out on his brow.

"We can't," Whyborne protested. "The seal—this is our only chance to get it."

"We don't even know where it is," Christine said. "Maybe we can meet up with Niles on the street outside, and come back in with enough force to fight, but—"

The words died on her lips as we finally stumbled through the staff door and into the back of the grand foyer. The door slammed shut behind us of its own accord, as if to block off any retreat. As for the doors, there was no hope of escape through them after all.

Nephren-ka was waiting for us.

CHAPTER THIRTY

hyborne

MY HEART POUNDED from our run, so loud I could barely hear, and my lungs wheezed from lack of breath. I felt light-headed, whether from the exercise or from horror, I didn't know. The hunting dead had been terrible enough, but this...

Nine years ago, I'd nervously entered through the great doors, stammering to the ticket taker that I had an appointment with the director, Dr. Hart. I'd been to the museum before, first as a child trailing after my godfather Addison Somerby and his son Leander, later by myself as a youth. It was here I'd first realized my facility with languages might have a practical application, first glimpsed the possibility of a future other than the one Father had planned for me.

When I'd interviewed that day, I'd been so afraid Dr. Hart would see my last name and hire me for that alone, under the mistaken impression my father would donate to any museum I worked for. But that hadn't proved the case. I'd been offered the job due to my own skills.

Finally, for the first time, I had something that was just mine. The work brought me joy. Before I moved in with Griffin, I'd been happier in the Ladysmith than anywhere else on earth.

And now Nephren-ka had rendered it corrupt. Tainted. Violated.

The risen pharaoh had reconstructed the grand foyer to his liking. Torches illuminated the scene, giving it an air of something out of antiquity. His golden throne had been removed from its exhibit in the Isley Wing and placed before the hadrosaur skeleton. The other skeletal exhibits had been brought forward from the back of the huge hall: three saber-toothed tigers, an Irish elk, and a prehistoric armadillo whose enormous carapace I could have curled up inside.

But of course he had done far more than simply rearrange the exhibits. Greenish mist crawled along the floor, and blood stained the marble. The air reeked of death, and flies buzzed in the thousands. Things slithered and flopped through the mist. My stomach rebelled at the sight of a partially dissected rodent that had escaped its specimen jar. A scream of repulsion and rage rose in my throat, locked behind my clenched teeth.

Before the throne lay a pile of bodies, most of them wearing the uniform of the museum guards. I feared to look too closely, certain I would recognize some of them. The bloated, black flies swarmed most closely around them, and they'd swelled hideously in the summer heat.

When the librarian, Rath, had spoken of Dr. Hart confronting Nephren-ka, I'd held out some slim hope the director might have survived the encounter. That hope was now dashed, in the most terrible way.

Dr. Hart's corpse hung from the wires which had once supported a heavy portrait. The walrus mustache of which he'd been so proud was wet with his own blood, and a heavy blow had staved in his temple. His shattered spectacles had slipped sideways, and one eye seemed to stare at me, as if asking why I hadn't done more to stop this.

Iskander made a choking noise, and Christine swayed on her feet beside me.

"Why?" I whispered. "Why would anyone do this?"

"Because he defied me," said a deep voice.

There came a rustling sound from the shadows clustered in the hall behind the throne. Two shapes stepped out, one to either side of the throne.

The first was Mrs. Creigh.

Curse the woman—she must have used her sorcery to escape the fire. But it had not left her unscathed. She moved as though in great pain, and bandages swathed her entire head, save for her nose, mouth, and one eye. They vanished beneath her dress, and though one hand appeared unscathed, the other was similarly bound. She looked as though she was in the process of becoming a mummy herself.

The other was Nephren-ka.

When Blackbyrne had been resurrected, he had been mostly normal, save for the stink of death that hung around him, and his need to feast on human blood and flesh. But no one would mistake the pharaoh for anything living. His body was little more than dried skin over bone, the flesh stained from the resins used to preserve him. He wore a tattered linen skirt, and had adorned himself with the jewelry from his tomb: earrings, an elaborate beaded necklace, cartouche rings loose on his skeletally-thin fingers. A gold funeral mask covered most of his face, save for his mouth. It was utterly featureless, and for a stupid moment I wondered how he could see, before recalling he shouldn't even be able to walk.

In one hand, he held an Egyptian sorcerer's wand like a staff: five feet of solid bronze cast in the shape of a serpent, its carnelian eyes afire with magic. It was apparent to me he was using it to funnel the power of the maelstrom, to disturb the sleeping dead and transform the museum into an abattoir.

And in the other, he held the bronze seal.

"Dr. Hart never hurt anyone!" Christine exclaimed, her voice trembling beneath a varnish of anger. "He could be a bit of an idiot sometimes, but he didn't deserve this."

"He would not surrender." The deep voice issued from somewhere within the desiccated husk, but his lips failed to move in sync with it. I wondered briefly how he spoke English, then realized again that there was no logic to any of this. This was ancient magic, fueled by the Outside, set in motion by Nyarlathotep thousands of years ago. "When I first awoke, he ordered his guards against me. I made him into a warning to any who would consider doing the same."

God. I tried not to look at Dr. Hart's dangling corpse, but the awfulness of it pressed down on me like a physical weight. Why hadn't he run? Why had he tried to fight?

But I already knew the answer. Dr. Hart loved the museum with his whole soul. He'd always aspired to making it the best museum in the nation—in the world. He wouldn't stand by when one of our own exhibits got up and started making threats. He'd probably told Nephren-ka to get back in his glass case and stay there.

Mrs. Creigh let out a racking laugh. "The looks on your faces," she said. Her voice was ruined from smoke and flame, but the glee in it sickened me.

"At least we have faces," Christine snapped back.

Frost raced across the floor, and Christine let out a cry of startled pain. I raised my hand, wind ruffling my hair as the spell formed. Iskander stepped defensively in front of Christine, witch hunter's daggers drawn.

The dead bodies on the floor began to stir. Slowly, one at a time, they climbed to their feet. Their injuries were many and varied, but blood no longer seeped from the torn flesh. The flies swarming on them went into a frenzy, and it was everything I could do not to gag.

"I will add your companions to my army of the dead, little spark," Nephren-ka said. My skin crawled; "little spark" was what Nyarlathotep had called me. "As for you, your heart has been found unworthy and shall be devoured."

Another shadow detached itself from the back of the hall. I'd never imagined to see such a creature in life, but I recognized it immediately from countless papyrus fragments, sarcophagi, and tomb walls. Part crocodile, part lion, and part hippopotamus: Ammit, the devourer of those hearts weighed in judgement and found lacking.

To the ancient Egyptians, she had embodied the greatest of all fears: to undergo the "second death" and be lost for all eternity.

Whether this was some creature of the Outside like the rat-things, which had taken on the form of the demoness, or if the legends sprang from her instead, I couldn't guess.

My heart pounded as the dead lurched toward us. Ammit's prowl was slower, but her red eyes fixed on me. "We killed your god," I said. Trying to bluff as I had with Mrs. Creigh. "Call off your army, give us the seal, and return to dust where you belong."

Nephren-ka laughed, a hollow sound that seemed to emanate from somewhere far away and merely echo through his mouth. "I think not." He lifted the seal, as if taunting me with it. "The Occultum Lapidem whispered to me of so many things. It told me of gods even greater than Nyarlathotep, who was but a servant to them. And now that he is gone, I will set myself in his place. When the masters return, I will stand at their right hand, and all the graves of the world will open to me."

"Whyborne!" Griffin shouted, and flung the lantern at the dead who had once guarded the museum.

The lantern shattered, and most of the oil turned instantly to flame. The little that didn't, I ignited with a word. Fire was a reliable way to destroy those resurrected by necromancy, and one of the guards fell.

Then Nephren-ka spoke a word in no language I knew, and the fire went out. The bodies were charred, ravaged—but still on their feet and moving.

This was extremely bad.

I couldn't call down lightning inside, and frost wouldn't stop the dead. I reached to reshape the very stone of the marble floor around their feet, but before I could do so, Mrs. Creigh laid frost across my skin. I tried to ignore it, only to be caught by a blast of wind and heaved off my feet.

I skidded across the marble. Griffin cried out, and I looked up, only to find Ammit upon me. I flung up my left arm to ward her off. Her crocodile teeth closed on my forearm, and pain blazed through me.

I tried to pull free, but her hold was implacable. I slapped my right palm against her neck, scars aching as I dragged arcane power through me. I'd set fire to her mane—

The power poured out of me, but not into the spell for fire. Instead, Ammit drank it down, her red eyes glowing in triumph.

I stopped drawing magic from the maelstrom, but that made no difference. Still she fed, siphoning off my power. And since the magic in my skin *was* me...

She was going to devour a soul, all right. Mine.

CHAPTER THIRTY-ONE

riffin

"Ival!" I shouted.

The monstrous creature fastened on him with its terrible teeth. Blood streamed down his arm, and arcane power rushed from below, feeding from the maelstrom and into him. For a moment, he burned in my sight—

Then the glow faded, passing instead into the creature. Its terrible eyes blazed with stolen power as it feasted on his very essence.

"Nyarlathotep warned against killing the sparks," Mrs. Creigh said.

"I'm not going to kill him," Nephren-ka replied. "I'm going to annihilate his very being. There will be nothing left of him to return to the maelstrom once Ammit is done."

I wasn't about to let that happen. Turning my back on the dead wasn't easy, but I had no choice. "Hold them off!" I called, and hoped Christine and Iskander would be able to do so.

The marble turned slick with frost beneath my feet, and I fell heavily, bruising hip and elbow. "What do you think you're doing?" Mrs. Creigh asked in her fire-withered voice.

Heat raced along my leg, and I rolled over, smothering the flame either she or Nephren-ka had tried to set to me. I had to get to Ival; I couldn't let them stop me.

I saw the spell shaping the marble just in time to move before it closed over my hand and trapped me. Mrs. Creigh cursed. Iskander let out a yelp of pain, but there was nothing I could do for him, so I lunged to my feet and crossed the distance to Whyborne.

My sword cane sank into the monster feeding on him, aiming for its heart. Either I missed, or its internal anatomy was as senseless as its external. But I was not wholly unsuccessful. Unwilling to simply stand there feeding while I stabbed it, the monster let go of Whyborne's arm and turned on me. The sudden movement ripped the sword cane from my hand. I scrambled back, but this time Mrs. Creigh's spell trapped me, my shoes sinking into the stone as if it were mud.

Like a boar maddened by its injuries, the hybrid creature was on me. I fell back, my ankle wrenching painfully as my foot was yanked from my boot. Its weight pressed down on my chest, and the acrid stench I associated with creatures of the Outside swept over me. Its jaws gaped, lunging at my face, a heart-stopping view of teeth and endless, yawning gullet.

Then it screamed.

Its head twisted back as it snapped furiously at the sword cane still embedded in its torso. Smoke rose from the blade, and a stink like burning offal filled the air. It stumbled away from me, thrashing and shrieking, until it collapsed into a heap a few feet away. Within seconds, its hide went to slime. My sword cane tumbled free, the blade still red from the fire Ival had poured through it.

He crouched where the beast had left him, his sleeve sodden with blood. But he'd drawn the maelstrom's power into himself, replacing whatever the creature had fed on and more. Blue fire shone from his eyes, and his right sleeve charred as power surged through the scars underneath.

"This. Ends. *Now!*" he shouted, and surged to his feet.

The great doors exploded open, cool night air pouring inside, whipping into a gale. Mrs. Creigh screamed and ducked behind the throne. Iskander dropped immediately to the floor, dragging Christine with him, and I just had time to note they were each holding one of his daggers, no doubt to protect them both from spells.

The wall of air slammed into the dead, hurling them back. The wires holding Dr. Hart's mutilated body sang in the wind, but somehow held. Nephren-ka staggered a step, but didn't fall.

The dead flailed broken limbs. Some staggered up, but Iskander and Christine were ready for them, rolling to their feet and slashing and stabbing. Whyborne called out, and the marble deformed beneath the dead, binding their feet so they thrashed helplessly.

The wind had blown some of the green mist away; Whyborne called it again, scouring away mist, snapping the ankles and legs of the dead held in the grip of implacable stone. Then they were afire, burning with such intensity that Iskander was forced to leap back.

"Fool," Nephren-ka said. "You exhaust yourself to no end. My army is almost here."

I turned, and saw that Ival indeed had begun to wilt. Channeling the maelstrom had a cost, even for him. He stumbled and went to one knee.

I ran to him. "Ival," I began, but a strange sound outside cut me off. After a moment, I realized it was the tramp of feet.

The open doors showed us the street in front of the museum. For a moment, the view was almost beautiful in a strange way. Night blanketed the world, the stars shining in all their glory in the heavens. The lumina and nereids glowed like those very stars come to earth, and had they not been our enemies, I would have been moved by the sight of them.

But a second glance revealed the ugly truth. The museum stairs led down to a wide avenue, now stained with blood. Fideles in their masks, alongside the Perfected, the lumina, and some nereids, had faced off against our forces. I glimpsed Niles amidst the crowd, as well as librarians, ketoi, and umbrae. But the battle had ground to a halt, silence falling across all of the living as an army of the dead approached.

Combatants on both sides fell back to let them through. Many of the graves in Widdershins held contents too old to be raised easily. But that left hundreds, perhaps thousands, of the town's dead to answer Nephren-ka's call. Skeletal remains, barely held together by tattered shrouds and dried tendons, stood side-by-side with bloated corpses in the first stages of rot. Their stench was astounding, and I found myself gagging as they drew up to the stairs leading into the museum.

At their head walked a single figure cloaked and hooded in white. One of the more recent dead, I assumed, as its movements were as natural as those of a living being. It climbed a single step, then stopped, and the army halted behind it.

There were too many of them. We'd never be able to fight them all. And for every one of our forces that fell, they would gain a new soldier.

"Yes." The hollow voice welling from within Nephren-ka's dried husk rang out in the silence. "My destiny is at last fulfilled, despite all your pathetic attempts to thwart it. I am the Lord of All Lands, awakened from my long slumber remade by the masters, and herald of a new world." He pointed a sticklike finger at Ival. "Destroy the rest, and bring the little spark to me."

For a long moment, nothing moved. Then the figure clad in white lifted pale hands and pulled back her hood.

"The dead of Widdershins don't answer to you, necromancer," Miss Lester said, her eyes flashing fire. "Widdershins knows its own, and you do not belong here."

She raised her arm and let it fall in a silent command. And the army of the dead attacked.

CHAPTER THIRTY-TWO

hyborne

AT MISS LESTER'S COMMAND, the rotting army at her back fell upon the Fideles and their allies. Shrieks of terror and revulsion filled the air, and some of the cultists broke and fled. The Perfected, nereids, and lumina had no such choice, however. No expression showed on their blank faces: no horror, no fear, not even disgust at the stench.

Some of our own side fled as well, and I couldn't say I blamed them. Their own family members had risen to defend the town, but to see them in such a state, let alone smell them, was simply too much for some to bear.

Most remained, however. "Forward!" Father roared from their midst, and lantern light glinted off his saber.

"No," snarled Nephren-ka. "No! Obey me!" With an inhuman sound of rage, he lifted his hand to the featureless mask covering his upper face and ripped it off.

A host of tentacles squirmed where he should have had features.

"He didn't look like that when we unwrapped him," Christine

remarked. "Though if he had, I doubt I would have been able to publish a paper on his mummy in any reputable journal."

Nephren-ka began to chant. Griffin gripped my good arm and helped me to my feet. "He's doing something to the fossils. I can see the glow of magic surrounding them."

Every inch of my body hurt, and exhaustion gripped me. My very bones felt hollowed out by magic, the scars on my good arm screamed with pain, and blood dripped steadily to the floor from the wound on my left.

The metal bars and wire holding up the hadrosaur creaked ominously. For a moment, I thought the heavy fossil was about to collapse.

Instead it turned its head and looked at us with empty eyes.

One of the saber-tooths tore free of its own display, and the huge armadillo swung its heavy tail as it shrugged off the sleep of ten-thousand years.

"Whyborne?" Christine said, backing up. "How do we fight these?"

I didn't know. Fire certainly wouldn't work on them; rock and bone wouldn't burn like desiccated flesh. Neither would knives, or a sword cane. The smartest thing to do would be to flee outside—but that would expose others to danger. And we still didn't have the seal.

Iskander tore off his tie and wrapped it around the bite on my arm to stop the bleeding. "Will killing Nephren-ka again have an effect?" he asked.

"It might," I said.

Christine nodded. "Leave that to me. I took him out of the ground, and I'll put him back in it."

I wanted to beg her to be careful. But at this point, "careful" was a dot on an unfamiliar map, a place we'd left behind long ago. "Taking the staff from him will cripple his ability to funnel the power of the maelstrom, too. If nothing else, get the seal from him and run." I swallowed. "Leave the hadrosaur to me."

"Ival," Griffin began, as though he meant to argue.

There was no time. Griffin's sword cane would be of little use against the glyptodont and the saber-tooths, but he could do even less against the hadrosaur. I at least had some chance against it.

I hoped.

The great dinosaur tore itself free from its metal armature. "Go!" I shouted. Griffin and Iskander moved to block the other fossils. Christine faded toward the back of the hall, even as Iskander let out a blood-curdling war cry surely meant to call Nephren-ka's attention to him. As for where Mrs. Creigh was, I was no longer certain—hopefully still cowering behind the throne, waiting for us to die.

I wrenched my focus back to my own predicament; distraction right now would surely mean death. In life, the hadrosaur had been a plant-eater, but its toothless jaws were stone now, and would surely be powerful enough to crush any body part it fastened them on. Claws tipped its feet, front and back, and its long tail curled and lashed behind it. The floor trembled as tons of heavy stone began to move in my direction.

If this didn't work, I'd surely be crushed or bludgeoned to death.

Nephren-ka held power over the fossil dinosaur because it had once lived, and still bore something of the shape it held in life. I had made no deep study of paleontology, but I did know what bore down on me was not bone, but stone.

I had no power over bone. But rock was another matter.

The earth spell had always been the most difficult for me, though I'd gotten far better at it over the years. I focused all of my will on the charging behemoth, shutting away doubt and fear, concentrating on nothing save the spell.

I could sense the magic wrapped around it, animating it and giving it a mockery of life. If I'd had time, the curse-breaking spell might have worked against it, but Nephren-ka's resurrection spell was far too complicated and layered for me to destroy with simple force. So I ignored his necromancy and focused on the stone itself.

Distantly, I heard Griffin shouting my name. I glimpsed the flash of skirts at the back of the hall, past the charging fossil, but had no time to make certain who they belonged to. The marble floor trembled beneath the soles of my shoes as the hadrosaur drew near. The maelstrom howled like a damned thing, rotating endlessly beneath us.

The hadrosaur's jaws opened, preparatory to crushing my skull like a grape. I lifted my head and stared at it unblinking as arcane fire broke open the scars on my arm.

Stone fractured, then turned to sand, raining down in front of me. The snout crumbled first, then the neck, then the rest of its body, the skeleton coming unstrung, steel and wire crashing to the floor. Momentum carried some of it forward, and grains of fine sand just brushed the toes of my shoes.

I turned slowly. Iskander's knives had proved effective against the necromantic spells on the other skeletons, but one of the great cats had torn open his shirt and vest with its claws, and blood stained the ruined cloth from the wounds on his chest. Griffin had dropped his sword cane and snatched up a nightstick from one of the fallen guards; the heavy blows had managed to break bits off the giant armadillo's shell. Even as I watched, it swung its tail at him, the ball on the end enough to shatter bone if it connected. But the armadillo was slow, and Griffin danced back, well out of reach.

Nephren-ka stood before his throne, the squirming mass that had taken the place of his upper face sickening to behold. The eyes of the serpent staff blazed with power, and his withered lips drew back from teeth sharpened into points.

"You are nothing, little spark," spoke that hollow voice. "I am the Great Pharaoh Nephren-ka, the Lord of All Lands! I have defeated death and made it my slave, and when the masters return, I will be raised to godhood and take Nyarlathotep's place."

I stared defiantly at where his eyes should have been. "I am Percival Endicott Whyborne, philologist at the Nathaniel R. Lady-smith Museum. And you, sir, are trespassing."

The tip of a witch hunter's dagger burst through the stained leather of Nephren-ka's chest. Christine's face twisted into a savage snarl as she withdrew it, then buried it a second time in his back.

"You like the dead so much?" she asked. "Then rejoin them."

The thing that spoke through Nephren-ka let out a hollow wail.

His jaw sagged open—then the dry flesh cracked, and the bone fell away, disintegrating before it hit the floor.

The tentacles sloughed off, revealing the human face beneath, before it too went to dust. Skin flaked away, bone turned to ash. The wand tumbled from his hand, the serpent eyes cold and dark.

The remaining dead things stopped moving, the skeletons collapsing, the crawling things on the floor relaxing with a sigh, following the necromancer who had raised them back into peace and silence.

Christine stood triumphant. Her hair hung in disarray, and grime streaked her face, but her victorious grin lifted my heart. "Well done, Christine!" Iskander exclaimed, and for a moment I expected her to run to him.

Instead, she staggered forward with a startled shout of pain. A round, silvery blade projected from the back of her right shoulder. "You'll learn to serve your masters," Mrs. Creigh growled. "One way or another."

A cry tore from my throat. I'd let myself be distracted, just as Nephren-ka had been distracted, and Mrs. Creigh had taken advantage. I should never have let myself lose track of her; I should have made certain I knew who the skirts I glimpsed belonged to.

As Christine slumped to the ground, Mrs. Creigh ran for the great doors. She didn't make it.

Rage roared through me, blasting away aching weariness. The pain in my scars grew intense, but I no longer cared. The marble floor turned liquid at my will. It flowed over her feet, and she stumbled. Held fast, she twisted around with a snarl, the words of a spell on her lips.

Griffin's sword cane slid between her ribs, into her heart. She crumpled, dead before she hit the ground.

I ran to Christine. Iskander had already reached her side. "Christine?" he asked frantically. "Dearest?"

Her eyes squeezed shut, and her teeth gritted with pain. "Devil take that woman," she managed to say. "What did she stab me with? It burns."

"Hold still," I said, and reached for the strange knife. At least it didn't look to have hit anything vital. "Griffin, do you have anything to use as a bandage? It's going to start bleeding as soon as I pull the blade out."

When Griffin didn't answer, I turned back to him. He'd stopped a few feet away, the expression on his face one of despair mingled with grief.

"Griffin?" I asked uncertainly.

"Pull it out," he said. When I only stared at him, he shoved past me, grabbed the blade, and yanked it free.

Christine shouted and cursed him. But the wound failed to bleed.

"What's happening?" Iskander asked. His gaze darted from Griffin to Christine and back.

Griffin held up the weapon. Now that it wasn't sunk halfway into Christine's flesh, it was easier to make out. It wasn't a knife at all, but more some sort of hollow tube, like an over-large needle.

"Syringes are used to transform humans into Perfected," Griffin said, his voice shaking. "But this… it's what they use on the ketoi and the umbrae. I saw one like it in the memories of the Queen of Shadows."

Iskander's skin went gray with fear. He grasped the edges of the hole the weapon had left in Christine's shirt and ripped it open, exposing her back.

Already, the infection had begun to spread. The skin around the wound had gone sleek as a dolphin's, and a strange glow radiated from just beneath.

The infection would turn a ketoi into a nereid. What it would do to someone purely human, I couldn't guess. I only knew that, once it spread far enough, Christine and her baby would be lost to us forever.

CHAPTER THIRTY-THREE

hyborne

I SANK DOWN SLOWLY in front of her, my mind dazed. Iskander made a choked sound and put his arms around her. "Christine," he said into her hair. "I can't...our child..."

Would the infection cause her to lose the baby? Or would it visit some unspeakable transformation on it instead?

"Hold on, Christine," I said. "Just h-hold on."

Christine's dark eyes met mine, and I saw my fear reflected in them. "I don't think that's an option, old thing."

"No." This couldn't be happening. This wasn't happening. "We can stop this. I-I'll burn it out. It didn't work with the woman on the farm, but it will with you."

"Christine received a much larger dose of the infection," Griffin said quietly. "It's moving fast. I can see it."

"I don't care!" I shot him a venomous glare, then clasped Christine's hand. Her skin felt strange under my touch, but I told myself it was just a trick of my mind. "Fenton was able to fight its control, and he didn't have a tenth of the willpower you have, Christine."

Of course, Fenton hadn't been turning into a completely different species. But surely that wouldn't matter. I wouldn't let it.

"I am fighting," she protested. "I will. But we don't have time for this, Whyborne. It's getting on toward dawn. Sirius will be up soon."

I shook my head. "I don't care." Let the masters come; let the world burn.

"You have to." Her hand tightened on mine. "The whole world is in the balance, Whyborne."

"I won't sacrifice you."

"I'm not asking you to." She drew me to her. "Because the choice isn't yours. It's mine. And I've made it."

Tears burned my eyes, and I could feel Iskander's body shake with sobs. My heartbreak was surely nothing compared to his. But she was my best friend, and I was going to lose her, and it wasn't *fair*.

None of this had ever been fair.

I hated the maelstrom. I hated it for bringing her here; I hated it for making me; I hated it for existing at all.

Christine drew away, swiping angrily at her eyes. "W-We don't have time for this." Her shoulders straightened, and her mouth set with determination. "There's no point discussing it. You have to go on without me."

She rose to her feet and went to the desiccated pile that had once been Nephren-ka. She knelt for a moment, running her hands through his ashes, before holding up the seal in triumph. "Here. Take it, Whyborne. Take it and go."

I took it from her. Her hand had already acquired a strange texture, and the nails begun to transform into claws. It was taking her so fast. "Christine..."

"I'm sorry, Whyborne, but I can't come with you this time. You understand." She strove to put on her usual brave face, but I could see her lip trembling with suppressed emotion. "I don't know how long I have until my mind isn't my own." Her human hand slipped down to rest on her belly. "This isn't...this isn't how I wanted things to end."

My throat tightened, and I choked on a sob. "Neither did I."

"Go," she swallowed hard. "You must get to the bridge and the eye of the maelstrom before Sirius rises, or this will have all been for nothing." She met my gaze. "Stop the masters, and send the Fideles screaming to hell for me."

"I promise."

"Good." She stepped back and waved at us. "Now go on. All of you."

Iskander shook his head. "I'm not leaving you."

She closed her eyes and took a deep breath. "Kander, don't. If I'm to lose my mind, my will, I don't want you to see it happen."

"As Whyborne pointed out, Fenton kept some part of himself." Iskander took her hands in his own. "Maybe you will, too. And if not…I vowed to stand by you in sickness and in health, until death do us part. I made an oath to you, and I mean to keep it."

She nodded, and he put his arms around her. Over her head, he met Griffin's eyes. "Good luck, Griffin. And good-bye."

Griffin put out a hand and rested it briefly on Iskander's shoulder. Then he turned and made for the open doors. I followed, pausing just once to look back. Christine and Iskander stood wrapped in one another's arms, the ruin of the grand foyer all around them. The last torch had begun to gutter, and soon it would go out.

CHAPTER THIRTY-FOUR

hyborne

I SET foot on the stairs and looked over the scene before me. The army of the dead had collapsed, whatever magic animated them finished. The battle between the living was still ongoing, but it seemed to have moved closer to the docks, and nearer to the Front Street Bridge, where the masters would emerge. The glow of lumina lit up the night sky there, eclipsed now and again by umbrae.

It was Griffin and me now. We hurried through strangely deserted streets. As we went, I saw in real life what Nyarlathotep had shown me in visions atop Carn Moreth. Burned out houses, rifts in the earth, the electric trolley torn from its track on River Street. Dread filled my veins at the sight, but I tried to shove it aside. Tried to block out the final vision, of Persephone and myself dead on the Front Street Bridge.

Most of all, I tried not to think of Christine. Of Iskander. Of the raw wound in my heart that felt like it would never heal.

"Percival!" Father called.

He emerged from the stone edifice of First Esoteric Church, accompanied by Mr. Quinn, Miss Lester, Miss Parkhurst, and Persephone. Rupert and Hattie followed them out; apparently they'd made it from Boston and into the harbor here.

"What were you doing?" I asked, baffled. "It seems a strange time to go to church."

"Using the bell tower to get an overview of the battlefield, of course," Father said, not bothering to hide his annoyance. "We've managed to drive the Fideles to the waterfront, but they've dug in around the bridge."

"They'll fight to the death to hold it until the masters come," Rupert said. His ordinarily neat clothing was grimy and spattered with blood.

Miss Parkhurst looked about anxiously. "Where are Dr. Putnam-Barnett and Mr. Putnam-Barnett?"

I couldn't bring myself to say it. Griffin had to speak for us both: "They aren't coming."

She leaned against Persephone, who put an arm around her shoulders. My sister's tentacles hung limp around her face, and the scars the mask of bone had left on her face had begun to blister. I hadn't been the only one channeling arcane fire, it seemed. "Did you get the seal, brother?"

I held up the bronze bar. Such a plain thing; it hardly seemed worth the high price we'd paid to get it. "Yes." My voice sounded almost as if it belonged to someone else.

"Now all that remains is to break through the Fideles and reach the center of the maelstrom," Father said. "How much time do we have left?"

I didn't know, precisely, only that it wasn't long. I could feel the shift in my bones, in the air, as if the universe itself was drawing in a long breath. "Not long."

Persephone freed herself from Miss Parkhurst and held out a clawed hand to me. "Then we have no time to waste."

I looked out over the desolation of what had been—was still—my home. The decaying bodies of the long dead, the fresher corpses of friend and enemy alike. Whyborne House was in ashes, the museum torn apart, and my best friend and her baby lost to us. Possibly Iskander as well; I couldn't believe he would put up a fight if she attacked him.

We'd struggled so long and so hard, but at that moment it all felt futile. I'd asked for none of this. I wished the masters had never come to this world. That the Fideles had never risen. That the maelstrom had never been created.

"Come to me."

"I'm coming, you bastard," I whispered under my breath. My body still ached from my earlier channeling of power, but that didn't matter. It couldn't matter.

I'd never wanted this fight. But by God, I meant to win it, or die trying.

I stretched out my arm and took Persephone's hand in mine. And the arcane fire poured through us both.

CHAPTER THIRTY-FIVE

riffin

THE TWINS LIT up like flares in my shadowsight. Wind whipped suddenly down the street, and frost spread across the stones where they stepped.

Mr. Quinn watched avidly, his hands clasped to his chest. "And the town will rise to their hands," he said. And, though the line wasn't as I'd first heard it so long ago in the prophecy, the town did rise.

The twins began to walk, their steps in perfect sync, and the world lit up around them. Arcane fire infused the stones of the street, the houses, and throbbed in the very air. Lumina swooped down from the night sky, only to be blasted apart by lightning. Nereids raced at us, and the cobblestones rippled like water, sucking them down into the earth. Persephone's tentacle hair fanned out around her head, and Whyborne's locks stood on end. The smell of sea and ozone drove back the stink of death.

Maggie and I ran after them, and the rest followed us. "What happened in the museum?"

I kept my eyes fixed on Whyborne and Persephone. I didn't want to answer her, didn't want to think about the bleeding wound in my heart. I loved Christine, and Iskander had been a brother to me. He'd been so excited about becoming a father, and I'd let myself dream of playing with their child, watching it grow.

And now it was all gone, dreams turned to ash.

Even as I told Maggie what had happened, in as few bleak words as possible, I felt a new fear growing in my heart. Ival and Persephone were spending power recklessly, and though the capacity of the maelstrom was infinite, their ability to channel it through their very mortal bodies was not. He'd already been stumbling, and that had been before the fight with the hadrosaur.

They might collapse before they reached the bridge. Or—and my heart stuttered at the thought—they might burn up, scoured from the inside by the enormous power of the great vortex.

As we drew nearer to the waterfront, we came at last to the fighting. Ketoi boiled from the river, swarming up the bank, across the fronts of houses, battling nereids and cultists alike. The police and the old families stood side-to-side on the streets, while overhead umbrae and lumina battled in the sky. Mr. Quinn climbed atop an overturned omnibus, his book held high like a banner.

"To arms, Widdershins!" he shouted. "Rise up and fight! Fight for your home! Fight for your families! Fight for your lives!"

"For Widdershins!" I shouted, and those around me took up the cry, until it became a roar. *"For Widdershins!"*

In the midst of it all, the twins burned. The very stones of the town responded to them, the ocean smashed nereids against the rocks, and currents of wind tore lumina from the sky.

The Fideles barring the bridge wavered, and first one fled, then another. One of their lieutenants, some underling of Mrs. Creigh, fought to rally them. "Stand your ground! The masters draw near! Hold fast, and the cities of the world will be yours to rule!"

I slashed one Hound, then skewered another as it emerged

through the Veil. The ketoi in the river swarmed up the pylons, even as our army of the land closed in to either side of the bridge. More and more cultists broke and fled. Some threw down their weapons, and others leapt into the water, preferring to take their chances with the ketoi than with the twins.

The river churned, whether from the ketoi or magic, or both, and the wind whipped my hair, first from one side, then the other. Blood and ichor spattered my face, and my mouth tasted of iron. As the ranks of the enemy crumbled, I sprinted past the stragglers, striving to stay close to Whyborne and Persephone.

How long they could keep channeling the arcane fire, I didn't know. And surely it would take something out of them to seal the Veil before the masters could breach it. If they reached the point of collapse, I wanted to be close enough to render aid.

And if their hearts gave out, or their bodies burned...

They stopped. Without exchanging a word, they each took one end of the bronze bar, and lifted the seal high over their heads. And the magic pouring through them began to flow into it.

CHAPTER THIRTY-SIX

hyborne

THERE WAS no part of me that didn't hurt. There was no part of Perse-phone that didn't hurt, either. I could feel my sister, just as I'd sensed her in the Draakenwood, as though we shared the same nerves. Our hearts labored, and the taste of burning copper filled our mouths. The only thing keeping us on our feet now was the same blaze of power that threatened to overwhelm us.

But we had made it.

I could sense the pressure on the Veil, as if reality were an over-filled balloon, ready to burst. Something enormous loomed just before us, separated only by the thin skin of our world. The earth rotated, and the stars spun, and beneath our feet the great maelstrom turned eternally widdershins.

We lifted the seal, and it came to life at our touch. The priests had crafted it four-thousand years ago, to hold back Nephren-ka both physically and magically. The images of the two ka, of the heart on the scale, began to glow as we funneled arcane power into it. We let go, and it floated in the air, slowly rotating to show first one side, then the other.

Otherwise, nothing happened. The Veil felt no stronger than it had a minute ago.

Panic touched me. Were we doing something wrong?

Perhaps it simply required more magic.

I'd already let down every barrier to join with Persephone, but perhaps we could become even more of a conduit. I tried to release every thought, all the fear and the hope and the rage and the grief, and let the magic flow through me and into the seal. The scars on my arm and on Persephone's face began to bleed, and I couldn't seem to get enough breath. My pulse stuttered, grew slower, then faster, then stumbled again.

It made no difference. On the very edge of the horizon, Sirius crept into the sky like a distant, burning eye.

A howl of rage and despair joined the magic, ringing through us, tearing our throats. A huge beam of light erupted from the eye of the maelstrom, hurling us back. Persephone's hand was torn from mine, and I fetched up against the iron rail.

"Ival!" Griffin's hand closed on my bloody one, and I cried out weakly. I couldn't run; I couldn't even stand. Mr. Quinn joined him, and between them they heaved me to my feet. Father and Miss Parkhurst had gotten Persephone up, but like me, she was spent. Her tendrils hung limp, and blood ran down her face from her scars.

My own shirt was sodden, and the bite on my left wrist had begun to bleed again as well. Griffin's touch felt like fire against my skin, and tremors wracked my muscles. It distantly occurred to me that I might be dying.

If I was, then Nyarlathotep had indeed been lying. Because we hadn't won.

The sky split open, and reality tore like a painted backdrop. Even as Griffin and Mr. Quinn dragged me back, something stepped through from the Outside and into our world.

Griffin began to scream.

CHAPTER THIRTY-SEVEN

riffin

THE THINGS that stepped through the Veil defied all description. They blazed in my shadowsight, much as Whyborne and Persephone had. But whereas my gift showed me the hidden beauty within the twins, in this case it revealed horror beyond my ability to comprehend.

Perspective became meaningless. The masters were enormous—then my eyes shifted, and they were the size of a human. I couldn't tell if they were near, or far, or somehow both at once. They had things that were eyes, and appendages, and faces—and yet were absolutely not any of those things at all.

They were madness incarnate, and my brain could not encompass the sight of them.

My throat ached, and I became aware I was screaming at the sight. Hands gripped me, and Ival's weight nearly dragged me down. "Griffin!" he shouted. "Griffin, what do you see?"

I couldn't tell him. The masters were simply too alien to any kind of earthly life. I could only scream and weep.

I wasn't the only one screaming, though no one else could have beheld them the way I did. Still, whatever the Fideles had expected the masters to look like, it couldn't have been this.

Then the light of the maelstrom rose up and closed around the two figures, shielding them from my view. I caught my breath on a sob, my mind reeling. I blinked, then blinked again, as they settled into the masks they used when dealing with earthly life.

The forms they chose were human-like, though utterly androgynous. Both towered above us, easily fifteen feet tall, and every inch of them was as white as plaster, without pore or flaw. One had webbed feet and fins, and the other seemed more suited to walk the land.

Comprehension began to seep back into my bruised mind. The seal hadn't worked. We hadn't succeeded in keeping them out, and we had no weapon with which to fight them.

We had failed, and the world was doomed.

Ival clung to me, and I to him. His skin was worryingly cold, and he was bleeding badly, but at least he seemed able to keep his feet for the moment. "I'm sorry, Griffin," he whispered. "We tried. I must have made a mistake, must have misunderstood…"

I pressed my lips into his hair. "It isn't your fault. None of this is your fault."

"At last," one of the cultists called, his hoarse voice filled with glee. "Welcome home, masters. We the Faithful have awaited your return."

He bowed before them, and the remnants of the Fideles rushed to do the same. Would their reward be worth the cost, even to them? But no cost must have seemed too high, for I glimpsed smiles on the faces of those who had removed their masks. Like the Brotherhood before them, they were ready to sell the world to ensure their own power.

"And yet you have failed us," the Master of the Sea said. It didn't speak in English—I wasn't sure if it spoke at all, or if the words simply imprinted themselves directly on my brain. Its human-like mouth curled into an expression of disgust.

The smiles dropped from the faces of the Fideles. Their leader straightened. "These rebels have caused trouble from the moment the Beacon was sent, but they were unable to prevent your return. We have served you faithfully, and—"

"Failed the Restoration." The burning eyes of the Master of the Land swept across the waterfront. The stunned armies, the smoking buildings, the blood and misery and death. "We expected to return to a world restored to the order it was meant to have. To take our places as the sole rulers of this world, this dimension."

"Instead we return to this *chaos*." The other master spoke as if the word were the vilest oath imaginable. "And you try to claim it as success?"

The Master of the Land shook its head. "I suppose we'll just have to deal with this mess ourselves."

It stretched out a hand tipped with sharp nails. The power of the maelstrom surged through it, shooting out of its palm in a beam of pure arcane energy.

The beam fell on the leader of the Fideles. He began to scream, thrashing madly as the magic burned him from within. His eyes glowed blue, and then he began to crumble, clothing flaking away into ash along with his body, until nothing remained.

Oh God. How were we to fight such power?

Ival straightened, then took a staggering step toward the masters. Out of the corner of my eye, I saw Persephone do the same, shaking off Maggie's hands. "Run," Persephone grated. "Run, and we'll hold them off for as long as we can."

It was absurd—they could barely even stand up—but so like them both. I drew my sword cane and firmed my stance, because there would be no more running. No more retreat. Everything would come to an end here.

Persephone's movement caught the attention of the masters. "What do we have here?" one asked.

The other cocked its head. "These must be the pale imitations Nyarlathotep told us about. What do you think the maelstrom meant, creating these little mockeries?"

As it spoke, it reached out a hand toward Whyborne, like a child reaching for a doll. "No!" I shouted. "Don't touch him!"

How I meant to stop such a creature, I didn't know. I only knew that I had to put myself between him and the beings that would surely destroy him. But even as I moved, the master withdrew its hand and rose. "Enough of this," it said, and spread out its arms.

The other mirrored its movement. "Agreed."

Before any of us had time to react, thousands of thin, needle-like shards shot out from the masters. My skin stung as some of them struck me, and I flung up my arm to protect my eyes.

"Griffin!" Ival reached for me, his eyes wild. Though it was hard to tell, I didn't think any of the slivers, whatever they were, had struck him. Then again, he was covered in so much blood it was hard to tell.

One of the glowing needles had buried itself in the back of my hand. I started to pick it out, then froze, as the shine of magic flowed down from it and into my own body, leaving behind an empty, glass-like sliver.

No.

I glanced wildly about. The masters' reach was far, and almost everyone in sight had been struck by the slivers. Whyborne made a choked sound, and I turned to see him staring at my hand.

Above us, the umbrae began to glow. The ketoi in the river and on the banks changed, their hair becoming spikes, their colorful swirls vanishing as they transformed into nereids. And the skin on my hand took on a familiar waxen texture.

I had been hit multiple times. Even as the magic flowed through me like poison, I found myself surprised that it didn't hurt.

Nothing hurt, actually. I had been angry about something...or perhaps I'd been grieving?

The very concept of grief felt alien. As did joy. Love and hate were simply words.

I had been broken and put back together. But now, I no longer had to worry about society's censure. I would never again have a nightmare, or even a dream, for that matter.

I'd spent my life struggling to be what those around me most wanted me to be. But the struggle was over now.

I was finally Perfect.

"Griffin?" said the man in front of me. He seemed familiar; perhaps I had once passed him on the street. "Do you still know me? It's Ival."

"Who?"

CHAPTER THIRTY-EIGHT

hyborne

I COULDN'T MOVE, my limbs gone numb with shock. Griffin stood before me, his question hanging on the air.

But it wasn't Griffin, or not the Griffin I knew. The freckles I loved were wiped away, and his eyes were a pure, unearthly green, untainted by threads of blue and russet. All of the tiny imperfections I'd never even truly noticed were fixed: his nose ruler straight, mouth perfectly aligned rather than tugging slightly to one side, the weathering of sun and wind banished. Everything that had given his face character and life was simply…gone.

"No," Persephone moaned. "Maggie, please. Look at me."

This was the cost of our failure. *My* failure. It had been up to me to translate the Codex, to find the answers that would save us. I had misread, or misunderstood, and this was the result.

My town lost. My husband a transformed stranger. My family, my friends, still here and yet gone in every way that mattered.

"Much better," said the Master of the Land with an air of satisfaction. "Now, find any others who have escaped and bring them to us."

"And the rest of you, clean up this mess," the Master of the Sea added.

Persephone spun on them with a snarl. Or, rather, she tried to. But her frog-like feet tangled, and she stumbled. I caught her on my shoulder, and we leaned heavily on one another.

We were both dying. We could channel the arcane fire as no one else, but even we had our limits. Limits which we'd surpassed, and for which we now paid the price.

The attention of the masters turned again to us. It had an almost palpable weight, and it was everything I could do not to collapse beneath it. I saw myself as they saw me: tiny, insignificant, meaningless. They had traveled through vast dimensions, seen things I could not imagine, lived for eons.

I was nothing to them. Dust, and less than dust.

So close, the masters radiated cold. They were something more than ice, more than any winter. Their cold was that of the empty places between the stars, the absolute stillness waiting at the end of the universe, when all else dies.

Even masked as something that could walk among the creatures of the earth, they were terrible. Perfect, and pale—and evil, because they could look at my town and my love and my friends, and see something that needed to be remade to fit their desires.

The Master of the Sea shook its head in disgust. "They're horrible. I don't want to look at them anymore."

"What about Nyarlathotep's caution?" asked the other.

"We're here, now. We've returned, and the maelstrom can do nothing more to thwart us. Whatever danger it foresaw has passed."

"Then let's not waste any more time." The Master of the Land reached out to one of the lamp posts lining the bridge. The metal stretched and bent at its command, transforming to a jagged bolt of black steel.

On instinct, I put myself in front of Persephone. But she had no strength to flee, not that I believed for an instant she would. "You'll never prevail," I said, despite the evidence all around me.

The Master of the Land arched one perfect brow. "We already have."

The heavy blow nearly knocked me from my feet. But something held me up, preventing me from falling to the bridge. Persephone made a strange, gurgling sound behind me.

There was something black before my fading vision. The rough spear of iron jutted out in front of me, but it took a moment to realize the blow had been it striking me through the chest.

I tried to lift my hand, but I couldn't. I couldn't even hold up my head. As my vision blurred into gray, the last thing I saw was the masters standing triumphant.

Then there was nothing.

CHAPTER THIRTY-NINE

iddershins

WHERE ONCE A THOUSAND sparks of life created a mosaic of color and joy, now there remains only an empty gray sameness.

They are still here, walking the streets, performing the tasks assigned them by the masters, and yet they are lost: to me, to one another, even to themselves.

Mr. Quinn goes to his library. He must cull the shelves, remove anything that might contain dangerous knowledge. The fact that he'd once relished such knowledge seems strange to him. Almost as much as recalling he'd once cared deeply about the fate of the maelstrom beneath his town. The vortex is only a tool of the masters; he'd been deluded to imagine it as anything more.

Miss Lester walks indifferently past the dead. She spent most of her life struggling against one thing or another: society, her grandfather, the Fideles. If she had only given in, everything would have gone so much more smoothly. How had she failed to see that before? At least now the masters have opened her eyes.

Rupert Endicott feels a peace such as he has never known, all the doubts and burdens of being the Seeker of Truth lifted in an instant. The Endicotts had been so vital to him, but what was serving his family compared to the greatest honor of all: serving the masters?

Christine slips beneath the surface of the river. Her life of the land is already a fading dream. Something within her twitches, pressing against her organs. There was a man, handsome as the pharaohs of old, but the memory of his face slips away, unimportant.

Griffin walks past people who seem vaguely familiar: an older man, a young woman. A man with the same green eyes as himself. None of them truly look at one another. They are together, but all utterly alone.

Their victory secure, the masters turn to reshaping the town, as they've reshaped its inhabitants. The Master of the Sea wades into the bay and raises up three great, black spires of stone, each on one of the huge arcane lines arcing beneath the waves. It etches the spires with its words and fills them with magical power. Now they are like the summoning stones of the ketoi, but much larger. As the conquest continues, the spires will help transform and command ketoi farther and farther from Widdershins, until only nereids remain in any ocean.

The Master of the Land raises up similar spires at each of the three major arcane lines, where before there were only standing stones. These spires are of dark, glassy stone shot through with red veins. Like the Occultum Lapidem, these will control umbrae and lumina, and ensure the conquest of the land.

Then the masters rejoin one another at the very eye of the maelstrom. The bridge collapses into the river, and in its place rises the great tower from which they will command their servants as they spread out across the earth, until the world is theirs once again.

As night falls, worker lumina gather in a horde and begin to excavate and shape the new tower, carving out the rock into corridors, rooms, and ramps. Someday, it will stretch deep underground, just as the masters' city in Alaska once did. They will live in splendor amidst their servants, and this time the mistakes that cost them the world will be avoided.

Away from the flurry of activity, cast aside and forgotten on the river's edge, lie two bodies. The water washed some of the blood from them, but they are both very pale, and very still. Their chests and backs gape, where the steel spear impaled them both through their hearts.

At last, they have come back to me.

CHAPTER FORTY

hyborne

I OPENED my eyes and sat up.

To my shock, I found myself in the grand foyer of the museum. It was no longer a place of horror, as it had been under Nephren-ka's reign. The marble floor and walls were spotless, polished until they shone.

All of the exhibits had been removed. Though the lamps were on, most of the illumination came from a diffuse, blueish glow which seemed to emanate from everywhere and nowhere all at once. The ticket seller booths were closed and the doors shut. Except for myself and one other, the place was utterly empty.

A lone figure stood with its back to me, facing the doors. It was the same one I'd seen in my dream aboard the *Melusine,* though I could perceive it more clearly now.

It was tall and slender, and for a moment I thought it a ketoi man. But the longer I stared at it, the more details came into focus. Its skin was like parchment, or a paper lantern filled with bluish light. The ketoi-like markings weren't solid, but rather formed from thousands of closely written words.

I knew somehow that this wasn't a dream, or a delusion of my dying brain. It might not be literally real, but it was certainly happening.

I climbed to my feet. Nothing hurt, and my scars were no longer open and bleeding. I was dressed in one of my plain brown suits, the sort I might have worn if I'd come here to do my daily work at the museum.

"Hello?" I said tentatively. "Who are you?"

It bowed its head but didn't turn toward me. "You know the answer to that."

I supposed I did. "You're the maelstrom. Or a representation of it my mind has come up with."

"Yes."

My hand curled into a fist. I wanted to scream at it. To rail against it for its grand scheme, for bringing Griffin and Christine and Iskander to Widdershins. I longed to blame it for everything that had happened, everything that had gone so terribly wrong.

But I couldn't.

The maelstrom hadn't wanted the masters to return. That had been the fault of the Fideles, of Bradley and my accursed brother Stanford. The maelstrom had done what it could through the centuries, weighting the dice of fate, shaping people and events. Shaping my bloodline, so Persephone and I would be born to stand against those who would enslave or destroy us all.

The rest had been up to us. To me.

And I'd failed.

The weight of it pressed down on me, until I longed to collapse beneath it. Griffin, Christine, Iskander, Mother, everyone and every-thing I'd loved was lost. I hadn't been smart enough, or fast enough, or bold enough. Maybe if I'd been able to strike down the Perfected without qualm, or not tried to save anyone from Whyborne House, I would have gotten the Codex sooner. Would have had time to discover my mistake.

I'd failed everyone, including this inhuman being. What a bitter disappointment this moment must be, for all its centuries of scheming to have resulted in *me.*

"I'm sorry," I said heavily. "I couldn't be what you wanted me to be."

It lifted its head, though it still watched the doors. "What is it you think I want you to be?"

When I died, I'd expected the spark of myself to be reabsorbed seamlessly into the maelstrom. Not this strange conversation. Maybe it wished to understand what I'd done wrong, so that in some far future, should there ever be a second rebellion against the masters, it would avoid making the same mistakes.

"A hero," I answered. "A leader. Someone who would have done a better job of everything." A bitter laugh escaped me. "Forget leading the armies you brought here to fight for you; I couldn't even translate the Codex correctly. The one thing I thought I was truly good at, and I got it wrong."

The maelstrom shook its head. "I didn't bring them to fight for me. I brought them here to fight for themselves. To fight for one another."

It wasn't the answer I'd expected. "Even so. Either I translated the Codex wrong, or we didn't use the seal correctly. If only we'd been fresher, perhaps we could have drawn enough magic through our failing bodies to seal shut the Veil."

"There was never enough magic to do that."

The devil? "What are you saying?"

"I already have all the magic anyone could wish for. I *am* magic. Through the rivers and streams of the arcane, I span the globe." It shrugged. "This was never about power."

I didn't understand. Hadn't it created me to be its hands, its voice, its heart? To lead the army of the land and defeat the masters in battle? "Then why did you make me at all? If not to lead an army, if not to use the seal, then *why?*"

"I created you to do what I could not." It finally turned to me, and its features were familiar, because they were the ones I saw in the mirror every day. As it crossed the marble expanse toward me, its glow faded, its parchment-skin took on color, its tentacle hair darkened and became human, and clothing appeared. When it finally came to a halt less than a foot away, it was a perfect duplicate of myself.

"I made you to be you," the maelstrom said in my voice. "I made you to know love and hate, grief and joy. To hope. To laugh. To *live.*"

I'd always thought of the maelstrom as being of singular purpose. A thing of cool strategy, gathering who and what it needed to defeat the masters. I'd told Griffin it wasn't moral, and maybe it wasn't in any way I would understand. But I'd been wrong when I assumed I knew its purpose.

I recalled the dreams Persephone and I had, me in the empty valley and her at the bottom of the sea. The loneliness that had engulfed us both.

And I finally understood.

"You didn't collect people to raise an army," I said slowly. "You collected them because you wanted a family."

Morgen had put something of herself into the maelstrom when she created it at the order of the masters. Something they had either never noticed, or had discounted. Her actions had given rise to the sentience before me, but they'd shaped it as well. Imbued it with some of her own longing, perhaps.

Or maybe it had learned how to be lonely all on its own.

"Yes," it said.

"I see." Through the grief and despair, my mind had begun to work again. To analyze. "The seal. It wasn't meant to keep the masters out. It was supposed to tell us how to defeat them."

I clasped my hands behind me and paced a few feet, thinking furiously. "The ka is the part of the soul that exists in the context of society. You can't do that on your own, can't interact with people. But Persephone and I can. The two ka on the seal are meant to represent us."

I stopped pacing and stared at the doors, my mind racing. "On the other side of the seal, the weighing of the heart is depicted. You made us to have—well, *human* hearts isn't the right phrase at all, but close enough. To be a *part* of the life of Widdershins as you couldn't be. To have families and friends. But how will that help..."

I trailed off. Hadn't I seen one person who was able, at least in small part, to resist the compulsion of the masters, even after he'd been fully Perfected?

Fenton had stood behind Mrs. Creigh's chair and silently signaled to me that Father wasn't in the mansion. And when my life was threatened, he'd managed to break free of Mrs. Creigh's orders long enough to sacrifice himself.

Our other servants had been loyal, yes, but Fenton's devotion to Father—his love, even—was exceptional. He hadn't been able to disobey because he was particularly iron-willed, or some sort of genius, or a perfect specimen of humanity, but because of the bond he had with Father. A bond that moved him to save me, because it was what Father would have wanted most of all.

If the key was to be part of the life of Widdershins as the maelstrom could not be, to have families and friends and lovers, then the bonds between us must be the solution. And if it was just such a bond that allowed Fenton to disobey...

The woman in the farmhouse had wanted to be Perfected. To be worthy of love, just as Griffin had spent so many years struggling to be the perfect son, the perfect Pinkerton. To earn his place; to earn love.

But Widdershins didn't demand perfection, and all Griffin had to do to earn love and the bonds of family was to be his flawed self. We were all defective, and some of us were broken, but that was all right. Griffin didn't have to be whole and healed of all pain before I loved him. Christine could barge into my office, and swear to make a sailor blush, and be disowned by her parents, but she meant more to me than anyone except for Griffin.

Heavens knew, Persephone and I had enough flaws between us to fill a novel. But we were loved, deeply, even when it was sometimes hard to understand why.

I looked back at the maelstrom and found it smiling at me. "Do you understand?" it asked.

"Yes." I put my shoulders back. "I know what I have to do." There was one problem, though. Mainly that I'd been killed. "You healed me once before, when Bradley sent the Beacon. Can you do it again?"

"Of course. You are a part of me." It paused. "Though, if you are disintegrated, or die far enough away from my eye, I won't be able to save you."

"Then I'll do my best to avoid disintegration." I looked around. "Where is Persephone? Are you speaking with her, too?"

"I am. You will rejoin one another when you leave here."

It made sense; the Ladysmith would have far less meaning for Persephone, and I wouldn't recognize whatever undersea room or grotto held her heart.

It was extraordinarily odd to embrace my double, but I did it anyway. When I stepped back, the maelstrom had returned to its semi-ketoi form, though it still wore my features. "You are a part of me," it said, placing its hand over my heart. "But you belong only to yourself. Remember that."

"I will." I stepped back. "Good-bye for now."

I walked to the great doors without looking back. They opened easily at my touch, and I stepped through into blinding light.

CHAPTER FORTY-ONE

riffin

THE SUMMONS CAME, not as words in my head, but as instinct. It was time to gather, so the masters could send us out to fulfill their glorious plan. We walked silently through the streets in perfect order, with no one bumping into anyone else, the fast moving around the slow like water around rocks. The great tower loomed in the eye of the maelstrom, and there was surely no more fitting place in all the world for the masters to make their new home. I had a dim memory of having some sort of emotional attachment to the great vortex, but it seemed far away and unimportant. Just a silly dream I'd briefly indulged in, to be set aside now in the face of the work to be done.

Only, as I drew closer to the tower and the heart of the maelstrom, a blaze of light from the river caught my eye. I stopped, squinting. Though the rush of the rivers of arcane power into the massive vortex nearly blinded my shadowsight, I could still make out this strange imperfection, flowing not toward the tower of the masters but rather counter to the current. As it reached the level of the street, I saw there were two of them.

The sight disturbed me, though I didn't know why. Perhaps it was because they were not Perfect? The man was tall, his hair laughable, one side of his mouth slightly higher than the other, his skin scarred… and that wasn't even taking into account the mix of blood, river water, and mud on his clothing.

And yet he burned, like a beautiful, clear flame. As did the ketoi woman whose hand he held.

For the first time since the masters had so generously calmed my mind and my heart, I didn't know what to do. Should I shout an alarm? Stop them?

Though most of the crowd moved on, some had halted. I looked to my fellows, but they seemed as unsure as I. There was a young woman, whose name I didn't recall, and a pregnant creature not quite nereid or human, and a man with brown skin. Nereids in the river came up as well, three of them, as though some force had drawn them here.

The man filled with flame extended his free hand to me, and I found myself unable to look away. His eyes were lit from within, and his imperfect features achingly familiar.

"I see you, Griffin," he said. "I see your nightmares, and your doubts, and your regret, and your fear."

I shook my head, though I wasn't certain what I denied. I'd struggled to be the perfect son, then the perfect Pinkerton, and even after Chicago and the asylum I'd tried to present the perfect image. And now I'd finally succeeded, and this man, this being, was reminding me of my past flawed self.

"I see you," he repeated. "And I love you."

I tasted the dry dust of Fallow, the bitter sting of rejection, the despair of the asylum. But I remembered now. In those dark days, in all the days after, I had been seen. The maelstrom found me, and brought me here, and I…

I was flawed, just like any other human.

And I was loved.

"Ival?" I whispered, and took his hand.

I cried out, fire whipsawing through my nerves. But I didn't let go, only gazed steadily into his eyes, holding on to the memory of him—onto the memory of myself—as it became firmer with every passing second.

Then the young woman—Maggie—took Persephone's hand, and the pain lessened, some of the arcane fire that had burned through me raging through her as well. Her features shifted, became less symmetrical and more human, her hair losing its unnatural shine.

"Christine," Whyborne said urgently, "you've never let anyone tell you what to do in your life. Good God, woman, don't tell me you're going to start now!"

A clawed hand gripped mine, and I finally looked away from the twins, in time to see Christine regain her human form, the infection burning away before the onslaught of arcane fire. "Come here, Kander," she said in her ordinary voice, and he took her hand.

With every link in the chain, the pain grew fainter, though the magic didn't seem any less effective. Jack took Iskander's hand, and then Niles, then Mr. Quinn and Dr. Gerritson and more and more, until the chain included people unknown to me, though not to those who held their hands.

A worker lumen crawled from some subterranean hole, and Christine and I put our joined fingers onto its jelly-like surface. The glow inside it died as it became an umbra once again. Another linked with it, then another.

On Persephone's side, the chain extended from Maggie to Heliabel to Stone Biter and Calls Dolphins, all restored to ketoi form. Soon the line extended down into the river, vanishing beneath the water, only to climb back out to loop in Rupert, Hattie, and Basil.

My mind was clear once again. The arcane fire flowed through us all, but rather than scorching, it filled me with a fierce sense of joy. "Ival," I said in wonder, tightening my fingers on his. "Are you all right?"

I'd seen the masters spear them both on the jagged steel. His clothing bore a ragged hole, stiff with blood, but there was no wound. His scars had closed and faded back to silver, and the crocodile bite on his arm was gone without trace.

"Yes." His grin showed his teeth. "But we still have work to do." He looked away from me, up at the tower. "They've noticed us."

CHAPTER FORTY-TWO

iddershins

COLOR SURGES BACK through the mosaic I created, all the stolen pieces restored one after another, until it becomes a virtual cascade of light, hue, and joy. Chains of being spiral off in all directions, each link seeing the other, and being seen in return.

Even those few who touch no chain are restored, because even if no one else sees them, *I* do. I know them for all that they are, and their value is no less than any other.

Righteous fury thrums through Mr. Quinn. These monsters turned him against his beloved library, against *Widdershins*. He longs for a book large enough to beat their tower into dust.

Miss Lester snarls. Her ancestors swore they would be controlled by no creature of the Outside. Not Nitocris, or Nephren-ka, and certainly not these beings who care about nothing but their own glory.

Rupert Endicott narrows his eyes in anger. These foul things meant to break the Endicotts apart, to sever the bonds of loyalty that hold them together. The Endicotts are slayers of monsters, though, and now every last one of them aches to see the masters die screaming.

Christine pulls her husband's ripped shirt over her head. It isn't long enough to reach her knees, not with the baby in the way, but modesty can go to hell. She eyes the great tower, its curving stone, the carved bas-reliefs so similar to those she saw in Alaska and Carn Moreth. Even if she had her rifle, the masters are too high up for a clear shot. Better go along with whatever hare-brained scheme Whyborne has hatched, then.

Griffin stands beside the love of his life, awe and joy piercing him straight to his heart. They form the bedrock from which determination springs, as he turns his gaze reluctantly from Ival to the creatures who had enslaved his mind.

They're ready. They're going to fight.

No—*we're* going to fight.

Together.

CHAPTER FORTY-THREE

hyborne

I STOOD in the center of the world with my sister, arcane fire pouring through me. I didn't know what she had seen in the maelstrom, if her conversation with it had been as strange as mine. But when we awoke on the riverbank, a single glance was all that was needed to communicate we both knew exactly what had to be done.

Now we were connected with all of Widdershins: human, hybrid, ketoi, and umbrae. Power surged through me; my heart pounded; my teeth ached as though I'd bitten an electrical wire.

We'd taken away the masters' toys. And now they weren't just coldly annoyed. They were furious.

"How dare you?" the Master of the Land demanded. Its eyes flashed white fire, and the mask it wore for our reality trembled.

Persephone and I spoke as one, and the rage of the maelstrom rushed through us. "How dare *you?* We are the fire; we are the beating heart; we are this world's magic." The wind picked up, howling in from the ocean, and the ground beneath our feet shook. "We are Widdershins, and we will never bow to the likes of you."

The masters flung the thin, glass-like needles again, seeking to convert our people back to theirs. But this time, we were ready. Wind scattered the needles harmlessly, and arcane fire seared them the moment they touched the ground.

"You think you can fight us, you weak, mewling thing?" said the Master of the Sea, and its words were like a scream of metal on glass, horrible to hear. "We have already taken steps to make our dominance complete."

I couldn't see the spires they'd raised at such a distance, but I *felt* a pulse in my bones. To my alarm, the ketoi dropped their arms as one, weapons falling from nerveless fingers. The umbrae froze as well, whatever strange will their species possessed suspended by the spires on the land.

Thank heavens, the influence of the sea-spires didn't seem to affect Persephone and me; perhaps the sheer amount of arcane power coursing through us shielded our minds in some fashion. But Mother stood glassy-eyed, and the ketoi in the river sank beneath the surface. With a single blow, the masters had removed both umbrae and ketoi from our ranks, leaving only our human forces to fight.

The situation was bad. But then it became worse.

"Now learn your place, maelstrom," the Master of the Land said. "You may be able to influence some earthly forces, but you have no sway over those of the Outside."

It made an imperious gesture, and the Veil between realities ripped like a rotting curtain. Byakhee poured through on their mold-eaten wings, along with Hounds, rat-things, and even a scattering of yayhos.

My heart banged against my ribs, as if acutely aware it might stop beating again at any moment. Persephone's clawed hand tightened on mine convulsively.

A clawed hand. A ketoi hand.

In Balefire, Morgen had shown me how to move my consciousness not only through the Needle, but through the very stones of Carn

Moreth. There, it had been a terrible struggle, with all the magic diverted away from the tidal island.

Here, we had magic to burn.

"What do you need us to do?" Griffin shouted over the howls of the things pouring into our world. Father stood behind him, along with Mr. Quinn and Rupert Endicott. All looking to us, their eyes betraying their faith that somehow Persephone and I would know what was necessary.

And, for once, I did.

I tightened my grip on Persephone, calling up arcane fire and letting it spill between us. Showing her wordlessly what Morgen had taught me.

"Hold them off," we told Griffin.

Persephone and I closed our eyes as one. As the vortex roared around us, we sent our consciousnesses down into the very earth, just as Morgen had been able to send hers throughout Balefire. Persephone's task was the sea; the sense of her presence vanished instantly. I turned my attention toward the land.

The perspective was dizzying. I sensed the umbrae frozen in place beneath the streets, while the battle raged above. I moved through the town itself, along one of the vast rivers of arcane fire, streets, houses, shops, and more unspooling above me. I noticed a yayho skittering toward a house where children and the elderly cowered. I reached out; the cobblestone street lifted, formed into a hand, and smashed the yayho like a cockroach. Then I moved on, speeding through the line toward the filthy spire the masters had built on it.

The spire sang, just on the edge of my hearing. Its stone gleamed, a sort of dark purple shot through with red, just like the Occultum Lapidem.

The masters meant to trap those who had rebelled against them long ago, to return the umbrae and ketoi to captivity. To silence the songs of the Mothers of Shadows, of the dwellers in the deep, and smother the will of every species.

I let the fury add fuel to the magic. The spire shivered—then a huge *crack* like a thunderclap rang out as it split from top to bottom.

Not enough. The masters might still use it, or some sorcerer might find the remains and try to make their own Occultum Lapidem from it.

The arcane line surged, its flow momentarily disrupted as a huge burst of power channeled into the stone. When I was done, only dark sand remained, fine enough to scatter on the wind.

I sent my consciousness back the way I'd come. The worker umbrae were moving now, burrowing with a speed I'd never imagined. But the influence of the other two spires were still too great for the queen and soldiers.

Damn it. I needed to hurry.

A byakhee, brought to the ground by Rupert's magic, charged Griffin. Wind tore at his overlong hair, and he bore a cut across his forehead that hadn't been there before. His eyes widened at the sight of the byakhee, but he held his sword cane firm, putting himself between it and my prone body.

I split the earth open beneath it, a gaping mouth into which the byakhee tumbled, before it snapped shut again.

"Ival?" Griffin asked. God only knew what his shadowsight had shown him.

I couldn't stay, even though I wished to. I raced past, along the second arcane line. If I saw an enemy threatening someone, I turned the town itself against them, but otherwise I didn't pause.

The spire jutted high from the island in the center of the lake, where the Brotherhood had once opened a portal to the Outside. Where Griffin had nearly been sacrificed, and I'd had to put a knife in the resurrected thing that wore the face of my childhood love. Where later I'd accidentally channeled arcane fire through Griffin, knocking him unconscious even though it saved us from the Fideles.

So many memories of desperation and anguish surrounded this place, and I shattered the spire into dust in an instant.

Only one left. I was beginning to flag, though, my strength slowly eroding. How long could I survive like this, tied to my body with only a tenuous thread?

Hopefully long enough to destroy the final spire. I let the flow of arcane power carry my consciousness back into the town, and my heart leapt to see the soldier umbrae were now free. They streamed from below the ground, up from basements and collapsed tunnels, their bodies flattening into stingray-like shapes as they took to the air. Acid feelers lashed from their underbellies, snatching up Hounds, rat-things, and more, dissolving them into slime and bones. Others tangled with the byakhee; a pair of combatants plummeted into the river, locked together in death.

And still more creatures of the Outside flowed into our world through the rift in the veil.

CHAPTER FORTY-FOUR

riffin

MY ARMS ACHED, and the cut on my forehead leaked blood into my eyes, but I refused to falter. At my back, Whyborne and Persephone lay collapsed, their hands still linked together, motionless except for the shallow rise and fall of their breath.

They'd gone into Widdershins, as Morgen had once reached out through the stones of Balefire. She had made bas-reliefs look at Whyborne, or blinked painted eyes at him. But, typical of my Ival when it came to magic, his use of the skill wasn't nearly so subtle.

Heliabel suddenly stumbled, as whatever locked the ketoi into place was disrupted. She turned on the nearest Hound with a snarl, leaping onto it and stinging it with her hair, even as her claws and teeth wreaked bloody vengeance. Calls Dolphins thrust her spear into the air, and more ketoi emerged from the river to join the fight.

A few seconds later, soldier umbrae appeared above us, and my heart leapt at the sight. Somewhere in the back of my consciousness, I could sense the Queen of Shadows still writhing in her bonds, but Ival and Persephone were systematically breaking the hold of the masters on their former slaves.

Fury distorted the faces of the masters. They stood with their arms lifted, their clasped hands mimicking Whyborne and Persephone. But in their case, the masters sent their will through the vast tear in the Veil, calling forth a seemingly unending stream of creatures to fight for them.

Ival and Persephone might destroy the spires, but then what? We couldn't fight forever. Even with the umbrae and ketoi joining the battle, we'd ultimately be overwhelmed by sheer numbers.

Christine had found a pistol somewhere. If any Fideles sorcerers remained, they weren't interested in fighting for the masters now, and she could use it in some measure of safety. She picked her targets and fired with cool aplomb, even though she was dressed in nothing but Iskander's torn shirt.

The triumphant cry of the Queen of Shadows sounded in my head. *"I am free!"*

Whyborne and Persephone had succeeded in breaking the hold of the masters on the ketoi and umbrae. But now what?

I turned, just in time to see twin flames return to their flesh. Persephone was on her feet in seconds, and Whyborne immediately after. "We did it," she said. "The spires are gone."

Rupert hurled a flask at one of the yayhos. It exploded, liquid fire igniting on contact, and the yayho let out a horrifying, chittering scream. "Good show," he said, "but it only delays the inevitable."

"Nothing's inevitable," Christine said, felling a rat-thing with a single shot.

Whyborne flushed bright red at the sight of her attire, or rather, lack thereof. "Christine's correct."

"As always."

He ignored her. "We have a plan. We'll draw the attention of the masters to the two of us. The rest of you, just keep fighting."

"Draw the masters' attention?" I grabbed his arm. "They've already killed you once!"

"And I mean to try to avoid it a second time."

I tightened my grip. "Then I'll stand beside you."

To my surprise, he gave me a soft, sad smile. "You can't, darling. Just keep fighting, and watch each other's backs."

He leaned over and brushed his lips over mine. Then he pulled free, and he and Persephone ran, straight for the tower of the masters.

CHAPTER FORTY-FIVE

hyborne

WE NEEDED TO GET THE MASTERS' attention focused on us, and away from either the rip in the Veil or our friends. As I tried to think how to do so, Persephone simply drew on the arcane power and pointed at the sky.

A titanic lightning bolt split the air, so close and bright it seared my retinas. It struck the masters full on, and smaller arcs blasted a flight of byakhee emerging from the Outside, killing them instantly.

As for the masters, the lightning seemed to have little effect, other than to draw their attention. They turned on us as one, and the chill of their gaze felt as though it stripped me to the bone. Once again, I felt so small. So insignificant.

And perhaps I was. But I wasn't alone. The people of Widdershins, umbrae and human and ketoi, had come together, and we were mighty.

"If you refuse to die, then we'll make you live," the Master of the Sea said.

Its twin added, "We'll pull you apart screaming, but there will be no escape. You'll hang behind our thrones for the next thousand years, begging for release."

"Never!" shouted Persephone. "For Widdershins! For the land and the sea!"

The earth beneath my feet trembled, and the waves from the bay battered the seaward side of the tower. For a moment, I thought we might have accidentally unleashed an earthquake that would kill us all.

A huge form exploded out of the earth, at the same moment a hulking figure rose from the sea.

The Queen of Shadows latched onto the Master of the Land, her sinuous body wrapping around it, feelers and legs tearing into its pallid, white flesh. At the same moment, the dweller of the deep's tentacles seized the Master of the Sea, wrenching it into a kneeling position and squeezing.

Sickly green light spilled from the masters' injuries. The dweller's tentacles strobed with white and red bands of luminescent fury. The Queen's single orange eye burned like a beacon in the night.

"How dare you!" the Master of the Land howled. "You will all perish."

"No," I said. "You will. *Now!*"

The Queen of Shadows whipped away, arcing gracefully back to the tunnel she'd cannoned forth from. The dweller released its prey, sinking into the bay.

And the heart of the maelstrom came alive as Persephone and I stepped into it.

For once, we didn't channel it, only offered it direction. A torrent of magic blasted forth, twisting with the rotation of the vortex until it formed a fire devil. It lifted me off my feet, as though I weighed nothing, but the blue flame didn't burn me or Persephone.

Everything else, it consumed.

Had the masters not been unaware and off-balance, they might have escaped. But they were injured just enough, slowed just enough, by the Queen and the dweller.

So instead, they burned.

The arcane force blasted away the masks they'd donned to walk our world, and I prayed the sheer brilliance of the maelstrom would keep Griffin from being subjected to them a second time. Lacking his shadowsight, I could see only parts of them, but even that was horrible enough.

Even worse was their scream. As their forms began to blacken and flake to pieces, they shrieked as nothing else I'd ever heard, a sound that seemed to transcend our reality. The rent in the Veil snapped shut, cutting off any hope of escape to the Outside.

And still the maelstrom scorched them. The vast rivers of magic flowed faster and faster, as if the very world rejected the presence of the masters and embraced the chance to be rid of them once and for all.

They tried to turn toward us, reaching out what might have been limbs in some insane reality. But before they could touch Persephone or me, the final collapse came upon them. The masters disintegrated into ash, then dust, then were scoured entirely from our world.

All around, the creatures they'd brought from the Outside plummeted from the air, or collapsed on the ground, screaming and thrashing before they dissolved into green slime. The tower they'd raised broke into pieces, falling away into the river and crushing what remained of the bridge.

The fury of the maelstrom began to die away, the arcane fire devil to lose coherence. I felt hollowed out, light as a feather that might blow away on the wind. Persephone and I lowered to the ground as the magic buoying us faded. Dust from the tower's collapse billowed around us, settling slowly, until we could make out the crowd gathering beyond.

Cheers broke out, and within moments it was pandemonium. People hugged, clapped one another on the back, laughed and shouted in relief and victory. Human and ketoi embraced, and the soldier umbrae retracted their acid feelers so they might be safely petted.

As the dust cleared, I saw all of my friends before me. Christine and Iskander, Mother, Miss Parkhurst, Jack, Father, Mr. Quinn, Miss

Lester, and so many more. And of course, Griffin, his face bloody but his eyes jubilant, his mouth smiling as he ran to me.

"We did it," he said when he reached me.

"We did," I replied. Then I took him in my arms and kissed him before the cheering crowd.

CHAPTER FORTY-SIX

*W*hyborne

ONE YEAR Later

"I KNOW the last twelve months have been difficult," Dr. Gerritson said. He stood at the head of the room used for all-staff meetings, wearing a sensible green dress and matching hat.

I surreptitiously checked my pocket watch. Only ten more minutes before Saturday's half-day at the restored Nathaniel R. Ladysmith Museum ended.

My work over the last six months since the museum reopened had helped re-establish my flagging reputation in the field of philology. It was amazing how much I could get done without having to fight cultists every few weeks. But today, I needed to get home as quickly as possible, and a staff meeting that threatened to over-run did nothing for my nerves.

"I want to impress upon you all, how proud I am of each and every one of you," Dr. Gerritson went on earnestly. Some people clapped. In her chair beside me, Christine rolled her eyes.

I'd never enjoy all-staff meetings, though admittedly they were much less dry now than they had been under poor Dr. Hart. Mr. Mathison, the museum president, and most of the board of trustees had survived the coming of the masters. Once their own affairs were in order, they'd turned their attention not only to helping to refurbish and repair the museum, but to choosing a new director.

My opinion carried weight, so when they asked it, I gave it honestly. As a result, our new director, Dr. Gerritson, had been installed in time for the grand reopening. The last six months had demonstrated the wisdom of my choice, as Dr. Gerritson pursued his new role with all the zeal, but considerably less of the stuffiness, as Dr. Hart once had.

"The memorial for Dr. Hart will take place tomorrow afternoon, in front of the statue," he went on. "Those who wish to share some memory of him, please meet me there at two o'clock. After the public service ends, we'll come inside the museum for a private memorial and drink to his memory." He looked around. "If there's no further business, then the meeting is ended."

Thank heavens. I hurried to my office, stopping in only long enough to snatch up my coat and hat. A few minutes later, Christine met me in the grand foyer.

Returning to the museum had been difficult, to say the least. Most of the staff had been spared the sight of the horrors unleashed by Nephren-ka, but for those of us who had stood here amidst death and destruction, the memories were hard to set aside. The first few months, I'd shuddered to set foot here, bile creeping into my throat as I recalled Dr. Hart's body. I'd considered sneaking in through the staff door in the back, but since I didn't intend to give up my job, I decided time and repetition were my only recourse. The memories had softened a bit, and been overlaid by new ones, but I was still uncomfortable within the foyer.

"There you are, Whyborne," she said. "Do hurry; we don't have all day."

I didn't bother to reply, as she'd stated the obvious. We hastened through the doors and down the marble steps. On a plinth outside, the new statue of Dr. Hart gleamed in the sun. The sculptor had done excellent work capturing every detail of his walrus mustache.

We took the omnibus to Water Street, then walked the last few blocks to home. Saul sprawled on our walk, the sun on his belly. He cracked an eye, but didn't move out of the way, forcing us both to step over him.

"Kander!" Christine bellowed as soon as she crossed the doorway. "We're here! Time to pack up and go home, so we can get ready."

I rubbed my ear and glared at her. She ignored me, in favor of following Iskander's call of "in here" from the parlor.

Griffin and I had come home to find the house thoroughly ransacked by the Fideles. No doubt they'd imagined I had all sorts of sorcerous secrets hidden here. If so, they'd been sorely disappointed. At least they'd left things mostly intact, so a few weary days of straightening up had set our home to rights again.

Iskander had taken over Griffin's desk to tinker with photography equipment. Griffin had developed a keen interest in some of the newer, smaller cameras for use in his detective work, and Iskander eagerly agreed to assist. I suspected it gave him a sorely needed excuse to leave the house, and offered Griffin an excuse to watch little Nathaniel and Alexandria while Iskander worked.

We'd all been surprised when Christine gave birth to twins—or at least I had. I suspected Griffin's shadowsight told him more than he ought to know at times, though in this case he staunchly denied it.

"How was the museum?" Iskander asked.

"The day ended on a staff meeting, so it can only improve." Christine bent and swiftly kissed him. "Were you able to work?"

"Quite well, thanks to Griffin. He's upstairs with the twins."

"I'll fetch them," I offered.

Griffin sprawled on the couch, eyes shut and breath rising and falling in the evenness of sleep. Tucked securely against his chest slept two brown-skinned babies. At nine months, Nathaniel Griffin Putnam-Barnett and Alexandria Hatshepsut Putnam-Barnett were seldom still, preferring to crawl, play with toys, and babble nonstop. Neither had yet spoken anything I recognized as an actual word in any of the languages I was familiar with, but Christine assured me the day wasn't too far off.

I paused, looking down on my godchildren and my husband: the babies' chubby little faces and thick black hair, and Griffin's handsome features peaceful in repose. I reached down and tenderly stroked the line of Griffin's nose, and his lips curled even as his eyes fluttered open. "Noon already?"

"Almost one, now."

"Can you take Alexandria, so I can sit up?"

I still felt horribly awkward around the children. At least they could hold up their heads on their own now. After they were first born, I'd been terrified to touch them less something go wrong.

She woke as I picked her up. Brown eyes, fringed thickly in lashes, blinked at me.

"Ba!" she shouted and waved an imperious arm. I assumed she took after her mother, and was practicing directing an excavation.

"Yes, right away," I replied.

Nathaniel was more soft-spoken. "Ga?" he asked as Griffin sat up, cradling him.

"Hello," I replied. I held out a finger, and he grabbed it in one small hand.

"He likes you," Griffin teased.

I snorted. "He's a baby. He likes anyone who smiles at him."

"That isn't true, and you know it."

I hesitated. It was probably foolish to ask, but... "Do they still glow?"

The prenatal transformation the children underwent had left them marked. They'd presumably been turned into something like a nereid along with Christine, then exposed to the arcane fire of the maelstrom when they transformed back. Christine had nothing of the nereid left in her, according to Griffin's shadowsight. But, as Persephone and I knew all too well, small babies were far more malleable.

We'd first seen them a short time after their birth. While Christine slept, exhausted by her ordeal, Iskander presented the cleaned and swaddled newborns. Griffin's eyes widened at the sight.

"They're glowing," he whispered, almost in awe.

Iskander, naturally, was alarmed. "What do you mean?"

Griffin touched one tiny, scrunched face in reverence. "The transformation they underwent...I can see traces, as if they're hybrids now. It stayed with them...and so did some of the arcane fire that passed through us that day."

My lips had gone numb. "A spark of the maelstrom?"

"Yes."

"It's not my fault!" I said frantically. "I didn't mean to do it!"

Iskander had been rather take aback to receive this news. When informed, Christine only shrugged and said, "You have to wait until they're at least ten before you start teaching them spells, Whyborne. I won't have toddlers burning down the house, or summoning windstorms every time they throw a tantrum."

Now Griffin gave me a bemused look. "I don't think it's the sort of thing they're going to grow out of, my dear."

I sometimes wondered if Nathaniel and Alexandria had been the maelstrom's final hedging of its bets. If Persephone and I failed, it might have been able to try again in a few decades. But then I recalled my conversation with it. Perhaps instead it had seen a chance to continue to be a part of the fabric of life in Widdershins, to have a family, and taken it.

Maybe it was a bit of both.

"I suppose not," I agreed.

"Whyborne!" Christine yelled from downstairs. "What's taking so long? You aren't up there teaching Alexandria how to summon rat-things, are you?"

"Ba!" Alexandria shrieked joyfully. She'd inherited Christine's lungs.

Griffin carried Nathaniel down the stairs, and I followed with Alexandria. "I promise there will be no unsupervised magical lessons," he said, passing Nathaniel to Christine. The child gurgled happily to see his mother, and immediately launched into a long, babbling speech. I gratefully gave Alexandria over to her father's care.

"Yes, yes, tell me all about your day," Christine said, bouncing Nathaniel absently. "We'll see you in a few hours, gentlemen. What time is the carriage to arrive?"

"Six," Griffin said. "Plenty of time."

"Plenty of time when one isn't wrangling a pair of nine-month olds," she muttered. "Come along, Kander."

GRIFFIN and I dressed in white tie and tails, and I wasted a good half-hour trying to tame my hair with oil. "You look very fine," he said, bending over so his face was in the mirror alongside my own.

I scowled at my hair and set aside the oil. "I suppose I'm as presentable as I'm likely to get."

Griffin, of course, looked as handsome as always. The formal wear showed off his trim shape to excellent effect, and a sapphire stickpin brought out some of the threads of blue in his eyes. I stood up and turned to kiss him. His hand slipped around to grip my backside.

"We don't have time. Father will be here soon," I reminded him.

He gave me a squeeze, looking up through his lashes. "Consider it a preview for later."

"Devil." I kissed him again.

As predicted, the hired carriage pulled up to our gate shortly thereafter. The driver was unfamiliar to me, and I thought of Fenton with a pang. "Percival," Father said when we climbed inside. "Griffin."

"Father," I said. "How goes the rebuilding effort?"

The loss of Whyborne House, and of Fenton, had changed my father. To my surprise, rather than immediately begin rebuilding the mansion, Father had cracked open the coffers and instead spent a small fortune repairing the damage done to Widdershins during the Dark Days, as they'd come to be referred to.

Of course, he'd also rented a palatial house on High Street to stay in for the duration. Some things would never change.

"Coming to an end at last," he said. He seemed frailer these days, as though age was at last beginning to creep up on him, but his eyes were still sharp and steady. "A good thing, too, as I go to New York next month. I've neglected Whyborne Railroad and Industry too long." He paused. "You know, son, if you ever tire of reading dead languages—"

"No," I said.

He shrugged. "Well, you can't blame me for trying."

I could, but was interrupted by the carriage coming to a halt. Christine and Iskander joined us, each one holding a child in a clean muslin dress.

"You're bringing them?" I asked in surprise.

"Of course," Christine said. "Don't be ridiculous."

"We were told this is less than a solemn occasion, though still formal," Iskander said. "Is that wrong?"

"No." Griffin pulled a face for Alexandria, who goggled at him as though she'd never seen such a thing before.

"Besides, Persephone wanted to see them." Christine glanced briefly at Father, then at me.

Father didn't know the twins carried their own fragments of the maelstrom. Christine and Iskander had decided it best to keep the secret among the four of us, plus Persephone.

Considering how sorcerers and cultists had disrupted my simple life, I agreed whole-heartedly. The children deserved the chance to grow up in peace, and to find their own paths once they were old enough.

The carriage took us along Cemetery Road, then over a bridge across the Cranch. Fins broke the water as ketoi swam upstream. The Draakenwood loomed on the horizon, and I asked Griffin, "Will the Queen of Shadows send anyone to join us? Or is that you?"

"I believe a worker will arrive once the sun is down, so as not to tax my human brain," Griffin replied. "Oh look—there's the house. I haven't seen it since the Endicotts came—they've done an excellent job of restoring it."

I'd offered the Endicotts Somerby Estate after the destruction of Balefire. Though I didn't know how long Rupert meant to stay now that the masters were gone, the very fact they'd undertaken the effort of restoring the mansion and grounds suggested at least some of them would remain on a permanent basis.

The carriage pulled up, and footmen hastened to open the doors. As we climbed out, Rupert himself appeared, dressed in a striking blue suit. "Welcome," he said to us all.

Father shook his hand. "Thank you for allowing use of the island. And for supplying the music and food."

"It's our pleasure." Rupert cocked his head. "The island is where you used to conduct your rituals, isn't it? We found...evidence...when we explored it."

"I'm sure you did," Father said. "But those days are gone."

I thought I detected a hint of wistfulness in his tone. No doubt he missed the days when he and the Brotherhood had been the great power in Widdershins, using dark magic to build their business empires and disposing of anyone who got in their way.

"Thank God," I said. "Are we to gather on the island?"

"Right this way." Rupert led us to the edge of the lake, where a small flotilla of boats waited. Each was decorated with garlands of ivy and roses, and bore a torch in the prow, to be lit at twilight. Basil waited with the boats; apparently he was to be one of the ferrymen, because he hopped into the stern as soon as we were seated. He murmured some words, and a moment later we glided smoothly forward, even without oars.

I tried not to look at the water until we reached the island. Griffin helped me out onto the dock and gave my hand a squeeze; no doubt he understood I'd never be entirely comfortable on this lake.

As for the island itself, the changes to it were immediately apparent. Its narrow beaches now glittered with sparkling sand from the remnants of the spire the Master of the Land had raised. The Endicotts had cleared the overgrown path, and we followed it easily as it wended through the small wood.

At the center of the island, where the standing stones had once loomed, and where the spire had risen and fallen, was a large clearing. The earth was covered in a layer of sparkling dust, shot through with wildflowers that had taken on some very odd hues indeed. Some of them had patterns that looked weirdly like faces, and I decided it was likely best not to examine them too closely.

The clearing was largely filled with white lawn chairs, an aisle covered in white cloth between them. At the end of the aisle stood the wedding arch, which sported an impressive number of skulls.

"How delightful!" Christine exclaimed at the sight. "We really should have taken Persephone up on her offer for our wedding, Kander."

Her husband looked rather pained. "Er, yes. What a shame."

Father stared at it for a long time, then sighed. "Come, Percival. We should greet the guests as they arrive at the dock."

I felt something of a fool, smiling and shaking hands, accepting congratulations on my sister's wedding as if I'd had anything to do with it. Most of the land-based guests were from the old families, and I let Father speak with them. Orion Marsh was there; he'd been Perfected early in the vanguard's assault, and spent the rest of the Dark Days under their control until Widdershins freed him. Police Chief Tilton had been badly injured, and survived only by hiding in the depths of the cannery, alongside Fred Waite. Though Tilton had made it through, Fred was less lucky, succumbing to a nereid bite.

Miss Lester arrived with Orion Marsh. For once, she'd dressed in something other than white, though given she'd chosen funereal black instead, I wasn't entirely sure how appropriate it was.

I took it upon myself to greet the guests from the museum staff on Miss Parkhurst's behalf. What remained of her family was in New Bedford, and she had sadly expressed her doubts that her mother would accept her marriage to a woman, let alone one with frog-feet and tentacle hair.

Dr. Gerritson and his wife arrived, wearing matching gowns that flattered them both. Mr. Durfree and Mr. Parr argued the entire time they disembarked, pausing only long enough to shake my hand before returning to their quarrel. Two secretaries, who I was given to understand were special friends, had also come. They giggled and one accidentally knocked off the other's hat when I greeted them.

Night fell. Candles floated across the lake on paper boats, making it seem that a thousand stars had come down to light on the water. As Basil brought over the last boat, Griffin joined us. "You'd better take your seats," he said to Father and me.

The clearing was now filled with humans and ketoi alike. An umbra worker appeared on the outskirts, its single eye fixed on a ritual that must seem incomprehensibly alien to its species. As we took our chairs in the front row, one of the ketoi blew a strange note through a shell.

A quartet began to play softly. Lights shone through the woods, and Persephone stepped into the clearing. She wore a shimmering cloak of golden mesh, its train held off the ground by Mother and Stone Biter. Jewelry weighed down her arms and legs, necklaces layered her throat, and on her brow she wore the tiara that formally declared her chieftess of the Widdershins ketoi.

At almost the same moment, Miss Parkhurst—I supposed I should get used to thinking of her as Maggie, as she would soon be my sister-in-law—entered opposite on Griffin's arm. She looked even more radiant than Persephone, her simple white dress shining in the torch- and candlelight, a bouquet of roses and ivy in her arms. At the sight of my sister, she broke into a smile of such joy it brought tears to my eyes.

They met beneath the arch. I took out my handkerchief and dabbed at my cheeks as they exchanged their vows. Persephone's were filled with promises to add the skulls of her new wife's enemies to their wedding arch, so I assumed she'd written them herself.

The exchange was short, and Persephone swept Maggie into her arms and kissed her. There was general applause, and then the crowd began to mill around as the chairs were rearranged and tables added.

The menu depended heavily on fish, and in place of the typical wedding cake there was a tower of waffles.

After dinner, I stayed in the clearing to witness the brides dance, made awkward by Persephone's ketoi legs. Griffin then danced with Maggie, and when they were done, I took his place.

"Thank you, Dr. Whyborne," she said. Her eyes bright, her cheeks flushed with happiness.

"It's just Whyborne now," I said. "Or Percival, but really, no one calls me that except my parents and Persephone."

She beamed at me, then glanced around. "Did you ever imagine...?"

"No," I said honestly. "And if I had, I should have taken myself straight to Stormhaven as delusional."

She laughed. "I would have made sure your correspondence was still delivered to you."

"I might have used the time to work on grant proposals."

The dance ended, and I handed her over to Jack. I'd meant to make my escape, but instead found myself dancing with Dr. Gerritson, then Mrs. Gerritson. Mr. Durfree and Mr. Farr seemed about to launch into a quarrel over which of them was to be my next partner, before Griffin swooped in and claimed me.

"You're quite popular," he said as we waltzed together.

"I haven't the faintest idea why."

"I don't know." He tilted his head back and pretended to inspect me. "Did you by any chance save a town around this time last year?"

"It wasn't me," I protested. "It was all of us, and you very well know it."

He smiled. "Then let's just say, people have the tendency to look outside of themselves for heroes."

"Then they can look somewhere else. I have no interest in the job."

"I'm not certain you have that choice." The music ended, but he kept hold of my hand. "Let's avail ourselves of the champagne."

Though the night was temperate for August, I'd worked up a bit of a sweat dancing, and was more than glad to follow his suggestion. We paused long enough to take glasses of magically-chilled champagne—

dear heavens, the Endicotts were determined to show off tonight. Christine and Iskander sat on a blanket under the eaves of the small wood, and we joined them. Nathaniel and Alexandria had slept through the ceremony, but were now awake and determined to crawl off in opposite directions.

"Oh good, you're here," Christine said as we lowered ourselves to the ground by them.

"What is it?" I asked suspiciously.

"We were just discussing whether it would be best to continue with my original plan to excavate the fane in Egypt, or should we take a look at this lost city of the masters in Australia?"

I gaped at her. "Dear lord, Christine, you can't seriously want to go to Australia!"

"Why ever not?"

I began to tick reasons off on my fingers. "For one thing, there are deadly spiders. For another, there are deadly snakes. Deadly kangaroos. Deadly—"

"Bah!" She waved away my concerns. "I'm certain we'll have no trouble whatsoever."

"There's also the matter of poking about in a city of the masters, if it even survives. Who knows what's down there?"

Christine absently picked up Alexandria, who'd been reaching for one of the strange flowers, no doubt intending to stuff it in her mouth. "It would also take a great deal of planning, even more than an expedition to the fane, as we'd have less idea of what we might be facing. Very well, the fane first, then the city."

"That isn't what I meant at all." I gestured to Alexandria. "Besides, you have two young children."

"Well of course we'll wait until they're old enough. Four or five should be fine." She brightened. "And that will give us plenty of time to research the possible location of the city in Australia."

"There is no 'us,'" I protested. Of course, she ignored me.

We sat for a while, drinking champagne and watching the dancers. In the presence of my friends, I felt any residual tension from earlier drain away. Talking with Christine, watching her and Iskander with their children, my heart seemed to loosen. We had gone through so much together, but we had come out the other side intact, the bonds between us stronger than ever.

After a time, Christine and Iskander went to dance, while we watched the little ones. Alexandria had given up on eating the disturbing flora and was now attempting to swing a small stick around her head. Nathaniel chewed on a stuffed bear, its cloth body soon soaked with drool.

Persephone bounded over to us. She'd taken off her cloak earlier, as it was impossible to dance in. "Brother," she said. "Brother's husband."

"Congratulations," Griffin said.

She grinned happily, her shark's teeth on full display. "Thank you."

Griffin rose to his feet. "I'll be right back," he said, and withdrew, leaving the two of us alone with the children.

Persephone dropped into a crouch. Alexandria released her stick, and Nathaniel lowered his bear, both of them staring at her with their big eyes.

Very softly, she began to hum, then to sing:

"Listen up little fish, little fish,
Let's make a wish, make a wish,
For a time not come but yet to be,
One for the land, and one for the sea."

"Not yet," I objected. "Not any time soon, surely."

"Not yet," she agreed. She extended her hands, and Alexandria grabbed the finger of one, Nathaniel the other. "Not until they're old enough to choose for themselves."

I shook my head vehemently. "No. I don't want them to have some —some destiny."

"Have you forgotten, Brother? They have the same destiny, the same purpose, as us." Persephone gently pulled free and rose to her feet. "To be themselves."

I sat silently for a few minutes after she left, except to rescue Alexandria from investigating the ground with her mouth. Christine and Iskander returned, Christine's cheeks flushed from exertion. "Thank you for watching them, Whyborne. I think it may be time for us to head homeward. I'll see you at the museum on Monday."

"I'll see you Monday, Christine."

As they departed, Griffin returned and extended his hand. "Walk with me?"

I let him help me to my feet. Hand in hand, we wandered away from the celebrations, until we reached the water's edge. Stars crowded the heavens, blotted out directly across the lake by the dark bulk of the Draakenwood. The dusty remnants of the spire glittered on the shore, and candles bobbed past in their boats, born by the current. Fireflies danced all around. A deep sense of peace descended over me.

"It's beautiful, isn't it?" I asked.

"Yes," Griffin said, but when I turned to him, he was looking up at me.

I bent to kiss him. "You're absurd."

"Perhaps. But you love me anyway."

"That I do." I moved to face him, slipping my arms around his waist, feeling him do the same to me. "There aren't enough words in every language I know put together, to express just how much."

His eyes shone. "I love to see you happy."

It seemed unspeakably strange to stand here on this island and think back to all that had happened since I first set foot on it. More; since I'd first set eyes on the man in my arms. I'd been anything but happy, then. I'd been miserable and alone, but too afraid to do anything to change my circumstances, lest they become even worse.

I was anything but alone now. My circumstances had changed beyond my wildest imaginings. I had a husband and a family. Most of that family wasn't related by blood, and some had tentacles or gelatinous feelers, but none of that mattered. What mattered was we'd faced the darkness as one, and together found a new dawn.

"I love you, Griffin Flaherty," I said.

His smile filled my heart with simple joy. "And I love you, Percival Endicott Whyborne. For all the days of my life."

We held one another in happy silence and watched the candles float slowly away.

Finis

SHARE YOUR EXPERIENCE

If you enjoyed this book, please consider leaving a review on the site where you purchased it, or on Goodreads.

Thank you for your support of independent authors!

AUTHOR'S NOTE

On June 1, 2012, I started to write what would ultimately become Widdershins, though the working title at that point was just "Whyborne" and the town was [creepy town name] in the text. (It became Widdershins within a couple of chapters, in one of those writing moments when you're not quite sure why your subconscious came up with that particular thing, but you roll with it and keep going. That happened a lot in this particular series.) I had no idea I was setting out on what has become the greatest journey in my life thus far.

There are a lot of things I could say, but I'll get right to the point: thank you.

Thank you for embracing an awkward, clueless, introverted philologist. Thank you for loving a troubled, scarred ex-Pinkerton searching for acceptance. Thank you for making an abrupt, bossy, opinionated archaeologist one of the best-loved characters I've ever written, and then asking me to give her a love interest. Thank you for welcoming into your hearts that love interest, whose saint-like levels of patience are probably even more handy than his skills at archaeology and knife fighting.

Thank you for coming on this journey with me. Thank you for allowing me to complete it, an astounding eleven books in.

Thank you for every email, every piece of fan art, every gift in my PO Box. I'm humbled and grateful beyond all words for the love and support this community has shown me.

And that's the greatest gift you've given me: that this has become a community. The fan group on Facebook has grown far past anything I'd imagined, and I'm overwhelmed by the support and love you show not just me, but one another.

Special thanks as always to everyone on my Patreon, especially Scott M., Shane M., Dusk T., Robin H., and Helen K. Thanks also for those patrons who helped me come up with names for ketoi characters and for Christine's twins: LaDa, Crystal C., Meredith M., Aurora G., Amy C., Colette, Kristin C., Elzbieta T., Jo G., Raven, and Angela R.

Enormous thanks to my wife, Beth, whose support has never wavered. Thanks also to my amazing editor Annetta Ribken Graney; Whyborne & Griffin owe her keen sense of story a debt of gratitude.

As much as you will miss reading new Whyborne & Griffin novels, I'll miss writing them. But as a storyteller, I believe endings are important. They give a story weight. An unsuitable end can ruin the memory of an otherwise wonderful series; a good one can mean years of re-reading in the future. I hope I gave Whyborne, Griffin, and everyone else the ending they deserved.

Widdershins lives within us now, and it knows its own. So instead of saying "farewell," let us instead say "welcome home."

Jordan L. Hawk
August 14, 2019

OTHER BOOKS FROM JORDAN L.
HAWK:

Hexworld
    "The 13th Hex" (prequel short story)
    Hexbreaker
    Hexmaker
    "A Christmas Hex" (short story)
    Hexslayer
    Hexhunter

Spirits:
    Restless Spirits
    Dangerous Spirits
    Guardian Spirits

ABOUT THE AUTHOR

Jordan L. Hawk is a non-binary queer author from North Carolina. Childhood tales of mountain ghosts and mysterious creatures gave them a life-long love of things that go bump in the night. When they aren't writing, they brew their own beer and try to keep the cats from destroying the house. Their best-selling Whyborne & Griffin series (beginning with *Widdershins*) can be found in print, ebook, and audiobook.

If you're interested in receiving Jordan's newsletter and being the first to know when new books are released, please sign up at their website: http://www.jordanlhawk.com. Or join their Facebook reader group, Widdershins Knows Its Own.

Find Jordan online:

http://www.jordanlhawk.com

https://twitter.com/jordanlhawk

https://www.facebook.com/jordanlhawk

CPSIA information can be obtained
at www.ICGtesting.com
Printed in the USA
LVHW111512260919
632369LV00004B/635/P